By Eliana West

A Paris Walk
Compass of the Heart
Dreidel Date

EMERALD HEARTS
Four Holly Dates
Summer of Noelle
Falling for Joy
Be the Match
A Homemade Hanukkah
Once Upon a Hike

MOCKINGBIRD BRIDGE
The Way Forward
The Way Home
The Way Beyond
A Hidden Heart
Ruby's Sparkle

RUBY'S Sparkle

MOCKINGBIRD BRIDGE

BOOK FIVE

ELIANA WEST

Published by
Second Press
info@secondpress.com

Ruby's Sparkle
© 2025 Eliana West

Cover Art
© 2025 Elizabeth Mackey
Cover content is for illustrative purposes only and any person depicted on the cover is a model.

Trade Paperback ISBN: 9781963011159
Digital ISBN: 978163011142
Trade Paperback published August 2025
v. 1.0

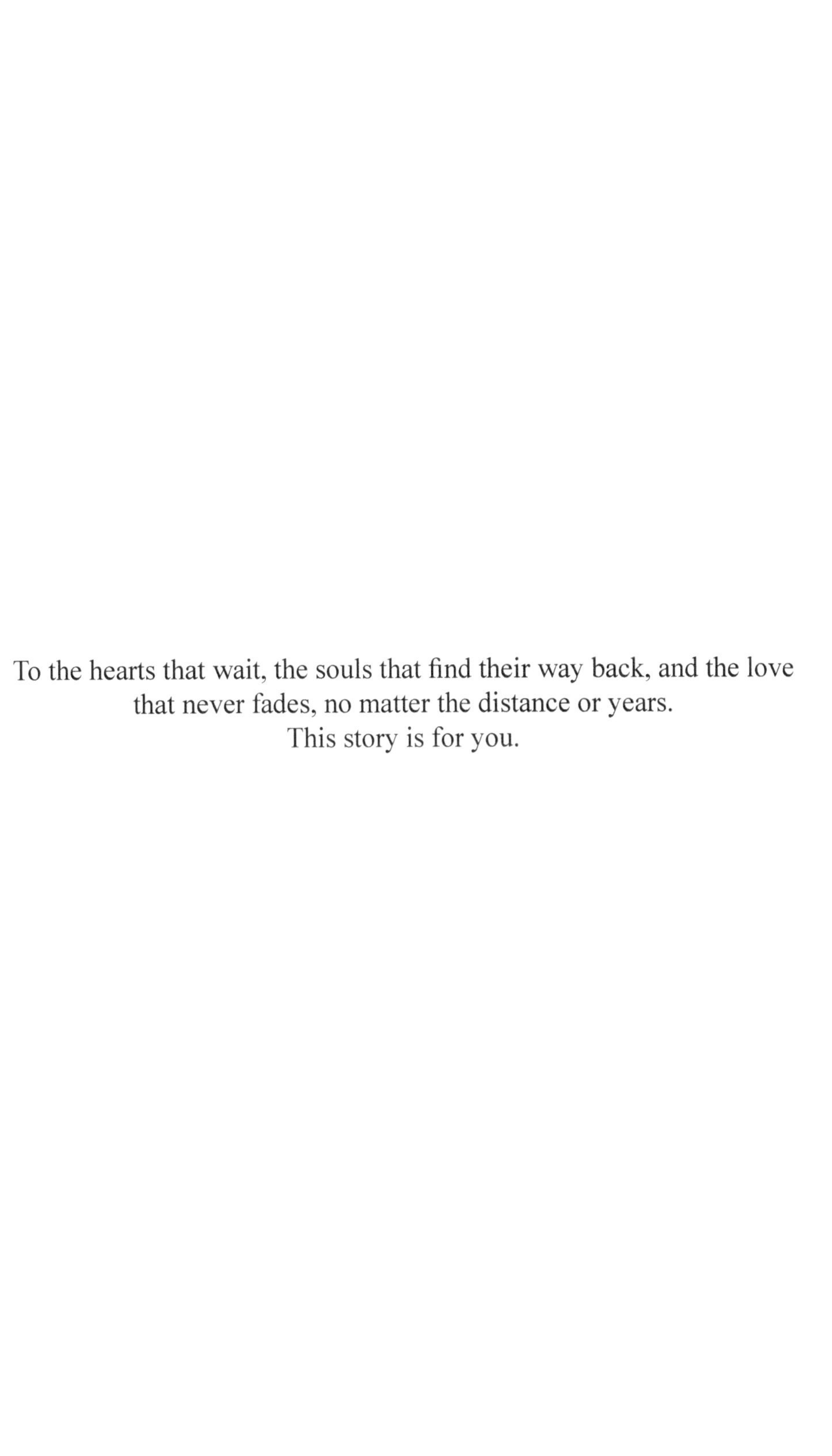

To the hearts that wait, the souls that find their way back, and the love that never fades, no matter the distance or years.
This story is for you.

Acknowledgments

To my sisters in words: Carmen Cook and Gina Knight, thank you for listening while I complained about how difficult Robert and Ruby were and for being patient with me.

To my big sister Neva, this is the story you've been asking me for.

To my legacy sister Reena, this is the South your father and my grandpa wished for.

To my husband David, who put up with many tears and bouts of self-doubt. Thank you for always believing in me. To Jackie and Satchel, you inspire me every day, and it is a privilege to be your mom. Thank you.

CHAPTER ONE

MAMA USED to say Colton was a town small enough for everyone to be all up in everyone else's business when they should have been minding their own.

Remembering the sound of her mother's soft, honeyed voice brought a smile to Ruby Colton's lips. Her mother was right, and it was one of the things she loved about her hometown. Ruby walked from the Craftsman bungalow her great-grandparents bought out of a catalog in the 1930s toward the Colton Community Clinic and watched the place she'd lived in her entire life come alive for the day.

Colton, Mississippi, a small town on the other side of a two-lane narrow bridge tucked away in the heart of the Delta. Once, it teetered on the edge of obscurity. For years, the number on the population sign remained unchanged. Now that number was rising, shifting almost weekly, as if the town itself had decided it wasn't ready to fade away just yet.

Richard Colton, who had dedicated his life to serving the community where his ancestors had once been enslaved, would have been proud. His granddaughter, Callie, served on the town council, and a new generation followed in Richard's footsteps, building a better town and a better South. The four blocks with a park in the center that made up the heart of Colton brimmed with a renewed sense of purpose.

Ruby waved to her cousin Nate, who was washing his firetruck outside the firehouse. Tillie Reynolds swept the sidewalk in front of the Catfish Café. Ruby chuckled with joy watching the town's mayor, her cousin Mae, and Mae's husband, Jacob Winters, fussing over their baby boy outside the town hall. Jacob kissed his wife on the forehead, their gaze lingering on each other for a moment before he walked across the street to open up his hardware store, Winters Hardware. They were fools in love, oil and water that somehow found a way to mix.

There was a lot of mixing going on these days in Colton, Mississippi. In the entire country. Times changed. What would have once gotten her in trouble, or even worse, was accepted now. Of course there were folks, both Black and White, who didn't. What was it she'd heard? *Down with the swirl*? Those same people didn't want any diversity in their world. They wanted everything, race, religion, and sexuality, kept in neatly labeled boxes. Ruby snorted and rolled her eyes. The world didn't work that way. It never had. But that didn't mean she was unaffected and didn't feel the sting of regret. A lot of people made sacrifices to bring about change. Hers might have been small, but it changed the trajectory of her life.

Ruby's footsteps grew heavier with the memory of her lost love. Robert Ellis.

She exhaled and straightened her shoulders. Revisiting the past wasn't going to change what needed to get done today. She continued on her way, ignoring the gazebo in the middle of the park as she passed. Town legend said a bride who said her vows under the gazebo would have a long and happy marriage. From all the brides she'd seen in her lifetime, that proved to be true. Ruby believed it would be true for her too. But she never got to say her vows in the gazebo or anywhere else.

The time for dwelling on past decisions and regrets ended when she arrived at the town clinic. Catching her reflection in the glass window, its cream lettering outlined in gold, Ruby adjusted her navy cardigan, the same hue as her scrubs, and wiggled her toes in her clogs. Somewhere beneath the layers, she still had a trim waist. Her brown skin remained smooth, untouched by time. Strands of silver threaded through her hair, a color she'd come to appreciate, if not the style itself. Too late to make any changes now. She'd arrived at her destination.

"Dr. Colton, you're here early," Ruby said, walking in to find the town doctor sitting at the computer behind the reception desk. Even though they shared the last name, Ruby and Dylan Colton came from very different places in history. Both Black and White residents carried the last name of the town's founding family. Ruby descended from people enslaved on the Colton plantation, who adopted the last name after emancipation. Dr. Colton and his kin carried the name through the DNA they shared with Colonel Absolem Madden Colton. In Ruby's eyes the town of Colton, and all the people who carried the last name, were special, the embodiment of America's complicated past and their hope for the future.

Dr. Colton continued to stare at the screen. "I couldn't stop thinking about our flu vaccine inventory. Reports are saying it's going to be a bad season. I want to make sure we have enough on hand."

Ruby put her hand on his shoulder. "Dylan, we have enough."

He stared at her for a moment before his shoulders slumped. "You're right," he said with a sigh.

"Come on, let's get a pot of coffee going," she said, leading him back to the small alcove where Dr. Colton's brother Taylor had built a mini kitchen with a refrigerator, microwave, electric tea kettle, and coffee pot when he remodeled the clinic. Having a sibling with a hit home restoration TV show had its benefits. Taylor and his wife Josephine had lovingly restored the old Colton plantation house, turning it into a trade school and historical site. Now, they focused on restoring other homes and businesses around town. Most small towns didn't have a state-of-the-art clinic, so Dylan and his brother had combined resources to create one.

Ruby leaned against the counter while the coffee dripped into the carafe, eyeing the doctor. "Dylan, you need a life. A hobby, something other than this clinic to take up your time," she said softly.

Dylan rubbed the back of his neck. "I could say the same about you," he said with a wry smile.

"I have my gardening and knitting clubs," she reminded him.

"Fair point."

"You're a good man and a good doctor." Ruby patted Dylan's shoulder. "You need to spend less time worrying and a little more time living."

"Thank you, Ruby. You're a wise woman."

The bell over the door signaled the arrival of their first patient and the beginning of their day. For the next eight hours, they took care of their community. Ruby didn't realize how much she'd missed nursing until Dylan asked her to return and help him at the clinic. She'd always been a caregiver. Even when she was a little girl, she'd beg her mama for scraps of fabric to make bandages for her stuffed animals. Nursing wasn't a career she'd chosen so much as she was pushed into it by her parents. It was the practical and safe choice. She patted the bun at the base of her neck. *Practical and safe were the principles that guided her life.*

Her sister Pearl dropped in at lunch. "I was over in Greenwood and figured I'd stop by Tony's. I thought you and Dr. Colton would like a treat," she said, holding out a box with the familiar logo.

Dylan's head popped around the corner. "Do I smell tamales?"

Ruby held up the box. "Pearl brought us a treat."

"Y'all going to knitting club tonight?" Pearl asked, balancing a plate in her lap while they all sat in the waiting room eating lunch.

"Someone's got to keep Presley from accidentally strangling herself with yarn." Ruby laughed with a snort.

"I thought she was doing better," Pearl said.

"I have to say, she surprised me with the job she's been doing as Mae's assistant." Dylan turned to Ruby. "You have to admit it was a great idea to set up an internship with the trade school for medical assistants, and she's been a huge help working with the college to coordinate the program."

"You're right. That girl has certainly surprised us all the past couple of years."

"I never thought I'd see this town thriving the way it is now," Dylan said.

Pearl nodded. "Neither did I. When Dax Ellis came back, I thought for sure he'd bring more trouble back home with him. But he showed us all what change can look like."

"And reminded us that everyone deserves a second chance if they're trying to better themselves," Dylan added.

Ruby set her empty plate aside. "I think we can all agree Presley Beaumont is the poster child for turning your life around. The former Miss Pickled Pigs Feet is now the mayor's assistant. That's a pretty big turnaround."

"More like a miracle if you ask me," Pearl said.

Ruby checked her watch. "Time to stop gossipin' and get back to work." She gave her sister a quick peck on the cheek and said goodbye.

"Thanks for the tamales, Miss Pearl," Dylan said, giving her a hug as she left. Dylan leaned his elbow on the reception counter, watching Pearl make her way across the park before he turned back to Ruby. "I admire how close you and your sisters all are."

"Don't be fooled. We spit and scratch every so often, the same way all siblings do."

"Yeah, but you're all so in sync with each other."

"They're my best friends." Ruby shrugged as if it were the most natural thing in the world. "I know they'll always be there for me, and I'll do the same for them."

"Y'all really are precious jewels," Dylan said affectionately.

That night, as she changed out of her work uniform, Ruby replayed their conversation at lunch. People changed. But she hadn't.

She reached into her closet for the pale blue cardigan she alternated with the pink one when she wasn't wearing scrubs. Catching her reflection in the mirror, she sighed. She looked as frumpy as she felt.

Lately, she couldn't shake the feeling of being stuck. She needed something new in her life—wanted it—but she wasn't sure what. And the one person she longed for? Well… sometimes, it was too late.

"I'm heading out," Ruby called as she gathered her knitting basket and handbag from the bench by the front door.

Her older sister Opal came out of the kitchen, wiping her hands on her apron. "Don't be too late getting home."

Ruby paused. "Opal, I'm a grown woman. I can walk eight blocks after dark."

"I'm looking out for my baby sister. There's nothing wrong with that," she said with a frown.

There was a lot wrong with her sister's overprotective and cautious nature, but Ruby bit her tongue. She wasn't in the mood to argue. Tonight she needed a glass of wine and a little knitting therapy. She was even looking forward to Presley's company.

Ruby may have been in the mood to relax and enjoy the night out, but it took one look at Jasmine Owen's face to see her young friend wasn't enjoying herself. Colton's new veterinarian and their sheriff Isiah Owen's little sister's chin quivered as she sat quietly on one of the sofas where they gathered for their weekly stitch and gossip session in the coffee shop next to the library. *Sniff, wrap, stitch.* Ruby watched the pattern repeat over and over.

Finally, she'd had enough. "Are you all right, honey?" she asked.

Jasmine let her knitting fall in her lap. "Yes—no. I don't know."

"Rhett's going to come around," Presley said, pushing a plate of cookies toward them.

Miss June offered up some of her homebrew bourbon-infused kombucha, which everyone wisely declined. Thank God for Presley's brother Ashton, who saved the day by pulling a bottle of wine from his yarn basket. Ruby loved it when her community rallied together for a good cause, but sometimes having too many folks caring all at once could be a little overwhelming.

When Jasmine burst into tears, Ruby put the lace shawl she was knitting for Pearl's birthday aside and went to Jasmine's side, putting her arm around her shoulder. Ruby guided her outside. "Come on, honey, let's you and I have a talk."

Ruby recognized a kindred spirit in the quiet young woman, who'd taken a leap of faith in moving to a new town and starting over after experiencing a crushing heartbreak and discrimination working as a Black veterinarian. Ruby may not have left Colton, but she certainly knew about heartbreak. She recognized the pain and longing she saw in Jasmine's eyes.

She understood more so than most. Her time for love had passed, but that didn't mean it was too late for Jasmine.

Chapter Two

Evenings when the air still held a hint of warmth and the leaves on the maple trees began to turn that deeper shade of green, holding on to the last bits of summer before they cloaked themselves in autumnal hues, were one of the things Robert Ellis missed the most during his time away from his hometown. There were a lot of things Robert had missed about Colton, Mississippi. The one thing he missed the most was still out of his reach, even after returning home more than fifteen years ago. Robert took his time to wander through the park after dinner and share a game of chess with his friends at Hank's Barbershop. His walk provided an excuse to peek in the coffee shop and spy.

He chuckled, laughing at himself. He wasn't really spying. Stalking? No that went against his moral code. Checking? Sure, he could lie to himself and say he was doing that. It wouldn't be untrue. He was always checking on Ruby Colton, making sure she was safe even though she didn't know it. He looked for any excuse to catch a glimpse of the only woman he'd ever loved. He stopped in his tracks when Ruby's voice drifted toward him. Following her voice, Robert moved closer, staying hidden behind one of the grand old oak trees in the park. Ruby and the new town vet, Jasmine Owens, were sitting on the steps of the gazebo that was the centerpiece of Ada Mae Colton Park. He hovered out of sight, listening. Hearing the tinge of regret in Ruby's words as she shared her sage advice left a bruise on his heart.

He had no business eavesdropping, and he was about to retreat when he heard Jasmine ask, "Are you sure it's too late for you?"

He took a step forward, holding his breath, waiting for Ruby's answer.

"I'm an old woman now. What man is gonna want me?"

Her answer landed like a punch in the gut. His body tensed. Robert's anger was directed at himself as much as it was toward what Ruby was saying about herself. They were both older, because he'd waited to damn long to claim the woman he loved. When he'd finally made it back to his hometown, nothing went the way he imagined. His backstory that he'd retired was a lie. He came home to Colton because he missed his home. Ruby Colton. Wherever Ruby lived was home, and she'd lived in Colton her entire life. His plans to make up for lost time went to hell in a handbasket the minute he set foot back in town. He'd returned to a town and a family in turmoil. Work and family kept him from living the life he really wanted. Things were finally settling down in Colton. Tonight there would be no more excuses. He stepped out of the shadows without hesitating. "I've always wanted you." The truth fell from his lips, his voice gruff with emotion.

Both women leapt to their feet, standing on the steps of the gazebo. Ruby's big brown eyes locked on him, while Jasmine's gaze flickered between them, as if debating whether to stay or flee back to the bookstore.

He pulled off his worn Biloxi Shuckers baseball cap and clutched it in front of him. He was tired of waiting. This moment had been a long time coming. "Ruby Colton, I've waited too many years to say things that I should have said a long time ago."

"What do you think you're doing lurking in the park, eavesdropping?" Ruby put her hand over her heart. "Lord Almighty, you about gave me a heart attack."

"I'll leave you two to talk," Jasmine said, making her way down the gazebo steps and hightailing it toward the bookstore and coffee shop. The minute she walked in the door, Presley Beaumont, the mayor, and the rest of Colton's knitting circle appeared at the window.

That was fine with Robert. If he had witnesses, then Ruby wouldn't have an excuse to deny what was happening between them.

Ruby threw her hands up. "That was a private conversation."

"Then you shouldn't have had it in a public place."

"Don't you dare." She shook her finger at him, coming down the stairs to stand in front of him.

"That's part of the problem. I haven't dared." He shook his head with a sigh. "What are we doing, Ruby? Why are we wasting what time we've got left?"

"You never wrote like you promised. You walked away, and I never heard from you again," Ruby exclaimed.

Robert frowned. "I wrote every week. You were the one who never answered."

Ruby threw her hands up again and started to walk away. Robert grabbed her by the shoulders. "You can slap me after if you want," he said and crushed his lips to hers.

Tears pricked at the back of his eyes. He'd dreamed about this, waking up with his face wet with tears of longing. Their years apart fell away and he was a young man again, kissing her on a starry night like this one. She remained unmoving in his embrace only for a second before she wrapped an arm around his shoulders and drew him in with a little whimper.

When his lips left hers, he cradled her face in his hands. His gaze held hers, looking for any regret in her eyes.

Her lips trembled. "Why did it take so long?" she whispered.

"We're gonna talk about that. You're coming home with me, Ruby Colton. I'm not letting you go again. That kiss was the first one of the rest of my life kissing you."

She lifted her face and pressed her lips quickly to his. "Okay, Robert, I'll go with you."

He closed his eyes and took a deep, shuddering breath. He'd wanted her to say those same words to him so long ago.

He took her hand. "Come on, let's grab your things."

Thank goodness the group in the bookstore was a knitting club and not playing at the tables in Vegas. Not a single one of them had a decent poker face. All of them stared with open curiosity when they walked in. Ruby bit down on her lip swollen from Robert's kisses, doing her best to hide her pink cheeks and avoiding eye contact with anyone as she gathered her things.

Robert offered his own words of advice to Jasmine about her love life, telling her, "Give him another week, and if Rhett hasn't come around by then, you have my blessing to go to him and"—his eyes flicked toward Ruby—"kiss some sense into him. Now, if y'all will excuse us, I'm going to escort Miss Ruby home." He took Ruby's arm and paused as they headed to the door, glancing back at the group. "My home."

Ruby remained silent at his side while he ushered her toward his truck. They'd crossed a mile down the road from Mockingbird Bridge before she turned to him and asked, in a quiet voice, "What letters?"

Chapter Three

Robert pulled into the gravel courtyard that spanned the space between the cabin and barn. He threw his truck into park and jumped out, jogging around to the passenger side to open the door for Ruby. She'd barely unbuckled her seat belt before he pulled her into his arms and kissed her. She welcomed his kisses with wonder at how easy it was to slip back into Robert's embrace. Kissing Robert would always be like coming home. She savored the slight trace of whiskey still on his lips. Even after all these years, they were in sync, their tongues touching in a familiar dance.

"I hope you understand, I plan on doing that a lot from now on," Robert said when they broke apart.

Ruby cupped his cheek, looking into his eyes. "I hope so too, but we have to talk."

Robert's brow furrowed. He nodded and took Ruby's hand, leading her up the stairs to the porch and guiding her toward one of the rocking chairs.

He pulled up another rocker, angling it to face hers and close enough that when he sat down, their knees pressed together. Ruby reached for his hands. He gripped hers, brushing his thumb over her knuckles.

Ruby gazed into his brown eyes. They might be a bit more faded, but they still made her heart flutter every time they fell on her. She took a shallow breath, and with a quiver in her voice, she said, "Tell me about the letters, Robert."

Robert's gaze scanned her face, his eyes clouded with confusion. "I wrote. I wrote about how much I missed you and how much I regretted leaving you. I poured my heart into those letters. I wrote until I came home, back to Colton. Back to you."

His confession pierced her heart. Ruby shook her head, blinking back tears. For a few seconds, she couldn't find her vice. "I never got them." She squeezed his hands. "Tell me what you said. Tell me you explained why you never showed up. Why?" Her voice broke. "Why I waited for hours in our spot and you never came."

Robert reached up, wiping away the tear that rolled down her cheek with the pad of this thumb, his own eyes watery with unshed tears.

"That night," he cleared his throat, "the night we were supposed to run away together." He turned away, his jaw tight. "I wanted to keep you safe. I realized even though I wanted to be a man, I was still a boy. I didn't have the means to take care of you."

Anger and frustration took up arms within her. "We agreed we would take care of each other."

"Yes, but…." Robert dropped his chin to his chest. "I put you in danger, Ruby. Before I joined the military, I was already working for the FBI as an informant. I was reckless sneaking out to see you. It was only a matter of time before someone... the wrong people saw us together. We became targets of folks involved with the Klan, but some Black folks weren't happy about us either. Even the minister at your church preached from the pulpit against interracial marriage."

"You think I didn't hear those sermons? I sat there, watching him glare at me from the pulpit while he tried to twist the Lord's words into an argument that races shouldn't mix. Do you think Reverend Evans didn't show up at the house to warn me? I was willing to take the risk, Robert."

The dim glow from the porch light cast shadows on his face, making it difficult to read his expression. Did what she said make any difference? What did she need to do to convince such a stubborn, strong man that she was capable of standing on her own two feet?

Robert's jaw was set. He sighed as if he were trying to convince a toddler to eat their vegetables. "Ruby, you were too young to realize how much danger you were in. I did what I thought was best. When Opal showed up at my house and told me what folks were saying, I took it as a sign I'd made the right decision."

With each word, Ruby's hackles rose. She pulled her hands out of Robert's grasp at the same time she drew her heart closed. Rising to her feet, she backed away. "You believed you made the right decision, but you took away my right to choose."

Robert jumped up and tried to reach for her. She moved out of his grasp. "Ruby, I had to make sure you were taken care of before I left. I pulled in every favor I had to make sure other agents kept an eye on you while I was away," he said with desperation in his voice.

A chill swept through her. "You mean I was being spied on?" she gasped. "Did your spies tell you when I went on dates? The times a boy would try to kiss me on the porch at the end of a date, and I pulled away because I missed you so much? All the times I sat on the flat rock at Turtle Pond crying because I wanted to run away and find you?" Her chin dropped, and her black clogs filled her vision. The same sensible shoes she wore for nursing, with baggy jeans and the god-awful pink cardigan her sister Opal had convinced her was the sensible option. Sensible and safe. As angry and frustrated as she was with Robert, she was as upset with Opal, the world, and herself. She'd put her life on hold, waiting… for what? To make everyone else happy? She'd trusted Robert with her heart and soul, a man who'd made a decision that affected both their lives without including her. For too long, she'd been letting others lead the way.

She backed out of Robert's grasp, shaking her head.

"Ruby, I did it all because I love you," he argued.

She hesitated. Robert Ellis wasn't a man who begged. Everyone in town thought he was invincible. The vulnerability she saw in his eyes told her he was human and as frail as everyone else.

"I never doubted that," she said, forcing the words past the lump in her throat. "And I love you. I thought we could pick up where we left off. That all the years would… fade away, and we'd be like we were before. But that's not how it works, does it? I'm not walking away from you, Robert. I longed for this moment, Robert. I've lost count of how many nights I fell asleep picturing us together and woke up with tears on my pillow. I still love you, but I am going to ask you to take me home." She pressed her hand over her heart. "This time I'll be the one who decides." She poked her chest. "I want to have a say in what happens in my life."

"I'm sorry," he said, the tremor of emotion in his voice revealing the depth of his regret.

Her heart softened. She reached up and cupped his cheek, his soft whiskers tickling her palm. "I know you are, and so am I. I'm not going to make you wait another fifty years, Robert, but I am going to ask you to give me a little time."

He nodded. "Can I call on you tomorrow?"

"Of course you can."

Robert's face was set in stone on the drive back into town. The dark shadows of the familiar landscape passed in a blur and Ruby didn't recognize any of it, lost in her own thoughts. She loved Robert. That was without question. She'd take her last breath loving Robert Ellis, even if she wanted to strangle him for being so stubborn right now. It wasn't fair to blame Robert for the situation she found herself in. Somewhere along the line, she'd forgotten to have a life of her own and love herself as much as she loved Robert. She bit her lip, blinking back tears. She reached across the bench seat for Robert's hand, needing the comfort of his touch.

Her voice was low and heavy with regret as she struggled to find the right words. "You wanted… tonight to be special, Robert, and so did I. I'm not keeping myself from you, I promise. But I want—I need to stand on my own two feet for a while. I need to figure out who I am before we take the next steps forward as a couple. And Robert, those steps will falter if you don't see me as your equal and not some precious, helpless thing you need to take care of."

"I—" He pressed his mouth closed, tightening his grip on the steering wheel. "I understand."

Ruby eyed him with doubt. He was trying, but he didn't understand. She didn't blame him. Ruby didn't understand what had come over her. She was seeing her world as if it were a clear blue sky after the rain clouds disappeared. Since the day she was born, she'd been a part of the Jewels. There was never a time when she was without her sisters, Opal and Pearl, at her side. She loved her sisters and Robert, but it was time to learn who Ruby Colton was and learn to like that woman. To love her with her whole heart.

Robert pulled up to her house and got out, coming around to open her door. Only this time, he didn't pull her into his arms when she unbuckled her seat belt. Instead, he tucked her arm over his and started walking toward her front door.

"I dreamed of doing this," he said, his voice full of longing. "Walking you to your door at the end of a date. Being able to kiss you on your front porch as bold as brass."

At the door, Ruby cradled his face in her hands and kissed him. "Tomorrow, Robert. And the day after that and the day after that. We'll walk and talk and you can kiss me on the porch anytime you want." She brushed her fingers over the lines at the corner of his eyes. "We'll laugh and I can assure you, we'll be loving when the time is right."

He nodded and pressed his forehead against hers. "I love you, Ruby."

"I love you, Robert."

He pressed his lips against Ruby's forehead again, brushing his thumb against the spot behind her ear that made her shudder and lean closer. With a heavy exhale, he stepped away and walked back to his truck. Ruby stood on the porch until his taillights disappeared.

Opal stood in the hall with her arms crossed and fire in her eyes when Ruby walked in.

She dropped her bag at her feet and folded her own arms across her chest. "Where are my letters?" she said between clenched teeth, fighting to maintain her composure. She'd be dammed if she'd let her sister use her being too emotional as an excuse for why she did what she did.

Opal's jaw ticked. Pearl came out of her room, walking down the hall toward them.

Ruby turned on Pearl. "Do you know where they are?"

Pearl glanced between her older and younger sisters. "Where what are?"

"The letters Robert Ellis wrote me."

Pearl gasped. "He wrote to you? All those years we thought he'd up and left without a word."

Opal lifted her chin. "I did what needed to be done to keep you safe."

"Opal, you didn't." Pearl's jaw dropped as she stared at her sister.

"How could you?" Ruby advanced on Opal.

"Someone had to be sensible. You were too lovestruck to think straight. I decided—"

"Damn it!" Ruby shouted, making her sisters both freeze. Shaking, her hands clenched into fists at her side, she took a steadying breath before she continued. "I decide what's best for me. Not you and not Robert. ME. Opal Marie Colton, you tell me what you did with my letters or I will tear down this house looking for them."

Opal's lips trembled. "I threw them away."

A tear slid down Ruby's cheek, and a soft, desperate keening filled the room. It took a moment to realize the sound was coming from her. When Robert left, Ruby thought her heart was broken beyond repair. Her sister shattered it.

Numb, Ruby turned on her heel and marched down the hall, forcing one foot in front of the other until she reached her room. She slammed the door shut with enough force to make the windows rattle and turned the lock. Pearl's and Opal's muffled voices came through the walls, Opal's resolute and Pearl's outraged. Ruby took in the room, unchanged since she was in high school, and a sob escaped. She didn't want to be here in this house, but she realized she didn't have anywhere to go. Colton didn't have a hotel, and she shared a car with her sisters, so she couldn't leave. She'd allowed herself to become trapped.

A door slammed in another part of the house, and then a quiet knock came on her door.

"Ruby, can I come in and talk?" Pearl called through the door.

She took a breath and wiped her eyes. "Not tonight, Pearl. My time for talking is done. I'll see you in the morning."

The shadow of her sister's feet hovered under the sliver of light at the bottom of her door for a moment before Ruby heard the soft click as Pearl's bedroom door closed.

For one reason or another, Ruby and her sisters had all stayed close to home. Opal moved away for a brief time when she married a boy from Greenwood. Dexter died in a car accident three years after they said their vows. Opal moved back home right after the funeral and never left again. Each of them found a reason to stay, and Ruby realized they had all lived in limbo since then. She never imagined her sisters would ever hurt her as much as Opal did.

Ruby lay on her bed, letting her tears soak her pillow, the gaping wound in her heart fresh and raw. She never imagined one of her sisters would betray her, break her trust and their sisterly bond in the way Opal had. She never would have lied or kept such a big secret from her sisters.

That wasn't true. She kept a lot from them. How much she loved Robert. How she grew tired of doing everything as a trio sometimes. She'd even let her hair grow longer than her sisters so there would be something to differentiate herself from her siblings.

A different hairstyle wasn't going to be enough. And she'd suffocate if she had to spend another night under the same roof as Opal.

"Ruby, you need to run away from home."

Chapter Four

"Uncle Robert, what brings you in tonight? We heard—" Robert's nephew Reid Ellis stopped wiping down the worn wood counter at the Buckthorn. The groves worn into the yellow pine came from the years of drinks sliding down the bar in the juke joint that had stood on the outskirts of town for longer than anyone could remember. His light brown eyes widened with surprise. "I thought maybe you'd have... company tonight."

Robert took a seat at the bar, thankful the picnic tables at the Buckthorn were mostly empty, with only a scattering of customers to share his misery.

"I dropped Ruby off at her house," he muttered.

Reid pushed the bar towel aside and rested his elbows on the surface. "Oh?"

Robert grunted. He wasn't in the mood for making conversation and pretending like everything was okay. "Can you ask Primus for a bottle for me?"

Reid hesitated for a moment, eyeing him with worry in his gaze. "Uh, sure, give me a minute."

Primus Wallace, the owner of the Buckthorn, was a master distiller, and only a very few could ask for and receive a bottle of his prime stuff. He listened to his nephew's muted voice and then a deep rattling cough before Primus answered in a hollow, thready voice. Reid came back out with a bottle and his fiancé, Dan Nguyen, at his side.

"Uncle Robert," Dan said with a nod.

Robert's heart softened at the greeting. He loved his nephews as if they were his own children, and he felt the same way about their partners. Dax and Reid had chosen well. He'd bonded with Dan over having careers in law enforcement. They'd continued to grow closer over the last year. Robert told him many times he could call him Uncle Robert instead of Mr. Ellis, but only recently had he started using it without hesitation.

Dan leaned in, his short black hair cut in a conservative, precise style, contrasting with Reid's curls that brushed against his neck. He whispered something in Reid's ear. Whatever he said made Reid's mouth tighten into a frown. He nodded, his expression clouded with concern,

"Primus isn't doing too well. I'm going to take him back to bed and sit with him for a spell," Reid said.

Robert nodded, taking the bottle Reid set on the bar and pulling out the cork. Dan reached behind the counter and slid a glass toward him.

"He going to be okay?" Robert poured himself three fingers.

"Reid or Primus?" Dan sighed, pressing his hands against the bar. "Primus is getting weaker every day. When it's his time, it's going to destroy Reid. Primus has been a mentor, friend, and like a father for him." Dan sighed. "For both of us. He's become an important part of our lives, and we care about him. I'd like to think we've been a surrogate family for him as much as he's been a father figure for us."

Robert drained his glass, letting the smooth, smoky flavor burn a trail into his belly. "You're fine boys. He's treasured the time he's had with you."

Dan turned his head, blinking back tears. "It's been an honor."

Robert refilled his glass, blinking back his own tears. Change could bring joy and pain. More often than not, all tangled up together in the adventure called life.

"How about we sit on the porch for a while?" Dan suggested.

Robert got up and trapped the bottle between his fingers, holding the glass with his other hand, and headed toward the open french doors.

"Willie, give a holler if anyone comes in," Dan called out to one of the men in the corner as he followed Robert outside. Willie waved, never taking his eyes off the chessboard he was seated at. "You want to talk about it?" Dan asked when they took their seats.

Robert drained his glass again. He stared into the forest beyond the Buckthorn. An owl hooted, and he lifted his head, searching the darkness for the source of the sound.

"We think we're doing our job when we protect our loved ones, but sometimes that…." He didn't know how to continue, how to explain, but if anyone would understand, Dan would. His nephew's fiancé also worked in law enforcement as an FBI agent.

Dan sat quietly for a moment. "The worst fight Reid and I had—" Dan chuckled softly, shaking his head. "Our first big fight, where I thought I might have messed up the best thing I ever had, was when we had the threat against the mayor. I completely flipped out when I learned Reid volunteered to go undercover to obtain information. I wanted to lock him away to keep him safe. I was ready to arrest him if that would keep anything from happening to him."

"What kept you from doing it?"

"Well, first Reid said he'd leave me if I did. Then he said something that made me stop and think. He said he understood I made decisions for people every day, doing what I thought was best for them without considering their feelings. That's the job. You can't think about protecting a witness's feelings. You've got to take action. We have to make their safety our priority. But Reid isn't my job. He's my partner, the man I'm going to marry. I can't make decisions that affect his life without his input. It's about trust and respect."

Robert stared into the amber liquid in his glass. "I don't regret the sacrifices I made in service to my country," he muttered.

"That doesn't make them hurt any less. I see the haunted look in my parent's eyes when they talk about relatives back home in Vietnam. They made a huge sacrifice and risked everything to come here with nothing and start over." Dan leaned forward, leveling Robert with the same gaze he used when he was working, intense, serious, and not willing to put up with any bullshit. "All those risks my parents took and the decisions they made, they did it together. One of them didn't make decisions that impacted the other without discussing it first."

Dan's words hit home, making him feel even worse than he did when he walked into the Buckthorn. Damn it, when did these boys get to be so wise?

Reid came through the doorway and leaned over Dan's shoulder, wrapping his arms around his neck from behind, and pressed a kiss to his cheek.

"Primus settled in?" Dan asked.

Reid leaned his temple against Dan's. "He's sleeping." Reid's gaze dropped to the half-empty bottle at Robert's feet. "You'll stay here with us tonight, Uncle Robert. You're in no shape to drive."

Robert's response was to fill his glass again. He had no desire to return to an empty cabin filled with shadows of regret.

"I didn't mean to overhear your conversation, but I caught the last part. Whatever happened between you and Miss Ruby tonight, Uncle

Robert, if you love her as much as half the town thinks you do, you can't make decisions for her."

"I'm learning that... now," he said with a grimace.

Reid straightened. "I'll leave you two. I'm going to go back and check on Primus and then I'll be at the bar."

"Proud of that boy," Robert said when Reid left.

"So am I. I'm most proud of knowing he can stand on his own two feet. Let me ask you a question. If, God forbid, something happened to you tomorrow, to Opal and Pearl as well, would you want Ruby to be left alone and feeling like she's helpless, like she can't do for herself?"

Robert bristled. "Of course not."

"Well, all right then."

"I don't like this," Robert grumbled.

Dan's lips quirked. "Being told you're wrong?"

"I'll admit it sure tastes bitter going down. I'm the one who doles out the words of wisdom to your generation, not the other way around."

Dan chuckled. "We still have a lot to learn, Uncle Robert, don't you worry." He shot a worried glance toward the tiny clapboard house Primus called home behind the Buckthorn. "I hope we can learn everything we need from our elders before we run out of time."

Robert tamped down the fear that bubbled up listening to Dan. Time was precious, growing more so every day. He needed to apologize to Ruby and make amends.

Late into the night, when even the lightning bugs had gone to bed, Robert found his way onto Primus's couch, although he remembered little about how he made it. A deep, rattling cough accompanied by shuffling footsteps woke him up as the sun was beginning to peek through the trees outside.

"Primus," he called out, rubbing the sleep from his eyes.

The older man put his finger to his lips and tipped his head toward the front porch. Robert followed him out. When Primus wobbled a bit, Robert took his arm and guided him into a rocker. Grabbing a blanket, he tucked it around Primus's legs.

He crouched down in front of his friend, taking in the way his eyes had sunken farther into their sockets and the deep lines that bracketed his mouth.

"Are you in pain?" Robert asked.

"No more, no less than I have been most of my life. But no, I've got medicine. I'm not planning on sleeping the rest of my days away." His deep baritone was gone, his voice thin and reedy. "Sit down, Robert. I have things I need to say."

"I expect the whole town will have things to say about Ruby and me."

Primus waved his hand. "I ain't worried about that. You two fools are determined to have the longest courtship in history." He leaned forward, his shoulders hunched. "If you take too long to figure it out, I ain't gonna be here to be a witness at your wedding." He put his hand up when Robert started to speak. "The boys will be up soon. I ain't got much time." Primus smiled. "They keep a sharper eye on me than a hen with her chicks. Those boys have been the greatest gift in my life. It's going to be hard for Reid when… it's going to be hard to say goodbye." He sat up suddenly. "He gets everything." Primus jerked his thumb toward the Buckthorn. "People are gonna come and want to take it from him. I got a safe deposit box at the bank. Ashton Beaumont will take care of it." Primus leaned even closer, his eyes darting around before he said, "I've got journals too. Everything that happened back in the day, it's all written down. You know how folks are about history these days, wanting to make it go away. They think if they ban a book, that will undo the history that's been wrote."

Robert snorted, shaking his head. "Fools."

"Pay attention," Primus snapped.

Robert sucked in his breath. He didn't want to face Primus leaving this earth, but he couldn't stop it. He owed his friend the honor of letting him speak his peace, so he clamped his mouth shut.

"I want the journals to go to the state archives. I've been talking to the archivist who takes care of Medgar Evers's files. She'll take care of my documents too. She's got your information and Callie's. Anyone who wants access to my journals will need approval from you or Callie. I figured Callie being the town librarian, she'd be the right person. Plus, her granddaddy's papers are at the archives. I've made sure there's a copy of everything for you too." Primus leaned forward. "I think most of the cases have been solved, but I wanted you to have a copy in case anything in the journals can help with any unsolved cases." Primus leaned back with a heavy sigh. "I'm glad the boys will have each other.

I always wished… I wish I'd been born in a time when I could have had what they have."

Robert did a double-take and took his time to choose his words carefully. "I didn't—I've never asked you about your personal life. I'm sorry for that."

"I've shared that part of my story with Reid and Dan. That's all that matters."

"I'm still sorry."

"It wasn't you."

The screen door creaked open. "Primus, what are you doing out here so early?" Reid asked.

Primus winked at Robert, the old twinkle in his eye returning for a flash. "I'm out here tradin' stories with my friend." He turned to Reid and reached for his hand. "You go back inside and catch a few more winks. We good, we still got time."

Reid squeezed Primus's hand. "Okay."

Primus's eyes shone with a combination of pride and unshed tears when Reid went back inside. "That's my family, my son. He's your kin by blood, but—" He tapped his heart with his finger. "In here…."

"That's where it counts."

"You'll be here to help guide them when I'm gone."

It was a statement, not a question. "I will," he answered with a solemn nod.

"It's going to be a lot. More than they expected. Reid needs to believe he can do it as well as I have. He's got to believe he's worthy. He's got to realize he can stand on his own and make peace with what his daddy done to him. It's a great comfort knowing he'll have Dan by his side, but he has to be confident he can do it alone too."

Robert scrubbed his face with his hands, a deeper understanding of how he'd undermined Ruby's confidence taking root. He stayed on the porch with Primus, talking and listening to the birdsong until his friend's eyes grew heavy.

When Primus tried to stand up and sank back down in his chair again, Robert got up and lifted him in his arms, ignoring his weak protest. Robert called out for Reid to open the door. He was at his side in a flash, a mask of worry on his face.

"He's okay," Robert reassured him.

Robert carried Primus into his room. Reid pulled back the covers and started fussing, plumping pillows and adding extra blankets as soon as Robert put Primus down. Primus exhaled, a weak wheezing sound as he sank against the pillows.

"He's not eating enough. I'm going to see if he'll eat some shrimp and grits when he wakes up," Reid said in a hushed voice as he and Robert left the room.

"Anything I can do?"

Reid shook his head. "We have a routine. I know what he likes and what he needs. Dan and I can make him comfortable and take care of him. You have your own life to put right."

Robert pulled his nephew in for a tight hug. "I'm proud of you." Reid nodded and sniffed. "Anything you need, I'm here for you."

Reid pulled back and wiped his eyes. Dan came out from the kitchen and wrapped his arm around Reid's waist. Reid sighed and let his head fall on Dan's shoulder. "Thank you. We're okay right now. Dan and I have shut down the distillery at the train depot for the time being. We're going to stay here until—" His voice broke.

"Until Primus doesn't need us anymore," Dan finished.

Robert watched his nephew with Dan. The love they shared was palpable. It reassured him that Reid had Dan to take care of him. Robert's jaw ticked as he mentally kicked himself. That was the kind of thinking that got him in trouble in the first place. Reid didn't need someone to make decisions for him. He didn't need a protector. He deserved a partner.

"I'll check in with you in a day or two," he managed to choke out.

He left Dan and Reid, taking comfort in knowing Primus was loved and cared for. But he was in rougher shape than when he started out. The reality of Primus's health couldn't be denied any longer, bringing his own mortality into sharp focus. He didn't have time to fuck around anymore. He needed to make things right with Ruby. Resisting temptation, he didn't backtrack into town and drive by her place. It wouldn't give him any advantage to show up with red eyes, stinky breath, and rumpled clothes, anyway.

No. He needed to go home, shower, change, and eat before he was ready to tackle the day. He had to face himself in the mirror before he could face Ruby again. The guilt for his actions gnawed at his gut. Ruby was right. He didn't have the right to decide for both of them, especially a decision based on fear.

Chapter Five

RUBY CRACKED an eye open with a silent curse at the birds chirping happily away outside her window as if today was another ordinary day. She stared at the ceiling, trying to find the energy to get out of bed. It wasn't the birds' fault. They didn't know her world came crashing down last night.

The same as she did every other day, Ruby got up, showered, brushed her hair back into a bun at the nape of her neck, and put on a pair of scrubs and her sensible clogs. Unlike other mornings, she didn't join Opal and Pearl at the kitchen table for breakfast. Today, she left the house and marched over to the clinic without a word to her sisters.

Dr. Colton put the stack of files in his hand down with a frown when she burst through the clinic door, letting it slam behind her.

"Morning, Ruby," he said cautiously.

"Morning," she grumbled, throwing her bag into the cubby behind the reception desk.

Dr. Colton tipped his head, studying her for a moment. "You want to talk about it?" he asked quietly.

"Not really, no."

He nodded slowly. "Alrighty then." He went over to the computer, his fingers flying over the keyboard for a second before he looked up at her with a sympathetic smile. "We have a light schedule today. I can call the trade school and see if they have someone from their medical assistant program who can come over and intern for the day. Why don't you take the day off? Or as many days as you need."

Ruby started to argue and then sank down into one of the chairs in the waiting room, burying her face in her hands. "I'm sorry," she said in a shaky voice. "This isn't very professional."

Dr. Colton pulled up a chair next to her and held her hand. "Ruby, I couldn't have revived this clinic without you. You came out of retirement, and you haven't missed a day's work since we reopened. I won't pry and ask what's going on, but you're more than a co-worker to me. I consider you a friend, and I hope you know I'm always here to listen."

"Thank you, honey." Ruby patted his hand. "Right now, I'm spinnin' like a top. When I get myself worked out, I'll tell you the story."

"I'll look forward to hearing it."

Ruby left the clinic, her footsteps faltering. She stood on the sidewalk, paralyzed for a moment after Dr. Colton shooed her out, unsure of what to do or where to go next. With heavy feet, she returned home once again, ignoring her sisters' hushed voices in the kitchen, and went straight to her room. If she wasn't going to work, she might as well get out of her scrubs.

She opened her dresser drawers with an angry grunt. "Frumpy. Ugly," she muttered, digging through her things. She finally settled on a pair of jeans, white t-shirt, and a navy cardigan. After tying the laces on her sneakers, she opened the door of her room, half expecting to find her sisters lurking in the hall.

The need for coffee outweighed her desire to avoid her sisters as she entered the kitchen, going straight to the coffee maker. She was waylaid when Pearl jumped up and came around the table to give her a hug. "Morning."

"Morning." Ruby patted Pearl on the back. Her eyes narrowed at Opal, who avoided her gaze and focused on stirring her coffee so hard the cream she put in was in danger of becoming butter.

"What are you doing back home? Shouldn't you be at work?" Opal frowned at her over a cup of coffee as she took a sip.

Ruby glared at her sister, refusing to answer. She had to accept that Opal didn't regret her actions and wasn't going to apologize. Like all siblings, they'd fought through the years, but Ruby had never intentionally hurt her sisters the way Opal crushed her hopes and dreams.

"How about I come by and take you to lunch today?" Pearl asked.

"I'm not going to work today."

Pearl's brow wrinkled.

Opal's head jerked up. "What are you going to do?"

"Whatever it is, it's none of your business."

Ruby shot Pearl a sad smile and turned away. Gathering her handbag, she walked out of the house and took a deep breath of the sweet morning air. She hesitated, looking up and down the street, unsure which way to go.

Her feet decided for her, and she found herself headed back toward the center of town.

The last drops of dew were evaporating as Ruby walked without a clear destination in mind, ending up in the park, her mind whirling. She picked a bench in a quiet corner of the park and sat down. "Ruby Anne Colton, you've been watching your life pass you by without participating in it. It's time for you to stop going along with what everyone else wants and do for yourself. So, what do you want?"

The familiar sights and sounds of Colton coming to life for another day surrounded her. Everything was the same as it was the day before, except for one important thing. She was different, and she couldn't go back to the way things were before. The cobwebs of her complacency disappeared as she viewed her world. She'd spent her entire existence in this sleepy town. Wide awake now, Ruby viewed her world clearly as the sun shone bright. She'd been living in limbo and too complacent for too damn long.

She was a grown-ass woman and free to do anything she wanted. The problem was she wasn't sure what that was. She wanted to be with Robert. But she wouldn't commit until she could show him and everyone else that she could stand on her own two feet. *You need to prove it to yourself too.* She pulled a pen and a scrap of paper out of her purse and started making a list:

- Place to live
- Car
- New clothes
- New hairstyle
- New Ruby

She tapped the pen on the piece of paper. Was that it? She'd need help figuring out the first step. The Catfish Café? No. Winters Hardware? No. Walker's Drug Store? Ruby snorted a laugh. Poor Emma Walker could barely take care of herself, let alone help her. She could talk to Dr. Colton, but… he might be a doctor, but that didn't mean Ruby wanted him all up in her business. No, she needed someone who would listen. Her gaze fell on the Barton Building. Dax Ellis was Robert's nephew and married to Ruby's cousin Callie. The former town bad boy had grown into a fine young man who'd left his wild days behind when he returned to his hometown. Sensible and smart, he was the right choice to help her with her list. She tucked the paper back into her bag and got up, heading toward Dax's office on the ground floor of the building.

Dax got up from his desk and greeted her with a kiss on the cheek. "Morning, Miss Ruby. What brings you my way today?"

"Good morning." She took a breath. "Dax, I—" Her eyes darted around the room. Even though they were alone, she still leaned in close. "I could use some help."

"What can I do for you?"

She handed him the piece of paper she'd scribbled the map of her new life on. "I've made a list, but I'm not sure where to start."

Dax's gaze flew to her face with surprise when he read the list. He opened and closed his mouth a few times, clearly trying to figure out how to respond.

"Let me explain," Ruby said with a heavy sigh. "All my life, I've been part of the Jewels. I've never really been on my own, and I need to do that before Robert and I—" She dropped her chin, feeling the heat rise in her cheeks.

Dax stared at her, tapping his lips with his finger before he finally said, "Uncle Robert and Opal are going to have a dyin' duck fit."

"If you don't want to help—"

"I didn't say that." Dax cut her off. "I'm trying to calculate how I'm going to handle the fallout," he said with a wry smile.

"I don't want you to catch any trouble."

"We both know I've gotten myself into much worse trouble back in the day. It's not the same, but I had to leave Colton and make my way in the world on my own before I figured out who I was. I admire your gumption, Miss Ruby." He tapped her list with his finger. "I can start with the first thing on the list," he said with a growing smile. "Come with me."

Ruby followed Dax to the third floor of the four-story Barton Building. The Beaux-Arts structure, once home to cotton traders in the early 1900s, had been transformed by Dax. He had converted the top two floors into apartments—four on the third floor, and one expansive unit occupying the entire fourth floor that Dax had occupied until he moved in with Callie.

"Isiah's moved up to my old apartment on the top floor since my brother and Dan moved into the train depot."

"I love that they've restored the old train depot and turned it into a distillery."

Dax nodded. "It's a smart move." He paused and smiled. "I'm selfish. What I'm even more happy about is that my brother decided to make Colton his home."

"When you find the people you love, you've found your home," Ruby said, patting Dax's arm.

Dax and his brother Reid had a rough childhood, growing up in a toxic environment, and it warmed Ruby's heart when Dax and his brother decided to return to their hometown and put down roots. The entire town was rooting for those boys, wanting them to find the happiness their parents denied them.

"I've got a new tenant moving in next week and someone else next month. Ashton Beaumont is occupying the other unit, and this is the one that's free," Dax explained as they continued upstairs. Stopping at one of the two doorways on one side of the hallway, he opened the door and stood back to let Ruby inside.

"It's just like the one Mae had before she and Jacob moved into their bungalow." Ruby's voice echoed in the empty room.

"All four units have the same open concept, with the exposed brick walls and pine floors."

The unit Dax let her into had grand arched windows like the rest of the building. The view from this unit overlooked the town hall, with a glimpse of one corner of the park. Cabinets along one wall and an island made up the small but workable kitchen space. Rustic pine floors with a warm honey finish glowed in the sunlight coming through the windows, bathing the room in golden light. The bathroom combined with the walk-in closet took up more space than her bedroom at home.

Home. She'd lived in the same place her entire life. Always with her sisters at her side.

"I'll take it."

Dax wrinkled his forehead. "Are you sure?"

Not really. The only thing she was sure about was the need to be on her own. "I'm sure."

"Do you want to hear what the rent is first?"

It didn't matter what amount Dax said. Her independence didn't have a price tag. She didn't have to worry. The rent was reasonable, and

Dax insisted she didn't have to sign a lease and could rent month-to-month.

"I can round up some of the guys to help you move your furniture in if you need," Dax offered.

Ruby frowned. "I don't really have any furniture. I suppose I could bring my bedroom set over. To be honest, I think I'd like to start fresh."

"Tell you what. I've got a jumble of furniture left over from previous tenants. It seemed like a waste to throw it away. I've been saving it in case anyone moving in needed anything." Dax took her down to the storage room on the second floor. "Mae left behind a full-sized bed frame," he said, pointing to the black metal, modern frame, completely different from the vintage carved wood bedroom Ruby had since high school. If she was going to start fresh, then she might as well try out a different style too.

When they finished, Ruby had selected couple of bar stools for the kitchen island, a small side table, and a loveseat as well as the bed.

"You can use the side table for a nightstand. If you get a couple of lamps and maybe a rug, you'll have enough for now."

Ruby nodded in agreement, apprehensions slowly being replaced with excitement.

"You can order a mattress and have it delivered by the end of the day."

They went back downstairs. With Dax's help, Ruby ordered a mattress, pillows, and new bedding. Everything would be delivered later that afternoon.

Ruby pulled out her pen and the list she'd made earlier. Crossing off the first thing on the list—place to live—she added towels, sheets, and dishes. The list had grown to an intimidating size quickly. That led her to the next thing on her list.

She gripped the paper in her hand. "I can't begin to tell you how much I appreciate your help. I hate to ask for more, but…." She pointed at the next item on her list. "Can you help me out with buying a new car?"

Dax paused before a slow smile spread over his face. "Well alright then. Let me give Callie a quick call and we'll head out."

Twenty minutes later they sat in Dax's truck, crossing over Mockingbird Bridge heading toward Greenwood.

"What kind of car are you thinking about, Miss Ruby?"

Ruby thought for a minute. "I want something fun."

"Fun can mean different things to different people."

"Maybe… maybe a convertible."

Dax nodded with a grin. "Got it."

Ruby took a deep breath. "Thank you, Dax."

He reached over and patted her hand. "I appreciate you trusting me with helping you spreading your wings."

"I was worried you might tell me I was being foolish."

"Everyone should know how to walk in their own footsteps before they walk alongside someone else's. I can sympathize with Uncle Robert's side of things too. I wanted to protect Callie, do everything to keep her safe. Wrap her up in bubble wrap if I could, but that's not how you love someone.

"No, it isn't, but I'm thankful you got to her in time when your mother—" Ruby sighed, shaking her head. "We all accepted that your mama was meaner than a wet panther, but none of us thought she'd gone so far off the deep end."

"No one did." Dax grimaced. "At the end of the day, I couldn't keep my mother from holding Callie at gunpoint. Dammit, Uncle Robert should have known better."

"It wasn't just Robert. My own sister, Opal, did something— unforgivable, interfering in my life." Ruby winced. "I never imagined she would do such a thing."

Concern clouded Dax's face. "I'm having a hard time wrapping my mind around the bond y'all have being broken. I don't want to stick my nose in when it's none of my business, but what did Opal do?"

Dax let out a low whistle when Ruby finished telling him about the letters her sister threw away. "You have every right to be madder than a wet hen."

"Thank you." Ruby appreciated Dax understanding and not dismissing her feelings.

The first two car lots they visited were a disaster. At the first one, the saleswoman was more interested in selling herself to Dax than selling Ruby a car. The sales agent at the second lot kept referring to her as the "little lady," and every time Ruby asked a question, he'd turn to Dax with his answer.

"Lord have mercy, is car shopping always this awful?" Ruby asked when they stopped for lunch.

"It is terrible, isn't it." Dax rolled his eyes.

After lunch they went to another big dealership. This time a young Black man with a charming smile greeted them, starting their visit on a positive note by asking "Which one of you is shopping today?" instead of assuming Dax was the customer the way the other two had.

The sales attendant's name was Jalen, and he asked Ruby thoughtful questions about what kind of car she was looking for. The convertible Mustang was a little too muscle car for her taste. The sleek German luxury convertible was beautiful, but….

"I said I wanted to spread my wings, but I'm not Icarus." Ruby chuckled, running her hand over the sparkling black exterior.

Jalen rubbed his hands together. "I think I have what you're looking for, Ms. Ruby." He took her over to another section of the car lot, and there it was.

Red, two-door, with a black ragtop.

"Oh my." Ruby leaned over the driver's side to run her hand over the smooth leather.

"The color is chili red, but I think this Mini Cooper convertible looks like ruby red to me. You said fun and not sensible—do you think this might fit the bill?"

Ruby glanced toward Dax to gauge his reaction. He'd walked around to the other side of the car and gave her a slight nod of approval.

She'd already decided to buy it before the test drive. Pulling back into the lot, she parked the car and turned to Jalen in the backseat. "How much of a discount will you give me if I pay cash?"

Jalen's smile grew into a grin. "Let's go inside and get you settled, Ms. Ruby."

Her hand shook a little as she signed the paperwork. It took a couple of hours going through all the fine print and calling the bank. She'd never spent so much money in her entire life. She'd never needed to before, and her bank account was more than healthy from living such a frugal lifestyle. Well, that was coming to a dramatic end today. Dax didn't interfere, but answered her questions and offered guidance when she asked for it.

She shook Jalen's hand and took the keys from him. Ruby walked toward her first new car—first car ever—with Dax. Before she got in, she gave him a hug. "Thank you," she said, fighting back tears.

"Miss Ruby, it's been an honor. I'll see you back in Colton. Don't you drive too fast," he said with a wink.

"I'm going to stop and pick up a few things on the way back, so it might be a minute. If it's all right with you, I'm going to spend the night at the apartment tonight."

"It's all yours now, of course it's okay. I'll take care of getting the furniture moved in for you."

Ruby gave him another hug with a peck on the cheek. "Thank you, sweetheart."

Her heart did a little flip-flop when she pressed the start button and her new car purred to life. When she finally arrived back in Colton, her little car was filled household supplies. She pulled up in front of the house she'd shared with her sisters and took a deep breath before she got out of the car and walked up the front stairs.

"Where have you been and what are you driving?" Opal pounced on her as soon as Ruby walked in the door.

Chapter Six

The time had passed when Opal could make demands.

"Where I've been and what I've been doing is none of your business." Ruby glared at her sister.

"Everybody's already saying you're moving into the Barton Building."

Ruby raised an eyebrow. "Everybody?"

"Mae's mama saw you driving out of town with Dax, so I went over to the library."

"Of course you did," Ruby muttered under her breath.

Opal pressed her mouth into a thin line, shooting Ruby a disapproving glare. There was a time when that glare would hold sway, but not anymore.

"You can't be serious about this. What will people think?"

"That I'm a grown-ass woman who's capable of living on her own."

"Quit being ugly," Opal spat out. "You can't leave."

Ruby took a deep, steadying breath. "Not yet, but as soon as I pack, then I'm leaving and I'm not coming back to this house."

Opal hesitated, and some of the vinegar left her voice when she started again. "You can't—"

"Why? Why can't I? Show me where the rules are that say the Jewels have to do everything together." Ruby took a breath. "Why should I follow made-up rules that you've imposed on us all these years? You picked up right where our parents left off. Where is it written in stone that I have to obey you when you don't respect me? You're not my mother, Opal, and you're not in charge of me."

That last part sounded petulant to her own ears, but Ruby was past caring at that point. Her hurt was taking charge over good sense. If Ruby thought her impassioned words would change her sister's point of view or earn an apology, Opal's reply was a disappointment.

"I did what I thought was best," Opal said with a slight lift of her chin and determination in her eyes.

Ruby threw up her hands with an exasperated groan and turned away, heading toward her room. She had one bag packed and halfway filled a second one when Pearl appeared, hovering in the doorway.

"So it's true." She shook her head. "Are you sure you want to do this?"

Ruby added another stack of shirts to her bag. "It's not a matter of want. I need to do this. Pearl, I can't stay here after what Opal did. I'm tired of people making decisions for me. Even Mama and Daddy, they wanted meet be a nurse. Opal wanted it too. They pushed and insisted that's what was right for me, so that's what I did. I love my job, but what would life have held for me if I'd been able to make my own choices?"

Pearl sighed and leaned against the doorjamb. "I didn't realize you felt that way. I wish you'd said something to me. I understand why you're angry. You have every right to be mad at Opal. I hate it when my sisters fight."

"I'm not angry about that. I'm not even angry at Opal. Well, I am, but I'm most upset with myself. I haven't spoken up for myself. I didn't fight hard enough for what I wanted. I'm not going to do that anymore. It's long past time for me to be on my own and figure out what I want and who I am."

"Can we meet up for coffee now and then?" Pearl asked in a shaky voice.

Ruby went over and gave her sister a hug. "Of course we can. I'm not going to the moon. The Barton Building is less than a mile away. It's got a rooftop deck we can sit on and drink sweet tea."

"It would be fun if it was the three of us gossiping on your rooftop," Pearl said with a hopeful look in her eye.

"That's up to her. When she can respect me, we can be friends again." Ruby eyed her sister for a moment. "What about you? Do the walls of this house ever seem like they're closing in on you?"

"I'm not like you, Ruby. You've always been brave, full of spirit. Opal is strong and determined and I'm… in the middle. Don't stare at me like that. I'm not some wilting wallflower either. You and Opal are like showy flowers in the garden, brightly colored. You're the ones who are picked to be the anchors of a bouquet, peonies and roses. I'm a filler flower like baby's breath or a daisy, happy to fill in the blank spaces when I need to."

Ruby put the sweater she was holding into her bag and sank down next to her sister. Perched on the edge of her bed, she wrapped her arm around Pearl's shoulder. "You are so much more than a filler flower."

"I know that. I was trying to explain that I'm happy where I'm planted. I'm not looking for more than what I've got."

"And I've always longed for more."

Pearl nodded with a sympathetic expression. She kept Ruby company while she finished packing. It didn't take long. Ruby realized she didn't have much she wanted to take with her. Everything seemed old and stale now. She was ready for fresh and new. The house would be here if she wanted to return; she had equal ownership with her sisters. If it turned out she wasn't satisfied with her newfound freedom, she could always come back. As she zipped her last suitcase closed, she knew in her heart she was leaving her childhood home for good.

"Are you sure that's all?" Pearl asked, looking at the clothes still hanging in Ruby's closet.

"I'm sure. You can borrow anything you want." Ruby picked up one bag and Pearl followed her out with the other. Opal was sitting on the porch when they came out.

"That thing isn't practical. I doubt it's even safe," Opal said, pointing at Ruby's new car. "How much money did you waste on that?"

"Opal," Pearl *tsk*ed, shaking her head.

"None of your business." Ruby kept moving, throwing her bag into the backseat of the Mini. Pearl was right behind her, adding the second bag to the first one.

Pearl jumped when the front door slammed. "I'll try to talk some sense into her."

"You're not your sister's keeper." Ruby gave her a hug. "Give me a few days to settle in and you'll come over for a visit. Okay?"

Pearl sniffed and stepped out of Ruby's embrace, wiping her eyes. "Okay."

Ruby got into her car and drove away before she gave in and started moving her things back in, unable to bear the hurt she was causing. But she'd been hurt too, and that wound wouldn't heal without time.

Less than five minutes later, she pulled up to the Barton Building, easing into one of the angled parking spaces out front before shutting off the engine. Ruby let out a frustrated groan, dropping her forehead to the steering wheel. It had already been a long day, and now Robert was waiting—sitting on the back of his truck, looking haggard and uncertain. She exhaled slowly, took a deep breath, and stepped out of the car.

"I like your car. The color's perfect for you."

"Are you going to tell me it's not practical too?" she grumbled.

"Nope," Robert said, dropping down from the back of his tailgate. He came toward her with slow hesitant steps. "I've been sending messages all day."

"And I sent you a message back saying I was busy and I'd call when I was done."

"I was wor—" He clamped his mouth shut.

"You were worried," Ruby finished for him.

"I can't help it." He came over and stood in front of her.

She reached up and brushed away the wrinkles on his forehead. "I understand. I don't like it, but I get it," she said, giving him a gentle kiss.

"But I'm gonna try to do better."

"Thank you."

Robert glanced toward the bags in the backseat of her car. "Can I help take your bags up?"

Striking out on her own and making a bid for independence was one thing, and Ruby might be stubborn but she wasn't going to turn down help when she was tired and hungry.

"That would be wonderful, thank you."

Robert hefted her suitcases out of the car while Ruby gathered her shopping bags. She admired the way he lifted her suitcases as if they weighed nothing, his muscles still strong and toned at his age.

Ruby took out her key when they reached her door, but Robert opened it before she could slip the key in the lock.

"Don't be mad," he said when she shot him a sharp look. "It wasn't me. The girls were over here all afternoon, buzzing around. Callie, Mae, Jo, Jasmine, and even Emma were all darting in and out whenever they had a break." Robert snorted a laugh. "Even Presley tried to help, but she was shooed out pretty quick when she kept suggesting adding more velvet and lace. Although I wouldn't mind a little lace." He winked.

Ruby's cheeks heated as she brushed past Robert into her apartment. "Well, I'll be," she said in an awed voice, taking in the scene. While she been gone, the furniture she'd picked out earlier was moved in. Crisp white sheets and a pretty pinwheel quilt in shades of pale green and blue covered the bed. The barstools were set at the island with two place settings and a votive candle on the countertop. A blue overstuffed armchair she didn't recognize sat by the window, with a blue-and-green throw pillow added and a floor lamp beside it. Another lamp sat on the small table next to it.

"They left a note." Robert tipped his head toward the kitchen island while he brought her suitcases in.

She put her bags down and went over to pick up the white envelope with her name on it. Opening it, she pulled out a sheaf of paper and read.

Dear Miss Ruby,

> *We think it's a wonderful thing that you are striking out on your own. (But please don't make Uncle Robert wait too long before you take care of his blue balls—Mae)*
>
> *We tried to do enough so you'll be comfortable until you can make this place your own. Emma stocked the bathroom with some homemade bath oil and soaps. Jo stocked the refrigerator, and Jasmine brought over the chair from Halcyon. The quilt is from me. Tillie sent over some catfish, greens, and pecan pie for dinner. She said to remind you, "Men spend half the time not knowing what they're talking about and the other half trying to figure out what they said wrong." (I'm not sure I agree but she made me promise to tell you.)*
>
> *We are well familiar by now with how stubborn and high-handed the Colton men can be, but it's because they love so fiercely. But they also need to learn they can't dictate!*

We love you,

Callie, Mae, Jo, Jasmine, Emma, and Presley
(even though she wasn't allowed to help)

Ruby held the card to her chest, blinking back tears. Darling girls, strong independent women. Here she was thinking she'd influenced them, and maybe she had, but now they were her role models.

"You okay, honey?" Robert asked, hovering at her side.

Ruby took a deep breath. "I am." She put the letter back in the envelope and set it on the counter where she'd found it and turned to Robert. "Would you like to stay for dinner?"

He shook his head slowly. "I would, but I think you should have the chance to spend your first night in your new place alone. You only invited me for dinner, but… well, I don't trust myself not to be able to leave."

Ruby wrapped her arms around Robert's waist and rested her cheek against his chest. "You're an amazing man, Robert Ellis, and I love you."

He lifted her chin with his finger and kissed her. "I love you too."

"It's Thursday. How about you give me one week? And then you'll come over for dinner and stay? We can still see each other. I can help you at the farmers' market this weekend, since I won't be helping my sisters."

Robert frowned. "I'm sorry, honey."

"It's not your fault. I—" Her voice broke. "I'm not ready to talk about what happened with Opal yet."

"You'll share when you're ready."

He kissed her, hesitant at first, but the spark that always connected them ignited quickly, and Ruby pressed herself against him as his hand snaked under the hem of her shirt. When he pulled away, leaving Ruby breathless, she tried to pull him back for more, but Robert shook his head and stepped back.

"You asked for a week, and that's what I'm going to give you."

The slight tremor in his voice gave her butterflies. It was a prideful thing, knowing he wanted her as much as she wanted him. He gave her another quick kiss and left before she could catch her breath.

"Well, shit," she muttered.

She'd bought herself some time for a reason. Ruby wanted to tackle the third item on her list. Robert's comment about Presley gave her an idea of how she could make it happen.

CHAPTER SEVEN

RUBY'S EYES fluttered open; she turned her head, taking in a new view, and marveled at how she could be only a mile from the house she grew up in, and yet everything could feel so different.

She smiled and stretched her arms over her head, reveling in waking up in her own apartment the morning after her bid for freedom. Yes, she was waking up alone, without Robert at her side, but that wouldn't be the case forever. She'd accomplished a lot in a short amount of time, but there were still things to check off the list she made.

The benefit of living next door to where you work was being able to take a few extra minutes to bask in bed before starting your day.

"How'd you sleep, Miss Ruby?" Dax asked when she came downstairs, ready to start her day.

"Like a baby," she said, giving him a peck on the cheek. "That's for you and for Callie. Thank you for everything you did for me yesterday."

Dax put his hand over his heart and bowed his head. "I meant what I said. It was an honor. You let us know if there's anything else you need."

"I think the rest is up to me now."

ROBERT WOKE up with a groan, looking at the familiar view outside his bedroom window.

He wanted to wallow in bed, but his crops weren't going to tend themselves. The field of corn he'd planted started out as part of his cover story. Moving back to Colton to live the simple life of a farmer. The field proved useful in other ways, mainly as a meeting place where local undercover operatives could relay information in person if necessary. He surprised himself, finding farming to be therapeutic. There was something about making something grow that gave him hope when the world challenged his spirit.

He reached over to the empty side of the bed he'd hoped would be occupied. There was no point in showering; he didn't have anyone to impress. He rolled out of bed with a grunt and shrugged on his overalls. With a mug full of the strongest coffee he could make, he walked across the road into his field. The corn was up to his shoulder in this section. He took a deep breath, inhaling the sweet green scent, and replayed what happened the night before in his head.

He'd messed up. Badly. If this had been an assignment for the military, he'd have been dead. "You're a damn fool, Robert Ellis," he muttered to himself.

"I don't think you're a fool. Maybe a little pigheaded sometimes, but never foolish."

Robert whirled around to find his nephew's wife, Callie, with their baby daughter, Amanda, on her hip with a sympathetic smile on her face.

"Well, if it isn't the two most beautiful women in the world," he murmured. He set his coffee down and plucked Amanda from her mother's arms when her chubby little hands reached out for him.

Callie raised an eyebrow. "Better not let Ruby hear you say that."

Robert chuckled, lifting Amanda high into the air, relishing the baby giggles he received. "She'll understand."

"I hope she's looking forward to being a grandma."

Robert swallowed past the lump in his throat, remembering the night Callie and Dax sat him down and asked if he'd be willing to take on the role of grandfather.

"You've been more than an uncle to me for a long time now." Dax held Callie's hand in his. "We want you to be Amanda's Grandpa Robert.

"You know my parents aren't going to be around. But you've always been here for us," Callie said, smiling down at their newborn daughter before looking at Robert with love and hope in her eyes. "Amanda is going to need her grandpa Robert to teach her all the things we can't."

"What do you think?" Dax said.

Robert would treasure the memory of that moment until his dying day. Callie and Dax would never understand the precious gift they gave him that night. Callie's question was her way of letting him know Ruby was included and welcome in the role of grandma. He couldn't help the brief pang of grief in his heart. His brother should have been the one hearing his granddaughter's giggles. His sister-in-law should have celebrated each milestone as the months passed by. His brother died before he had a chance to know his sons as the incredible men they turned out to be. His sister-in-law was too blinded by hate to love her children the way they deserved to be loved. They left Robert behind to clean up their mess and take care of their family legacy.

"We haven't had the chance to talk about it yet, but I know she'll be tickled pink," he murmured. He brushed his thumb over his granddaughter's rosy cheek. She had her mama's golden tan skin and her daddy's dark brown eyes. A sweet little girl he would do anything to keep safe.

"Robert?" Callie put her hand on his arm, searching his face. "What's got you thinking so hard?"

"Y'all would say something if I got too overprotective, wouldn't you?" he blurted out.

Callie's eyes widened with understanding. "That's what happened with Ruby, isn't it?"

"It started a long time ago, from the first time I realized she was in danger. A group of boys were following her home, and she didn't even know it." He stopped there, seeing Callie wince. She'd faced danger of her own when his sister-in-law, Dax's mama Dorothy, attacked her. Callie didn't need to hear the details. She could guess what those boys intended without needing to be told.

She sighed and patted his arm. "You and Dax could give Captain America a run for his money. You both want to save the world so badly. The two of you are peas in a pod." She hesitated, then blew out a shaky breath. "Don't take this the wrong way, but there's a fine line between being a savior and a dictator. Do you know what I think the difference is?"

Robert shook his head, biting the inside of his cheek as he waited for her answer.

"A savior—someone who truly wants to help—seeks guidance. They value and respect other viewpoints." Determination flared in her eyes. "And they don't make life-altering decisions for someone else without their say."

If they'd been boxing, Callie just delivered the knockout punch.

He leaned over and kissed her forehead. "You're a formidable woman. I pity anyone who underestimates you."

"I don't know the details, and I'm not asking for them. Whatever decision you made, I'm sure you meant well." She patted his chest. "It came from your heart. But you'll lose your second chance if you keep thinking you're the only one who knows what's best."

"You're absolutely right."

Callie picked up his coffee cup and looped her arm through his. "Come on, let's show Amanda how to collect eggs, and then you can make us an omelet."

"You don't have to get to the library?"

"I've got a solid group of volunteers. Mr. Lawrence is on duty this morning. Besides, you're family, and when your family needs you," she shrugged, "you show up."

A morning spent with Callie and his granddaughter was exactly what the doctor ordered. As they drove away, he stood in the driveway waving goodbye, feeling more optimistic that everything would turn out well in the end.

He had another visitor not long after Callie and Amanda left. He came out of the barn and stopped in surprise to see Rhett Colton with Rebel at his side sitting on the top step of his front porch.

"When did y'all get here? I didn't hear you pull up."

"Not long, maybe ten minutes ago. Didn't want to disturb you."

Robert stood in front of Rhett, studying the pained expression on his face.

"Stopping by isn't troubling me, son. I'm always happy to see you," he said quietly.

Rhett dropped his chin, his long blond hair hiding his expression.

"What brings you by?" Robert gently prodded.

Rhett's head jerked up. His blue eyes were bright with unshed tears. "I need help," he said in a low, strained voice.

Robert sat down on the step next to Rhett. "What can I help with, son?"

With quiet, halting words, Rhett told Robert about the argument he had with Jasmine and the ultimatum she'd given him. He listened without revealing any of what he'd overheard Jasmine telling Ruby when Robert saw them in the park.

"I want to show Jasmine I can ask for help. I don't want to keep secrets from her. I want to share everything, the good and the bad, because I know—" His voice broke. "I want to believe she'll love me anyway." Rhett turned to him. "Jasmine won't hate me." The question, a plea, and a prayer were clear in Rhett's voice.

Robert grabbed Rhett's hand and gave it a firm squeeze—a silent reassurance. He understood that sometimes, words weren't necessary.

He had spent countless moments with the men under his command like this, where comfort wasn't about what was said but about simply being there. He waited patiently until Rhett was ready.

Eventually, Rhett drew a deep breath and shared his plan to fix up his cabin. "Will you come out and help me?" he finished.

"Ain't no way I won't be there. I'm proud of you, Rhett." He let go of Rhett's hand and slapped his knee. "Hell, I could learn a thing or two from you."

Rhett shook his head. "I doubt that."

"None of us are perfect, Rhett. If you ain't got no problems, then you must be dead. Part of living is learning. You reminded me of that today. Thank you."

Rhett nodded, his hair falling forward again, a curtain between him and the world. Between him and his feelings. Robert didn't do anything to stop him; he understood. Rhett was still battling the ghosts of his past, the scars of severe PTSD left from his time undercover with the Klan. He had sacrificed his safety, his body, and pieces of his soul in service to his country.

Robert clenched his jaw, forcing down the rage that simmered beneath the surface. He hated what had been done to Rhett. Hated that the cost of his loyalty had been paid in blood and nightmares. It was an unspoken truth between them that the work they had both dedicated their lives to was unraveling. A new wave of so-called patriots had taken power, wrapping themselves in the American flag while tearing apart everything it was supposed to stand for.

After a period of quiet contemplation, their conversation turned to more mundane topics. What supplies would Rhett need for his projects at the cabin? How far did Robert think the Shuckers were going to go this season? Would they ever get a new ballpark? Had he heard Lucas Monroe's latest single? They talked about anything that made life feel normal.

With a long hug and reassurances he'd be at Rhett's place early on Saturday, Robert said goodbye later that afternoon.

Robert walked into the Buckthorn that evening, his eyes lighting up seeing Ruby sitting at the bar talking to Reid.

He took off his Biloxi Shuckers ballcap. "Excuse me, miss, may I buy you a drink?"

Ruby patted the stool next to her. "I don't accept drinks from strange gentlemen, but in this case, I'll make an exception," she said with a teasing smile.

Robert leaned in and kissed her on the cheek as he sat down, inhaling the intoxicating combination of whiskey and roses on her warm skin. "What brings you out here tonight?"

Ruby looked over her shoulder. "I've never been here by myself before." She turned back to him with a hint of mischief in her eyes. "I'm being bold and trying new things. Plus, I figured I might run into you here."

"Have you talked to Opal since—"

"Since I ran away?" Ruby chuckled, lifting her glass to her lips.

Robert leaned closer. "Damn, that was sexy the way your smile curves over the rim of your glass, and your eyes sparkle with mischief."

His head jerked up at someone clearing their throat and found Reid watching them with a smirk. "Can I get you something to drink, Uncle Robert?"

"I'll have what she's having," he said with a quick wink in Ruby's direction.

Ruby set her glass down, turning it between her fingers. "I haven't been back to the house or talked to my sister since I moved out."

"I'm sorry, Ruby, I truly am. I never wanted to come between you.

"You didn't. I've been feeling suffocated by Opal for a while now. Your letters, well, she went too far." Her voice trembled with a mixture of anger and anguish. "She threw them away. I didn't write you back because I never saw your letters. I didn't know where to write to you. Opal kept us apart. I can forgive a lot, but I can't forgive that."

Robert took a shallow breath. "She did what?"

Ruby put her hand over his, looking him directly in the eyes. "She threw away your letters, Robert."

"Why?"

"She said she was trying to protect me. It's no excuse. She didn't have the right to dictate my life for me. She made herself responsible for me when I never asked her to."

Shit. How could he be angry with Opal when she had the same motives he did? They'd both wanted to keep Ruby safe because they both loved her. Ruby wasn't the only person he tried to protect out of love.

"Don't get me wrong, I'm fighting not to drive over right now and give her a piece of my mind. I'm mad as hell, but I understand. I always felt responsible for my brother."

"Dad always talked about how much he admired you, Uncle Robert." Reid returned, refilling Ruby's glass. Thankfully, he'd only heard his last remark.

"I should have made more of an effort to see him."

"He understood. We talked about it," Ruby said quietly. Reid and Robert both drew back with twin looks of surprise. "He came to see me after you left," Ruby confessed. "He wanted me to know he was sorry things didn't work out the way we planned. He was so proud of you, but he also knew what you were giving up. The sacrifices you would be making. He accepted you wouldn't be around much anymore, and he hoped I understood too."

"I had no idea," Robert said with a tremor in his voice.

Reid reached for Robert's arm. "I'm learning to accept we'll never dig up all the secrets this family has buried." Robert glanced at Ruby. His wasn't the only family who had secrets.

"Thanks for sharing your memory with us," Reid said.

"I should have told you sooner,"

Robert reached for her hand. "We haven't exactly had much time, have we?"

"Life is a whirlwind, isn't it?"

"I'd say in our case, tornado is a better description," Robert said with a wry smile.

"Well, at least we know we'll all weather the storm together."

Reid smiled and leaned across the counter to give Ruby a kiss on the cheek. "Glad to have you under my umbrella any time." Two men came in and Reid stiffened, eyeing them warily.

Robert watched them as they took a seat at one of the picnic tables, frowning at the peanut shells under their feet. They tried to appear casual in their khakis and the sleeves on their Oxford shirts rolled up. To Robert, they stuck out like a sore thumb, and based on Reid's expression, he thought the same thing. The words of warning Primus gave him replayed in his head. He wasn't even dead yet, and the sharks were already sniffing around.

"You okay, son?" Robert asked.

Ruby tightened her grip on Robert's hand as they watched Reid approach the two men. Dan came out of the back room. The minute he saw what was happening, he made a beeline for Reid's side.

"Robert, what's going on?"

"Nothing you need to worry about," he said without thinking.

Ruby let out a low hiss, her grip on his hand growing painfully tight.

Robert's gaze flew to her, startled at the fire in her eyes. He instantly realized what he'd done. He tipped his head toward the men. "Folks are lining up trying to get their hands on Primus's business. They want his recipes."

Ruby started to get off her stool with a scowl. Before she could head over to Reid, Robert snagged her around the waist, holding her against his side. "Hold on there, mama bear. The boys are taking care of it. Watch."

Sure enough, Dan put his hand on Reid's lower back, a silent show of support as Reid leaned forward, saying something out of earshot to the men. Reid straightened, and the men got up, heading toward the exit as if a bobcat was hot on their tail. Dan put his arm around Reid, saying something that had Reid's lips curling into a smile. Everything Dan said to him about wanting Reid to be able to handle things on his own came rushing back to Robert.

He cupped Ruby's cheek. "I owe you an apology. My instincts kicked in just now. I was trying to protect you when I said you didn't have anything to worry about. I'm trying to do better. Can you be patient with me?"

Ruby closed her eyes and nodded. Robert relaxed. That was a close call. He had to do better for both their sakes.

Robert let Ruby go when Reid and Dan returned.

"Everything okay, honey?" Ruby asked Reid.

Reid smirked. "Everything is fine, Miss Ruby. Just had to take out the trash."

"They were pretending to be fans, asking about Primus, wanting to know if they could meet him."

"They didn't look like fans, more like executives to me," Robert observed.

"They weren't going to fool anyone around here," Dan agreed.

"Has this happened often?" Ruby asked.

"A few times."

Dan put his hand on Reid's shoulder, looking at him with pride. "Reid can handle it. They come in here all cocky and sure of themselves, and they leave with their tails between their legs."

"Primus warned me this was gonna happen, but I'm surprised at how they walked in here bold as brass," Robert said.

Reid and Dan exchanged a glance. "We're not," they said in unison.

"Uh-oh, y'all are finishing each other's sentences already," Ruby teased.

Reid waggled his finger at them. "Just wait. You're next."

"I hope so," Robert said under his breath.

Chapter Eight

Ruby focused on entering Dr. Colton's chart notes after her unexpected day off and didn't spot Rhett Colton hovering in the doorway of the clinic right away. His eyes darted around the empty waiting room, wary and uncertain. His trusted companion, Rebel, sat at his side, pressing himself against Rhett's leg. That dog was a saving grace and kept Rhett grounded, offering comfort and unconditional love.

Ruby didn't blame the young man for being so cagy. That poor boy had been through hell and back. Working undercover for the FBI embedded with the Klan did a lot of damage to Rhett. He'd sacrificed a lot to keep Colton safe, and the haunted shadow of exhaustion etched on his face revealed the heavy price he paid.

"Come on in, Rhett." Ruby waved him in. "You picked a good time to stop by. It's quiet today," she said gently, letting him know he would be safe. Rhett didn't do well in crowds, and some folks in town still had a hard time believing he wasn't the evil persona he'd had to present to the world.

He hesitated, glancing down at Rebel. "You sure it's okay?"

"Of course." Ruby opened a drawer behind the counter and pulled out a dog treat. "Do you have an appointment? I didn't see your name on the schedule," she said, coming out from behind the counter to pat Rebel on the head and offer him the treat.

"No, I came by to talk to Dylan, I mean Doctor Colton, and…." He took a deep breath. "I suppose I could ask you while I'm here," he said, his voice low and strained.

Ruby would never say it, but the man appeared like he'd been through the wringer—his clothes rumpled, dark circles under his eyes, and his streaky blond hair pulled back in a messy bun.

"What did you want to ask, honey?"

"The thing is…," Rhett said in a quiet, shaky voice. He cleared his throat. "The thing is, I need to ask for help." He winced and then, in a strong, clear voice without any hesitation, said, "I need your help."

Based on her conversation with Jasmine, Ruby instantly knew what Rhett was trying to do, and her heart went out to him.

Before she had a chance to respond, Dr. Colton came out with Primus Wallace. Reid and Dan brought him in that morning, frantic with worry after he'd had a particularly bad night. The older man was supported on each arm by Dan and Reid, both with grim expressions.

Rhett's face paled when he saw them. He rushed forward. "Mr. Wallace, Primus, are you okay?"

"I'm as good as can be," Primus said, his voice weak. The gray pallor beneath his dark brown skin made the silver strands in his hair stand out even more. The skin on his hand, that held Reid's in a tight grip, was paper-thin. "Ain't nothing wrong with me other than these two worrying over me too much." The complaint came with an affectionate nudge toward Reid.

"Rhett, it's been a while," Dr Colton said, holding out his hand.

Rhett shook it with a tight smile. "I don't have an appointment or anything. I—" He swallowed. Ruby gave him an encouraging pat on the shoulder, understanding how hard it was for him to speak up. "I came by to ask for your help."

Watching the two together, Rhett and Dylan, Ruby remembered they were cousins. Seeing them side-by-side, they were clearly kin. They shared the same blond hair and blue eyes and facial features, although Dylan kept his hair neatly trimmed and his face shaved. Trying to untangle the roots of the Colton family tree was as difficult as trying to untangle yarn a cat had its way with. Best Ruby could figure, Rhett and Dylan were second or third cousins. Robert and the Ellises were also in the mix somewhere. Ruby's Colton roots were as deep and tangled, connecting her to Callie's and Mae's families. All of them made up the colorful patchwork that was the town of Colton, Mississippi.

"If you'll excuse us, we want to take Primus home," Reid said.

They all said their goodbyes, and Dan and Reid ushered Primus out the door.

Rhett turned to his cousin, his forehead wrinkled. "He's not okay, is he?"

"I'm sorry I can't disclose anything, HIPPA laws and all," Dylan said as he slowly shook his head, the gesture speaking volumes.

Rhett blanched, and Ruby put her arm around him as Rebel whined, pressing against his side. "It's okay, honey." Rhett blinked rapidly and took a steadying breath.

"Rhett, why don't you tell us what you need help with," Ruby gently encouraged.

Of course, Dylan went into doctor mode, his eyes narrowing as he looked Rhett over. "Are you sick? Did you hurt yourself when—"

"No, I'm fine. Larry didn't hurt me."

"Damn fool," Ruby muttered under her breath. Rhett's cousin Larry was part of the White supremacist group Rhett was working undercover to take down. Larry viewed Rhett as the enemy, and his hatred had driven him into a reckless act. Thankfully, the incident ended without anyone being harmed, and Larry was now behind bars.

"I have work I need to do around the cabin and I, I'm putting together a kind of work party, I guess, this Saturday. Miss Ruby, I was hoping you and the Jewels could help plant some flowers or something, but—" He grimaced. "I heard y'all had a falling-out, so I understand if you didn't want to."

"Don't you worry about the Jewels. When someone you care about asks for help, you put your own troubles aside. We'll be there."

Rhett exhaled. "Thank you."

Dylan clapped him on the back. "Count me in."

"I appreciate it."

As soon as Rhett said his goodbyes and left, Dylan glanced at Ruby with a raised eyebrow. "What do you think that was about?"

"I think he's trying to win someone's heart."

"He deserves to find someone he can be happy with after everything he's been through."

"What about you, Dr. Colton? Is there someone you've met who can win your heart?"

Dylan folded his arms over his chest and leveled Ruby with a resigned look. "I think I have enough on my plate getting the clinic up and running again."

Dylan moving to Colton was a godsend for the town. Without a clinic, folks had to drive over an hour away to receive basic medical treatment. "You've done a fine job, Doctor. Everyone in town appreciates you moving down from up north."

"I couldn't have done it if you hadn't agreed to come on board and help out." He paused. "Will you be willing to stay on after you and Robert… well, whatever your plans are?" He shrugged, looking slightly embarrassed.

Ruby held her hand up. "I have no plans to go anywhere with anybody right now. I'm happy to stay on here with you for as long as you need the help."

Dylan grinned. "I'll keep you as long as I can have you. You're a wonderful nurse, Ruby. And I know it's none of my business, but I support your bid for independence. I think everyone should run away from home at least once."

Ruby snorted a laugh. "I didn't think of it as running away from home, but that is kind of what I did." She sobered. "It won't be for long. I plan on having the life I always wanted with Robert. I want a little bit of time on my own first."

Another patient came in, and in a blink the day went by. Ruby was thankful for the distraction. Back in her apartment, Ruby debated walking over to talk to Pearl and plan on what plants they could take to Rhett's. Seeing Pearl would mean facing Opal again, though, and Ruby wasn't ready for another confrontation with her sister. Instead, she sent Pearl a text inviting her over.

Half an hour later, Pearl buzzed to be let in. Ruby cracked her door open before pulling a bottle of white wine out of the refrigerator and opening it. A knock on the door announced Pearl's arrival, and she poked her head inside.

"Come on in," Ruby called out.

Pearl smiled, looking around the apartment. "Wow, you've already got this place fixed up. Where did the furniture come from?"

"Dax had some pieces in storage I could use. I didn't want to buy much since I'm not sure how long I'll be staying."

She ignored Pearl's raised eyebrow and stood by while her sister explored the apartment. Pearl wandered over to the windows and peered out. "You have a nice view of the town hall," she commented.

"And a little bit of the park. The rooftop deck has an even better view. You can see the whole town square from there. Want to go up?"

"Sure."

Ruby grabbed the bottle of wine and two glasses. "You can bring the cheese and crackers," she said, tipping her head toward the plate she'd set out on the counter.

Pearl followed her up to the deck. She set the plate down on the little side table between two rocking chairs and moved toward the railing surrounding the rooftop, looking over the edge. "It's like being up in a bird's nest."

"It is. I expect I'll be taking most of my meals up here when I can. It's so pretty, and the awning Jacob Winters built provides enough shade when it's so hot."

The sun was starting to set, and Pearl let out a little gasp when the market lights strung across the deck came on. "Oh, how pretty!"

"Isn't it lovely?" Ruby said, pouring two glasses of wine and handing one to her sister.

"Have you brought Robert up here yet?" Pearl asked, waggling her eyebrows.

"I've only been here a couple of days, and no, he hasn't come up here yet. But I expect in time he will."

"Is he as upset about you moving out on your own as Opal is?"

Ruby took a sip of her wine, contemplating Pearl's question. "More disappointed than upset. He… he was looking forward to us being together."

Pearl's mouth dropped open. "You mean you haven't?"

Ruby shook her head.

"Heavens to Betsy!" Pearl exclaimed.

"Don't. I'm already uneasy about… everything as it is."

Pearl set her glass down and put her arm around Ruby's shoulder. "We're well past the shy young virgin stage. You haven't gone on many dates over the years. And there's—"

"Please don't bring up Jerome. I'm not proud of how I led him on."

"You didn't lead him on," Pearl scoffed. "You were trying to move on with your life when you thought Robert wasn't answering any of your letters. It was a natural thing anyone in your position would have done."

"Getting engaged to someone I didn't love wasn't the right cure for heartache." Ruby sighed. Her moment of weakness all those years ago still hurt. She'd tried to love Jerome, the young man she'd met when she was at nursing school. They were both students at Alcorn State. Jerome was studying to be an engineer, and he'd tried to sweep Ruby off her feet.

Everyone loved him, including her parents and Opal. Over and over, they pointed out how he was handsome and polite, with the right drive, ambition, and temperament. And the most important thing, he was the right color. Her parents made no secret of the fact that they'd much rather Ruby give her heart away to a Black man and not Robert Ellis. "I hurt Jerome when I broke off our engagement, and I'll always regret that I wasn't honest enough with myself and how much it hurt him."

"We all have regrets when it comes to the choices we made with our hearts."

Ruby looked at her sister, realizing what she said didn't only apply to her. "I never thought of you as having regrets."

Pearl sighed. "I have my fair share."

"Do you want to talk about it?"

Pearl gave Ruby's shoulder a squeeze. "Not particularly. Someday maybe… but not today."

Ruby picked up her wine again and took a big sip. "Rhett Colton came by today and asked for help. He's having a work party over at his place on Saturday and I told him the Jewels would be there."

"Well, I'll be. I'm surprised on both fronts. You being willing to work alongside Opal and Rhett coming in and asking for help."

"I'll work alongside Opal because Rhett's struggle is more important than my fight with my overbearing mule of a sister."

Pearl *tsk*ed with a frown.

"Well, she is and I'm not taking it back. Now, let's figure out what plants we're going to take over to Rhett's. We've got some daylilies in the garden we can divide."

"A camellia could be nice."

"Roses," they both said at the same time and then broke out into laughter.

And as simple as that, they were back to the way they'd always been, finishing each other's sentences and knowing what the other was thinking. Ruby still felt a heaviness in her heart, though. Without Opal, the moment felt incomplete.

"Do you think Opal will ever come around?" Ruby asked.

"I think she already has. She's too stubborn to admit it."

"I never thought she could be so cruel."

" I still can't believe what she did." Pearl shook her head with a scowl. "She had no right to throw away your letters. Opal knows she owes you an apology."

Ruby bumped Pearl's shoulder. "When has our sister ever apologized for anything?"

"She loves you, so she will."

"She needs to accept I'm not going to be the person she thinks I should be."

"You're right." Pearl studied her with a worried expression. "Is that the same problem you're having with Robert? Is he wanting you to change somehow?"

"Yes and no. He doesn't want me to change. But he and Opal, the two of them are so damn overprotective. Both of them need to know their job isn't to protect me. I don't want that stifling kind of love. Would you?"

"No," Pearl sighed. "I suppose not. I'm also not a risk-taker like you are."

"I don't think of myself as a risk-taker."

"Not that you're going to go skydiving or take that new car of yours to the racetrack. Not that kind of adventuring. I'm talking about being willing to run away with Robert, to leave Colton if that's what it took to follow your heart." Pearl looked out over the park with a wistful smile. "I've never wanted to leave. I'd always hoped to find someone who would be content to stay. I don't want to take risks, but I do want to be carefree and not have to worry about what anyone else thinks. I don't want him to be so serious about keeping up appearances."

Ruby did a double-take. Pearl's comment sounded a little too specific. But if she didn't want Opal interfering in her love life, she shouldn't go around butting into Pearl's or anyone else's.

Pearl finished her wine and stood up. "I'd best be getting home." She gave Ruby a hug. "I'll see you at Rhett's on Saturday."

Ruby walked Pearl to her car and said goodbye. She stood on the sidewalk and watched Pearl's taillights disappear into the distance. What would happen on Saturday? Would Opal behave herself, be nice to Robert, apologize to her for what she'd done?

Slowly climbing the stairs back to the apartment that Ruby had already come to cherish as her refuge, a million questions ran through her mind, all of them circling back to: how did she put the past behind her and find a way forward?

Chapter Nine

Robert looked around at the family and members of the community who'd gathered to help Rhett. He might still struggle to believe it, but the people who showed up were more than folks who wanted to help out. Rhett had friends now and family who loved him. "Look what you did here, Rhett. This is more than trying to make things right with Jasmine. You've brought a community together. This is what Colton is all about. We take care of each other. People are happy to come out to support folks who ask when the time comes. I hope you'll keep asking for help when you need it."

Rhett looked at him with a mixture of hope and fear. "If I can't show Jasmine—if I can't prove to her that I can love her, that I'm not defined by this…." He winced as he reached behind his back. "Then I'm going to need all the help I can get, because I won't know how to go on."

Robert set his hands on Rhett's shoulders. He looked like a younger version of himself; their eyes may have been different colors, but they had the same crinkles at the corners that indicated they were probably related in the tangled roots of their family trees. Even the mixture of pain and regret in those eyes was familiar. If there was any way he could help Rhett avoid making some of the same mistakes he'd made, Robert was going to do it. "Son, I waited over forty years for the love of my life. I know what loss and longing are, better than most. You think you have obstacles keeping you apart, but I'm telling you now, I've seen the way Jasmine looks at you and the love in her eyes." Robert looked around at the folks gathering at Rhett's cabin, the place already bustling with activity. "When Jasmine gets here and takes this all in…. Well, it won't be long before the two of you are taking your vows under the gazebo."

Rhett dropped his chin to his chest. "Thank you."

"Come on now, let's get to work."

Robert turned in time to catch sight of Ruby's little red car zipping down the long drive toward Rhett's cabin. He wanted to run to meet her when she pulled in, but he was too damn old for running. He should follow Rhett's example and prove he could change, and that meant not hovering.

He didn't go over and offer to help Ruby unload the plants from her car. He kept his focus on helping his cousin Rhett, the one who actually needed the help. At the same time, he kept his eye on Ruby as she furiously dug in the dirt while she argued with her sisters. That wasn't entirely true; most of the arguing was between Ruby and Opal, with Pearl trying to play peacemaker. Watching the three of them, Robert felt a pang of empathy for anyone who fate had decided to assign the role of middle child.

He stayed away most of the afternoon, until Tillie called for lunch. Robert sidled up to Ruby as she loaded her plate from the trays and platters of food piled on a long table in the front yard. Her skin glowed from a morning working in the garden, and she had her hair piled on top of her head with a few curls escaping to frame her face. When he leaned closer, the scent of sunshine, earth, and flowers on her skin went straight to his groin, making him feel like he was a teenager again.

"Would it be okay to sit with you at lunch?" he asked.

She smiled with all her love for him reflected in her eyes. That never failed to make him weak in the knees. "Of course, Robert. You don't have to ask."

Robert glanced to where Opal was glaring at them from the other end of the table. "Are you sure about that?"

"Those daggers are for me. We're still locked at the horns." She sighed. "I'm afraid that's the way it's going to stay until she apologizes."

They carried their plates over to the porch steps and sat down. Robert couldn't resist pressing his thigh against Ruby's. She looked down at where their bodies joined, a bloom of pink appearing on her cheeks that tempted Robert to lean in and kiss the spot.

"How have you been doing?" he asked.

Ruby poked at the food on her plate. "Good and bad, I guess. Lately my feelings are all over the place."

"Understandable. I've been the same way.

"I'm sorry," Ruby sighed.

"Don't be. You're not doing anything wrong. None of this mess is your fault. I'm trying to give you space but I'm—I only got that one chance to hold you in my arms and kiss you and I'm—well, if I'm being honest, I'm itching for more time with you."

She leaned into him and rested her head on his shoulder. "I'm not… young anymore. I have a few more dips and lumps than I used to."

"And I don't?"

"It's different for men."

"In some ways, yes, but our bits wrinkle and sag too."

Ruby put her hand on his knee and squeezed. "I like your wrinkly bits."

"And I like yours." He kissed her temple. "When you're naked in our bed, I'm gonna love every wrinkle, dip, and lump because they're yours. They're a part of you, and I love all of you, Ruby. Inside and out. So will you let me love you?"

Ruby pulled back, frowning at him. "Robert, it's not a question of letting you love me. I've always loved you. I need to make sure I love myself as much."

He grasped her chin. "When did you stop loving yourself?"

Her eyes filled with tears. "A long time ago," she said in a shaky whisper.

"Uncle Robert." He jerked his head up. Dax, Reid, and Dan all waved him over toward the site of the new barn.

A grunt of frustration escaped. Couldn't those damn fools see he was with his woman?

Ruby gave him a gentle shove. "Go help the boys."

He got up and pressed a kiss to her forehead. He walked toward the barn, scarfing down the rest of his lunch. Now that he'd had a chance to talk to Ruby, he could breathe a little easier, but they still had a long way to go.

RUBY'S EYES followed Robert as he headed toward his nephews with a sense of calm and certainty she hadn't had in the last few days. They'd needed to talk. Some of the tension she'd been feeling drained out of her. They were as solid now as they were back in the day. She could share her hopes and fears with Robert, and he'd listen. He always did; it was another one of the many reasons she fell in love with him.

A hummingbird flew up in front of her, its little wings fluttering in a blur. It cocked its little head, looking at her.

"I'm no flower," she said and pointed toward the deep pink begonias she'd planted with her sisters.

The little bird with its iridescent green feathers and bright red breast hovered for another minute, blinking at her before it darted away. She'd been honest with Robert about her feelings, but not how she really perceived herself. Or how she saw herself now, after….

The memory of the day she overheard the Musgrove sisters in the Piggly Wiggly washed over her as if it happened yesterday and not three weeks ago. She'd stopped her buggy in the middle of the aisle when she heard them. She should have kept going, but instead, she wheeled her buggy closer and carefully shifted a stack of baked beans to catch a glimpse of the two sisters gossiping as they picked through a bin of green beans in the produce section.

"I can't believe that Ruby Colton thinks she's going to be able to keep a man like Robert Ellis interested, dressing herself like she's doin' some kind of reenactment from the pioneer days."

"Good gravy, if I see another one of those mock-neck long sleeve shirts."

"Ugh, and those print ones are gawd-awful."

"And that hair. Plastered against her head with that bun. And she's probably wearing granny panties to boot. What's Robert going to think when he sees that?"

The two women tittered as she stood listening to Marsha and her sister Roberta Musgrove ridicule her clothes and appearance. She pressed her hand to her mouth, biting back a sob. The Musgrove sisters were saying everything she'd been thinking but was afraid to admit.

"Ruby, what's got you so lost and far away."

"What did that man do to you now?"

Opal and Pearl's voices pulled Ruby from her memory. She looked down at where her fingers dug into the dirt, crushing one of the begonias she'd planted, and then up to find her sisters standing at the bottom of the steps, Pearl with concern in her eyes and Opal with her usual disapproving scowl on her face.

Ruby stood up, brushing the dirt from her hands. Rushing past her sisters, she went to another patch of ground in front of the cabin they'd been working on before lunch and started digging in the dirt with gusto.

"Ruby?" Pearl dropped down onto her knees next to her.

"I don't have to tell you everything," Ruby huffed, eyeing Opal standing over her. "I don't need your help or your opinions. We don't always have to be 'the Jewels,' saying and thinking the same thing all the time." She stood up and dusted her hands off on her baggy jeans. Looking down at them made her even more angry and frustrated. She surveyed the work they'd done so far and nodded. A pink camellia bush was planted on the corner, with azaleas under the window and a climbing rose bush by the stairs. Its dark pink blooms would climb up the porch post and eventually frame the front door. Pink and red begonias provided the finishing touch. On the other side of the front stairs were more azaleas and begonias. "I'm done for the day," she declared.

Ruby gave Pearl a quick hug and said goodbye. Pressing her lips into a thin line, she walked past Opal without a word. Bickering all day over the flowers, how deep to dig the holes, how far apart to plant the begonias, and whether the azaleas should be staggered or in a straight line—it all wore her down. None of mattered, and it wasn't about the flowers. The real fight was over who was in charge. Ruby marched toward the other side of the cabin, where Robert and Rhett were working on the roof.

"Miss Ruby, the cabin sure looks spruced up from flowers you and the rest of the Jewels planted. I can't thank you enough. I promise I'll take care of everything and do my best not to kill anything," Rhett called down from the roof.

"If something doesn't make it, it's not the end of the world. We can always plant something new," she said with a reassuring smile.

Robert climbed down the ladder. "Everything okay?"

"Yes, fine." Ruby forced a smile. "I'm leaving and wanted to say goodbye." The disappointment in Robert's eyes only added to her frayed nerves. She couldn't make anyone happy right now. Ruby took his hand in hers and gave it a squeeze. "I'll talk to you later."

He pulled her in and gave her a quick kiss. "I'm counting on it."

The town square was quiet since most folks were helping out over at Rhett's. That was fine with Ruby. She'd had enough socializing for one day. She parked and headed across the street to the park instead of going upstairs to her apartment. Delicate yellow blooms dotted the rose bushes surrounding the gazebo. Ruby sat down on the steps of the structure, admiring the arched latticework gracing the entrance. With all the weddings over the last few years, the gazebo was gussied up, looking as beautiful as the brides who'd stood under it. First Callie and Dax, then Josephine and Taylor. Jacob and Mae. Ruby chuckled, shaking her head. That was a wedding folks would be talking about for years to come.

Hopefully Jasmine and Rhett would make their way here soon. They deserved their own happy ending and so did she.

The days of imagining her wedding in the gazebo had faded a long time ago. In a fit of self-pity, she'd thrown away her bride book, the scrapbook she'd started when she let herself imagine saying her vows with Robert at her side. Hidden away in the back corner of her closet, Ruby pulled it out when she'd agreed to marry Jerome, thinking it would provide inspiration for her wedding. Looking through the clippings from bridal magazines she'd saved over the years had the opposite effect. A dream of one wedding didn't transfer to another, and no matter how hard she tried, she couldn't come up with a new dream with a man who wasn't Robert. Yet, when the time came, she still wanted the wedding she'd always dreamed of. Ruby would say her vows with Robert in this spot. She had a few foundational changes she wanted to make first.

Chapter Ten

"Psst."

Presley Beaumont stopped, looking around with a puzzled frown.

Good Lord, what had she been thinking? Well, it was too late now. She'd been foolish enough to think hiding behind the laurel bush in the Beaumonts' front yard, waiting for Presley Beaumont to come home from work, was a wise plan.

"Psst, psst."

Presley's eyes almost popped out of their sockets when she saw Ruby in the bush by the porch.

"Miss Ruby, what are you doing—?"

"Hush," she hissed, her eyes darting up and down the street before she stepped out from her hiding place. "I need to talk to you about something." Ruby leaned forward and whispered, "In private."

"Oh, well come on in, then." Presley gestured for her to follow her up the stairs leading to the porch.

Ruby danced from foot to foot, looking over her shoulder. The last thing she needed was people asking what she was doing talking to Presley Beaumont. Although that wasn't the scandal it would have been a few years ago. A lot had happened in Colton in a short amount of time. Buildings had been remodeled, the park had a new name, Mockingbird Bridge had a fresh sage green coat of paint. The town that had been on its last breath was breathing again. Things had changed, and that included people. And Presley Beaumont was one of the biggest transformations.

"Hurry," Ruby hissed, pushing Presley through the front door.

The Beaumont house had earned a reputation for being one of the tackiest houses in town. As soon as she entered the foyer, Ruby stopped and took in the walls stripped of their god-awful red velvet floral wallpaper and the muted, neutral paint strips taped to the walls.

"My goodness, Presley, what have you got going on here?"

Presley folded her arms, cocking her head and studying the tiny squares of color. "What do y'all think? Daddy likes this one," she said, pointing to a pale shade of white with a hint of a peach tinge. "He says it reminds him of daffodils. You know, the ones with the white petals and the frilly centers."

Ruby nodded. "Those are my sister's favorite. Well, your daddy is the judge, so if that's the one he likes, I'd say it's the right choice."

Presley bit her lip, tilting her head as she studied the swatch. "Will it be elegant?"

Poor thing, Presley was doing her best to change her ways. She'd come a long way from the worst of every Southern beauty queen stereotype—big blond hair, flashy clothes, and a healthy dash of racism. That part came from willful ignorance and hanging out with the wrong kind of people. Then, a couple of years ago, Presley had proved miracles really can happen. Now she worked as the mayor's assistant, joined the local knitting group, and organized town events from the Fourth of July parade to the Easter egg hunt in the park.

Ruby patted her arm. "It will be beautiful, honey."

Her compliment was received with one of Presley's beauty pageant smiles that showed all her teeth before she gasped. "Oh, I'm forgettin' my manners. Would you like something to drink? I've got sweet tea, water, or"—she hesitated—"Miss Ruby, would you like a glass of wine?"

"I would love a glass of wine." For the conversation she was about to have, she could use something a little stronger than sweet tea.

"Come on back." Presley waved her toward the kitchen. "I haven't figured out what I'm gonna do in here yet," she said, waving her hand toward the blue, red, and yellow striped wallpaper that strongly resembled an ice cream parlor.

"You don't have to do it all at once. Take one room at a time."

Presley took bottle of chardonnay out of the refrigerator, poured out two glasses, and set them on the island lined with barstools along one side. "Would you rather sit on the porch?"

Ruby sat down on one of the barstools covered in red leather. "No, I'd rather not have anyone overhear our conversation."

Presley joined her, and they each took a sip of wine. Ruby squirmed in her seat. The first part of her plan had worked. She'd gotten into the Beaumont house without being seen, but now she had to say what she came for.

"Miss Ruby, I don't mean to be rude, but what are y'all doing here?"

She took a large gulp of wine that went down the wrong way, leaving her sputtering and coughing while Presley thumped her back.

"Lord, this isn't going well," she wheezed, her eyes watering. She wiped her face and snorted a laugh. "I came to ask you a favor. It's… personal."

Presley's eyes grew round.

"The thing is… I was wondering if you would go shopping with me."

"Oh, of course, what are y'all shoppin' for?"

Ruby took another sip of wine. This was ridiculous. She was a grown-ass woman. She took a deep breath. "I need you to take me lingerie shopping."

In hindsight, it might have been a good idea to make sure Presley hadn't taken another sip of wine before she made her request.

Wine sprayed out of Presley's mouth with enough force to leave a splatter on the striped wallpaper. "What?" she gasped, her face turning beet red.

"I want to buy something frilly and"—her voice dropped to a whisper—"sexy."

"Don't you want to go with the Jewels?"

Ruby made a face. "Not this time. I need a break from my sisters. They'll want me in something buttoned up to my chin."

"Oh no, that won't do. Y'all should have something that'll make Robert drool. It's so romantic. Two star-crossed lovers torn apart and pining for each other for all those years. That night, the two of you in the gazebo…." Presley fanned herself. "I'd die of pure delight to have a man go all caveman the way Mr. Ellis swept you in his arms and kissed you."

"I forgot y'all were watching from the coffee shop."

"Best knitting club night ever," Presley said with a dreamy sigh.

It *was* a magical night. Ruby couldn't imagine when she went out to sit with Jasmine, hoping to console the young woman trying to soothe her broken heart, that she'd find her own heart stolen for the second time.

Robert Ellis, her first, second, and last love, had shown up at the gazebo and declared his love for her. Again.

"And it was so perfect that he kissed you in the gazebo," Presley continued. "Are y'all going to have your wedding there?"

"I—we—we haven't gotten that far yet." Ruby wanted to press her hands to her cheeks. Was she blushing again? Goodness, she'd blushed more in the past few weeks than her whole life put together. At her age she shouldn't be turning pink like a schoolgirl.

"I wouldn't get married anywhere else. I want to be a traditional Colton bride," Presley said with a wistful glint in her eyes.

Ruby took a moment imagining the same wedding for herself. She wanted to ask Presley if she thought she was too old for the big white dress with a train and all the bridal regalia the other gazebo brides wore. Would it be too silly for a woman of her age?

"Miss Ruby, you're blushin' again. Are you thinkin' about buying that lingerie?"

Ruby took a large sip of wine and shook her head. "No, honey, I'm a little heated, that's all. So, will you do it?"

Presley bounced in her seat. "Yes ma'am, I'd love to take you shopping." She tapped her fingers on her lips, narrowing her eyes. "Memphis is a bit farther down the road than Jackson. Both have shops that I like. Madame Cecile's has some dreamy French lace panties, but the Pretty Parlor in Jackson would also work."

"If it's all right with you, I'd rather go to Memphis than Jackson."

Presley's eyes lit up. "Yay, Madame Cecile's is my favorite." Presley cocked her head with a curious look. "What made you decide to do this now, Miss Ruby?"

Ruby gritted her teeth. "You know, I don't like to spread gossip, but it was that Marsha Musgrove. I overheard her in the Piggly Wiggly with her sister Roberta, talking about how she couldn't imagine how I'd be able to hold Robert for very long because I'm too old and frumpy."

"Y'all know, that Marsha Musgrove thinks the sun comes up just to hear her crow. Heavens to Betsy," Presley huffed. "She's been tryin' to fix her sister Roberta up with Robert for years, as if he'd want anything to do with that self-righteous biddy." Presley leaned close and said in a conspiring whisper, "Did you know there isn't a stitch of her real hair in that ridiculous beehive she insists on wearing? God forbid she gets too close to an open flame."

Ruby laughed until she was wiping away tears. "Thank you, honey. I needed that."

"Miss Ruby, you ever need to talk bad about one of those two, you come and sit by me."

They agreed to go that weekend and spend Saturday in Memphis. Presley would drive and Ruby would pay for gas and take her to lunch.

When she left, Ruby checked to make sure the street was quiet before she slipped out of the Beaumonts' front door.

The first part of her plan accomplished, Ruby strategized how she was going to slip away from her sisters and her beau on Saturday without any of them trying to get all up in her business. *Her beau.* Ruby did a little shimmy as she walked down the sidewalk. The idea still made her stomach do a little flip-flop.

Robert Ellis.

Ruby couldn't recall the first time she became aware of Robert Ellis. Maybe that's because he'd always been a part of her life. But her earliest memory of Robert and those piercing brown eyes must have been when she was about five. Robert was eight then and already had a knowing glint in his eyes and carried himself with a maturity beyond his years. Of course they didn't go to school together. School segregation might have been struck down by Brown v. Board of Education, but folks in Mississippi and other parts of the South figured out a cunning work-around. Black kids went to underfunded public schools, and White kids went to private schools.

From that first day she became aware of him, Ruby kept an eye on him from afar, until one day he looked back. Once their eyes met, a key slipped into the lock of her heart, and no one else had been able to unlock it since.

Ruby never blamed Robert for the distance between them. It wasn't his fault. The fault was hers for allowing herself to be convinced Robert wasn't good enough for her and she wouldn't be enough for him. Her parents made their disapproval clear. It was Pearl and Opal, the sisters who she'd always believed had her best interests at heart, who swayed Ruby, convincing Ruby that Robert leaving was best for both of them.

What would a young man in the Army do with a wife, a Black wife? How could she go to nursing school if she might have to up and move at a moment's notice to a new base in a new state?

Ruby chose her family, and Robert chose his country.

Chapter Eleven

THE END of the week found Ruby in Presley's convertible, trying to act calm as they sped down the highway toward Memphis.

"Since we have a bit of drive ahead of us, I was wonderin' if you'd tell me a story, Miss Ruby."

"What kind of story?"

"Everybody thinks they know what happened between you and Robert, but I'd like to hear the real story."

"Oh Lord." Ruby reached for the Jesus handle as the scenery went by in a blur of green. At the speed Presley was going, they'd be in Memphis in record time or in jail for speeding. "You'd have to keep driving around the world and back again for me to tell that story."

"Did y'all go to school together?"

"Schools were as much segregated then as they are now. The Black kids went to public schools, and the White kids went to private. But I'd seen him around town or in the park. And then one day, he was there. I was walking home from a friend's house one evening, and he appeared out of nowhere, offering to walk me home."

"How old were you?"

"Thirteen, and Robert was sixteen. I was so naïve I didn't realize until much later that Robert kept me safe that night. A group of boys had been shadowing me." Ruby pressed her lips together. "I shouldn't have been walking alone after dark. All of the sudden he was by my side asking, 'Mind if I walk with you for a spell?' I was so surprised I didn't say anything for a block. Then he asked, 'So, what do you want to be when you grow up, Ruby Colton?' I told him I was going to be a nurse, and he said it was a noble profession. Then I said, 'What about you, Robert Ellis? What are you going to do when you grow up?' He told me he was going to join the military. I wasn't surprised. He already had the discipline and that deep sense of right and wrong. I repeated his words back to him. A noble profession," she said, with a smile at the memory. "Each step we took brought us closer to my house, and I didn't want the moment to end. At the corner of my block, I couldn't take it anymore. I blurted out, 'Why are you walking me home, Robert Ellis?' If this was going to be my only opportunity to talk to Robert, I wasn't going to waste it."

"What did he say?"

"He stopped," Ruby chuckled. "Even at sixteen, he did that thing where he folded his arms across his chest, looking at me with those dark eyes. Even then, he'd already perfected that stern look that made you want to give up all your secrets. He said, 'Well, I've been thinking about that for a long time, and I have a feeling right here.' He pressed his hand over his heart. 'That you and I should be friends.'"

"Oh, how dreamy," Presley exclaimed. "What did you say?"

"It took me a minute to find my voice. He asked, 'What do you think of that idea, Miss Ruby?' I took a deep breath and lifted my face to meet his eyes and said, 'I think that would be all right with me.' I wanted to go up on my tiptoes and give him a peck on the cheek, but I was already being more daring than I'd ever been, walking down the street with an Ellis. And being seen kissing a White boy would cause a big ruckus. When I stumbled onto my front porch that night, I was out of breath and head over heels in love. I didn't want to admit it, but I was also scared. Falling in love with a White boy was going to change my life. I was willing to put myself in danger to love Robert Ellis."

Presley took her eyes off the road for a brief moment, looking at her with a frown.

"Yes," Ruby answered her unspoken question. "Things like that could happen and did. Even in the seventies, things were... difficult. Long before he started working for the government, Robert was working behind the scenes, helping Callie's grandpa and others with civil rights work." Ruby laughed softly. "That man was born to be a protector."

"It kinda seems like he's been undercover his whole life."

"In some ways he has. Robert had to hide his beliefs from his family, and what he was doing from everyone else. Except me. Maybe that's why we were so... bonded. I could always be my true self with him, and he could do the same with me. We were always safe in each other's arms. That's why he left, trying to keep me, keep us safe. There were folks around who weren't going to accept us and wanted to make an example of us, of me."

"It's hard to believe it. We didn't learn anything about this in the history books I had in school."

Ruby scoffed. "There will always be people who think if they keep a story out of the history books, they can make it disappear. Even now, we've got a big beautiful statue of Emmitt Till in Greenwood but folks still try to shoot up the memorial marker, and the state won't use eminent domain so the Bryant store can be preserved and turned into a museum. People think if the history gets buried under kudzu you can make it disappear. But folks like Mae, Taylor and Josephine with what they're doing with the Halcyon plantation house, and Taylor's home improvement show, are making sure history is preserved. We all need to be legacy keepers and tell our stories. You made me realize that. Thank you."

"I like knowing I'm working for a new South. A better South." Presley flexed her hands on the steering wheel. "I'm ashamed of how I behaved before. I'm not making excuses but I… I didn't know any better. I'm learning now." Presley chewed on her lip for a minute before she said, "Miss Ruby, can I tell you a secret?"

"Of course you can, honey."

Ruby expected Presley to confess her crush on a certain town sheriff. A crush that wasn't really a secret to anyone who was paying attention.

"I've been goin' to school. Real school this time, not the online bible college Ms. Dorothy insisted would be the right thing for me. They only taught how to be afraid of anything that was unfamiliar or different and how I should obey my future husband." Presley scowled. "I want to learn about real things. I want people to know I'm smart."

Ruby's heart went out for the young woman. It was true most folks in town didn't take Presley seriously. You couldn't blame them; Presley embodied every negative stereotype of a Southern belle, including serving as Miss Pickled Pigs Feet one year. Without a mama to guide her after losing hers to cancer early in her life, Presley threw herself on the influence of Dax Ellis's mother Dorothy. Under Dorothy's wings, all of Presley's worst qualities were encouraged rather than tempered. With Dorothy out of the picture, in jail where she belonged, Presley underwent a transformation. Sure, there were a few missteps along the way, but she seemed earnest in her desire to improve herself.

"Of course you're smart. Going back to school is a wonderful thing, and I'm proud of you. What are you studying?"

Presley straightened her shoulders. "I got my bachelor's degree in business administration, and now I'm studying government policy. I want to learn how to help Mae manage the town."

"Well, ain't that something. I expect you'll be running for mayor of Colton before you know it."

Presley's smile slipped. "I don't think folks would want me doing that. They wouldn't trust me after everything that happened."

"You mean how you helped save Mae when she was kidnapped? And how you welcomed Jasmine Owens into town? Or the way you've been organizing the farmers' market, making it bigger and better than it's ever been? Give yourself more credit, girl."

"Thank you, ma'am," Presley said in a shaky voice.

When they arrived in Memphis, Ruby expected to walk into something that could have been a bordello in a Mae West movie. To her surprise, not a speck of red or velvet was to be found in Madame Cecile's. Instead, she found whitewashed French antique furniture and a Persian rug in shades of pale yellow, cream, and pink, the same delicate pink that was on the walls. A round table sat in the middle of the shop with an enormous floral arrangement of pink peonies, pale yellow roses, eucalyptus, and curly willow. A circle of delicate lace fanned out around the vase. More satin and lace garments hung from gold hangers along the walls. Heavy floral embroidered curtains provided privacy for the two dressing rooms at the back of the store.

"Hey, Miss Cissy," Presley called out, waving to the woman behind the counter.

Ruby was surprised to see a petite woman with curly auburn hair and a smattering of freckles across her nose instead of the older French lady she expected. She came over and hugged Presley and eyed Ruby with an assessing gaze, but not an unfriendly one. Behind her dark red glasses, her bright hazel eyes studied Ruby with the experience and wisdom of someone who'd fitted hundreds of women from an A-cup to an H-cup and everything in between.

She clasped Ruby's hands in hers.

"It's nice to meet you, Madame Cecile." Ruby started to introduce herself and was cut off.

"Oh goodness, everybody calls me Cissy."

"Madame Cecile is the business. Cissy is the heart and soul," Presley said.

Cissy gave Ruby's hands a reassuring squeeze. "Come on in and let's find what you need. I'm gonna be your new best friend," she said with a wink.

Ruby took a deep breath and nodded. Any fears and misgivings she had disappeared in Cissy's welcoming presence. In the blink of an eye, she was ensconced in a cream brocade settee.

"Now, let's talk about what you're looking for today," Cissy said, taking a seat next to her.

"Well, I—" Ruby's eyes darted toward Presley, her cheeks heating.

"She's got a fella and they are burnin' up the sheets," Presley said, fanning her face. "Miss Ruby hasn't taken care of herself in a long time and she's ready to… to embrace her womanly wiles."

"Oh, I see." Cissy grinned and patted Ruby's hand. "Good for you, honey. I always say, if you think you're done, you're dead. Let's get you in the dressing room and see what we're working with."

Cissy got up and rolled a measuring tape from an ornate cast iron hook behind the counter and handed Presley a pad and pen. "You write down the measurements as I call them out, honey."

"Yes ma'am."

Two hours later, Ruby said goodbye to Cissy with a warm embrace and walked out of the shop having spent more money on underwear than she'd ever spent in her entire life without a blink of regret.

"Miss Ruby, I swear that new bra makes you seem taller," Presley said.

Ruby glanced at her reflection in the shop window they walked past. "You know what, honey, I think you're right." With the right size and lift, her breasts sat inches above where they were before, and she had the right amount of cleavage—not that anyone could see it underneath the frumpy shirt she wore. She'd thought it was the least dowdy item in her closet when she put it on that morning, but now…. She stopped, turning from her reflection to Presley. "Madame Cecile's was a fine start, but I'm thinking I'd like to pick up a few more things while I'm here. Do you think there are any shops we can find that would have some clothes for someone my age that aren't quite so…."

"Frumpy?"

"Exactly."

Presley bounced on the balls of her feet, her whole face lit up with excitement. She hooked her arm around Ruby's and started leading her down the block, exclaiming, "This is going to be so much fun. Come on, Miss Ruby, let's go find your sparkle."

With a little luck—and a lot of Googling—they found a beauty shop willing to take a last-minute appointment.

Ruby nearly turned around and walked right back out when the stylist appeared. He was young, with freckles scattered across his pale skin and hair dyed a soft lavender. Not exactly what she had expected.

But he was patient with her jitters. He introduced himself as Israel Silvera, his voice warm and reassuring as he explained, "I know I might not look like it, but my family back home in Texas is Latino. I've got a gaggle of nieces and nephews, half Black, half Latino, and I've been doing their hair since I was in junior high."

His easy confidence made Ruby pause. Maybe, just maybe, she was in good hands after all. When he turned her chair around with a flourish and Ruby saw her reflection in the mirror, she knew she'd made the right decision.

Presley jumped up from her seat in the waiting area, flinging her magazine aside as she rushed over. "Oh, Miss Ruby, look at those curls," she exclaimed.

Ruby watched Israel examining Presley's updo and could tell by his expression he was itching to get his hands on her overprocessed strands. "You know, I bet you have curls of your own if you styled your hair a little differently," he said diplomatically.

Presley's eyes grew wide and she took a step back. "I don't think—"

Israel smiled and reached into his pocket and pulled out a business card. "No worries, but if you ever change your mind."

"Maybe you'll come with me when I come back for a trim, because from now on Israel will be the only one cutting my hair." Ruby was already formulating a plan, determined to help Presley find her own sparkle when the time was right.

Israel grinned at her. "I'm glad you like it, Miss Ruby."

She leaned forward, fingering one of the perfect ringlets that fell to her shoulders. The frumpy bun was gone, replaced with soft curls. As he worked on her hair, Israel explained the techniques and products she could use to achieve the new style he created for her.

"I thought it would be too much work to wear my hair like this," she admitted.

"Maybe a little more work, but not too much," Israel said.

Ruby left the salon feeling lighter with a bag full of new styling products, a silk bonnet, and a special hairbrush designed for curls.

New underthings and a new hairstyle. Now it was time for a new wardrobe. At the end of the day, Presley's trunk was full of shopping bags and Ruby had put another dent into her savings, but she couldn't stop smiling on the drive home.

"Presley, I can't thank you enough for today. I couldn't have done this without you."

"I can't wait for you to make your debut with your new look. Those Musgrove sisters are gonna have a hissy fit. I should be the one thanking you. There aren't many folks around who think I can help them or want me to"

"That's not true, honey. Lots of folks see how hard you're working. I saw it, and that's why I asked you to help me."

Presley blew a raspberry. "You asked me because you think I'm a hussy."

Ruby grimaced. She was going to object, but honesty was the best policy. "You're right, and that's not fair to you."

"I was a flirt and a tease, but I didn't sleep around. I haven't even flirted with anyone since—" Presley pressed her mouth into a thin line.

"Since someone new came into town?" Ruby gently suggested.

"It doesn't matter. Nothing I do is ever good enough for him." She chewed on her lip for a minute before her expression brightened again. "Maybe if I can help more folks out, he'll believe I'm capable of doin' stuff."

Ruby raised an eyebrow, doubtful Presley's plan would work, but she didn't want to discourage her. She understood now how Presley had managed to win Mae over. Underneath the sparkles, the big hair, and the occasional thoughtless comments was a young woman with a big heart who'd earned a second chance.

"If he can't see the person you are inside, the kind and caring person I had the pleasure of spending the day with today, then he doesn't deserve you."

Presley parked in front of the Barton Building. She shut off the engine and threw her arms around Ruby. "I had the best day, Miss Ruby. Thank you for asking me." She jumped out and opened the trunk. "Let me help you take your packages upstairs."

Alone, Ruby stood amongst the bags scattered around her after Presley said goodbye. She was dog-tired but happy. Truly happy. Reuniting with Robert wasn't the key to her future happiness. She'd been right to take this time for herself. Eying her new lacy underthings, her lips curled into a smile. She and Robert would both benefit from the new and improved Ruby.

Chapter Twelve

"Good Lord, what have you done to yourself?" Opal exclaimed, marching down the aisle toward Ruby in Walker's Pharmacy.

Opal's gaze traveled from the tips of her toes, encased in bright green ballet flats, up her legs in slim dark jeans, to her green V-neck blouse with a hint of lace trim on the neckline and her new hairstyle. Her lips pursed, and disapproval glowered in her eyes. Ruby braced herself, ready for her sister's reaction. She looked good and felt good, and she wasn't going to let her sister make her think otherwise.

Ruby drew her shoulders back. "I think you meant to say, 'Good afternoon'. As for why I'm here, I came by to get some of the tinted lip balm Emma makes."

"Now you're going to start slathering makeup on your face." Opal rolled her eyes with a snort. "You're making a fool of yourself with all this nonsense."

"I didn't realize my happiness is nonsense," Ruby responded in a flat, cold voice.

"That's not what I meant."

"But it's what you said. My clothes," she reached up and tugged on one of her curls, "my hair, they make me happy. And so does Robert."

Emma came around the corner and let out a little squeak but retreated when she saw Ruby and Opal staring each other down.

"How much longer are you going to be bullheaded as a barnyard goat?" Opal demanded.

Ruby raised an eyebrow and shot back, "I don't know. How long are you going to be?"

Opal glared at her, but there was also something else in her eyes. Worry, fear, resignation? Ruby wasn't sure. Opal was saying a lot but not sharing what she was really thinking.

Opal clasped her hands in front of her as if she were about to give a solo in the church choir. "All I've ever wanted was for you to be happy."

"That's not true." Ruby shook her head. "If you wanted me to be happy, you wouldn't have thrown away my happiness."

"Those letters only would have made you more miserable."

"And that was your decision to make?"

"I—" Opal clamped her mouth shut.

There was no triumph in rendering her sister speechless. "You're not in charge of my happiness or my life, Opal. I stayed quiet and went along with what you, Mama, and Daddy wanted for too long." She fingered the lace trim of her blouse. "I like who I am. I wish you did too."

Before Opal could respond, Ruby turned around and walked away. "Emma, I'll come back later for that lip balm," she called out on her way out. She left the pharmacy and didn't stop until she reached the center of the park. Ruby leaned against one of the oak trees and took a deep breath, clutching her fist to her chest. She hated fighting with her sister. She loved Opal and knew what she said back at Walker's hurt her. The last thing she wanted was to spend the rest of her days estranged from either of her sisters. But if she gave in now…. Ruby straightened. No, there was no going back now, only forward.

ROBERT SHOULDN'T have been surprised to see Opal sitting on his porch when he pulled the tractor into the yard. He'd been expecting this visit since the night he kissed Ruby, but still, a part of him wasn't quite prepared to find her waiting there. He'd planned on knocking on her door soon enough, if it came to that—and had been ready for it. But seeing her here, unannounced, still caught him off guard.

Robert took off his hat, raking his fingers through his hair. He went over and sat down next to her on the porch in one of his rocking chairs.

They sat in silence for a few minutes, rocking in sync. A familiar figure arrived in a flutter of red, landing on the porch railing. The cardinal hopped along the railing, cocking his head and eyeing each of them, trying to determine which one would be the best candidate to give him his treat.

He stilled when Robert reached into the bucket of peanuts he kept nearby. The treat barely left his fingers when the cardinal snatched it and flew away.

"Greedy bastard," Opal said with a derisive laugh. She sighed, leaning back in her chair, looking at Robert. "White folks have taken almost everything from us at one point or another. I wasn't going to let you take my sister too."

Robert took a deep breath, weighing his words. "I wasn't taking her. There's a difference between taking and loving, Opal."

"I know that now. But at the time… I was so scared for her."

"And you think I wasn't?" Robert snapped. "You think I didn't get the same notes y'all got? Pictures of Ruby with a noose drawn around her neck?" Opal squeezed her eyes shut and shuddered. "I was young and naïve enough to think if I went away, if I fought this fight on a grander scale, I could fix the problem faster. I forgot how hate can be like a weed. You pull one and three more pop up. Every time I planned on coming back, I'd have a new assignment, a new mission that showed me how important fighting against hate, fascism, anti-Semitism, anti-gay, Muslim, and any other form of intolerance is. I put my country first. I can't regret that. I won't regret that."

Opal rocked for a moment, her expression a mix of compassion and regret. Finally, she spoke. "I don't know exactly what you did in the Army or whatever agency you were with, but I do thank you for it, Robert. I guess I never wanted to think of it as a sacrifice on your part, but that's exactly what it was." She twisted her hands in her lap, pain etched in her expression. "I'll never be able to undo what I did—keeping your letters from Ruby. I'm truly sorry, Robert. Part of me—I knew it was wrong when I was doing it, but I convinced myself I was doing it for all the right reasons, trying to protect my sister. Did you ever hear about our great-uncle?"

Robert shook his head. His gut tightened, anticipating what Opal was about to share.

Opal wrapped her arms around her middle, her voice dropping almost to a whisper. "I never met Uncle Louis. They said he'd taken liberties with a White woman." Opal turned to him with a pained expression. "That could have meant anything, but it was enough of an excuse for him to be—" Her voice broke. "—lynched."

Robert winced, drawing in a sharp breath. His heart broke for the family and some of his anger dissipated. Keeping his letters from Ruby hurt him deeply, but he understood the very real fear behind her actions. Three little girls had lost an uncle in the most horrific way.

"You must have been so scared."

"Pearl and Ruby don't know."

Robert sat forward. "What?"

"I wasn't supposed to know either. I overheard Mama and Daddy talking with my other auntie and uncle. It was late, and I got up to get a glass of water…. I never made it to the kitchen. I stood pressed against the wall in the hallway, listening."

"How old were you?"

"Seven."

"Opal, I…." Robert sighed. "You kept the secret to protect your sisters."

Opal nodded.

What could he say? How could he offer any words of consolation? Opal had saved her sisters from being traumatized, but at what price?

"I…." He cleared his throat. "I want to thank you for sharing that with me. We've both made sacrifices for the people we love. I have a lot of respect for what you did. I think if you shared with Ruby and Pearl what happened, it would go a long way toward mending your relationship."

Opal shot him an angry glance, then her face fell. "I don't want to fight anymore," she said with a heavy sigh.

"I'm not fighting. I never have."

Opal's mouth opened and closed a few times before finally saying, "Then I suppose it's up to me." She sighed. "I'm tired of being angry."

"It's exhausting, isn't it?"

"I miss my sister." Opal's chin trembled.

"I'm not taking her anywhere. We're gonna be right here."

"I know that. I miss… it's hard to let go. You'll be the one she shares her secrets with from now on. You'll be the person she shares exciting news with first, and you'll be the one she cries with. It's supposed to be that way. For a long time, we've been that person for each other, and it's hard to let go."

"I appreciate it wasn't easy, you coming here to talk to me, and I'm thankful to you for sharing what happened to your uncle with me."

Robert's phone rang and his nephew Reid's name flashed on the screen. "Excuse me, Opal. Reid doesn't call unless it's something important."

"You go right on ahead."

Robert answered and listened while Opal watched, her face lined with concern.

"I'm assuming you got the gist of that," he said when he hung up.

Opal sniffed, wiping away the wetness that hovered at the corner of her eye. "Those boys are a blessing for what they're doing. We'll take care of the flowers."

"I figured. Would you mind if I was the one to tell Ruby?"

Opal patted his arm with a sad smile. "That's the way it should be."

Robert followed Opal back into town, turning right when she turned left. He arrived at the Barton Building, parked next to her little red convertible, and buzzed her apartment.

CHAPTER THIRTEEN

"ROBERT, WHAT'S wrong?" Ruby said when she opened her door.

Whatever he was about to say flew out of his mind the moment Robert set eyes on her. No butterfly had ever undergone such a transformation. She had on a new outfit that showed of her curves instead of hiding them. The pastel shades he was used to seeing on her were replaced with a bright vivid green that made her skin glow.

He stepped inside and wrapped her in his arms. "I need to hold you for a minute." When he let go, Robert framed Ruby's face with his hands, his eyes roving over her features. Life was short, and he wanted to commit every detail to memory. "I like your hair," he said with a smile.

"I thought I'd try something new."

Robert reached up and hesitated. "Can I touch it?" She nodded. He wound one of the silky curls around his finger. The rest fell in a tumble of tight curls around her face, brushing against her shoulders. The black strands threaded with silver were soft, tickling against his fingers. He leaned closer, nuzzling the crook of her neck, tightening his hold on her.

"Robert, honey, tell me what's going on."

He squeezed his eyes shut for a moment before he met her worried gaze. "It's Primus. Reid called. He's… it's coming, Ruby."

She nodded and wrapped her arms around him. "I could see it in his eyes the last time Dan and Reid brought him to the clinic."

"The last time we talked, I sensed it too."

"What happened that brought you to my doorstep tonight?"

"The boys are asking for a favor, and I need your help. They need your help."

"Of course, what do you need me to do?"

"You'll have to work with your sisters."

Ruby frowned. "I'm not sure if I can do that. It was bad enough when we were working out at Rhett's place. Opal and I had a dust-up at Walker's today. It wasn't pretty. Opal owes me an apology and some respect."

Robert nodded. "She does, and she knows it."

"And how do you know that?" she said with a note of surprise in her voice.

Robert pulled Ruby over to the chair by the window and sat down on the footstool in front of her. He took her hands in his, rubbing his thumb over her knuckles. "Opal came to visit me."

Ruby's eyes widened with surprise and then narrowed in anger. "She must have come to you after our argument. What did she say? If she—"

"Don't get your dander up, darlin'." Robert stopped her before Ruby could get herself wound up again. "She's fixing to apologize. Opal might put on a tough act, but she's scared." Robert shook his head, blinking back the tears that pricked at the back of his eyes. "She had her reason for what she did. For the way she's treated you."

"That's no excuse for—"

"Sweetheart, let her explain and then decide."

"But—she—" Ruby sputtered. "No." Ruby shook her head, pressing her hand to her chest. "There's no excuse for what she did."

"Calm down, honey." He received a sharp look in response. "I shouldn't have said that."

"No, you shouldn't have. You're trying to help, but sisters... we're complicated."

"She was scared, Ruby."

"I know. But there's no excuse for what she did."

"There's no excuse but there is a reason. All I'm asking is that you give Opal a chance to apologize and show you she can respect who you are now."

Ruby sighed, letting her head fall on Robert's shoulder. "I can do that."

Robert tugged on her hand, pulling Ruby out of her chair, and sat in it, resettling her on his lap. Ruby draped her arm around his shoulder and rested her head against his.

"I thought we were the ones who were supposed to be older and wiser. Here I am fussing with my sister while...." She sniffed.

Robert kissed her temple. "I think we've all proven that's not true. Who would have thought that Dax, Reid, and all the other young folks in town would be the responsible ones?"

"Those boys are a treasure for giving Primus such a happy memory to leave this world with."

"I should get going. We've got a lot of work to do." A few moments ticked by before Robert moved, reluctant to leave the comfort of Ruby's arms.

Ruby tightened her hold on him. "Don't go, not yet."

Robert eased back down into the chair, shifting Ruby in his lap so they were face-to-face. "If I stay, I'm gonna want to kiss you," he murmured against her lips.

"I'm not saying no."

He cupped her face, inhaling deeply to savor the scent that was uniquely hers—sweet and reminiscent of spring lilacs and fresh rain. Her lips met his without hesitation, parting in an invitation he couldn't resist. A low moan escaped him as his hand slipped beneath her shirt, the need to kiss her overwhelming every thought. His tongue swept into her mouth, claiming her.

Ruby's fingers tangled in the hair at the nape of his neck, pulling him closer, her touch igniting a fire within him. His fingertips brushed the delicate lace covering her breast, the sensation electric. Her soft sigh against his lips spurred him on, and he deepened the kiss, losing himself in her completely.

"You better tell me to stop now or else I'm gonna take you to that bed and do everything I've been dreaming of."

Ruby pulled back, her lips slightly parted, looking at him through a haze of desire. "I was going to wait." She licked her lips and reached for the hem of her t-shirt. She hesitated, the corner of her mouth tipping up into a slight smile. "I was planning on seducing you."

"You seduced me the first time we kissed."

She let go of her shirt and leaned in to place a brief hard kiss on his lips before she grasped the bottom of her shirt again and whisked it over her head. "I didn't want reveal all of me and not feel sexy."

Robert sucked in his breath. With trembling hands, he reached up and caressed the delicate lace that covered her breasts. "Beautiful," he breathed. He unclasped her bra and slipped the lace off her shoulders, exposing her lush, full breasts. "Still beautiful," he said, brushing his thumb over her dusky nipple. "I don't give a damn what you wear, Ruby, you will always be beautiful to me." He kissed the freckle on the swell of her breast. "Every freckle, every scar," he pressed his lips to the half-moon scar on her shoulder, "every inch of your body is mine to worship."

Ruby shuddered in his arms, a tear leaving a thin trail of wetness down her cheek. Robert stood up, pulling Ruby up with him, and walked them toward the bed. When the back of her knees hit the mattress, he stopped.

"Is this okay?" he asked.

Ruby nodded with a soft smile. "It's fine. I'm not scared anymore." With trembling fingers, she reached for the hem of Robert's shirt and pulled it over his head.

Robert laid Ruby down on the bed, his touch tender yet possessive as he stripped away the rest of her clothes. Any remaining self-doubt disappeared as they relearned each other's bodies. Maturity brought a slowness to their lovemaking. The intimacy between them went beyond the physical joining, growing stronger as they explored each other's vulnerabilities and desires.

When they caught their breath and were lying wrapped in each other's arms, Robert covered Ruby's hand that rested over his heart with his own.

Chapter Fourteen

THREE DAYS later, Ruby arrived at the Buckthorn. Before she could even turn off the engine, Jason was at her car.

"I'll help you bring these in, Miss Ruby," he said, reaching into the backseat and lifting one of the buckets of flowers she'd gotten from Robert's yard.

"Thank you, Jason," Ruby replied, grabbing another bucket.

Before she could take a step, someone else appeared and lifted the bucket from her hands. The place was bustling with activity—people moving quickly, working together. Ruby didn't need to make a second trip to unload all the flowers from her car.

The floors had been swept clean, the usual peanut shells nowhere to be found. Along one wall, a row of picnic tables had been set up and covered with blue-and-white gingham cloths. Tillie, looking as focused as ever, fussed over a three-tiered cake while barking orders at one of her interns, a young man from the local trade school, who scurried around like a soldier under her command.

Twinkle lights crisscrossed the ceiling, adding a warm, welcoming glow to the space. Meanwhile, someone arranged the benches from the picnic tables in neat rows, leaving a clear aisle down the center.

Pearl beckoned Ruby over, while Opal shot her a wary glance from the back table, where she was arranging centerpieces. Ruby added her bucket of flowers to the others, claiming the last empty corner on the already crowded table, which was brimming with blooms from every garden club member's yard.

For the next hour, Ruby worked quietly, filling vases with yellow roses, bright blue hydrangeas, and cheerful daisies. The conversation was minimal—with an occasional request to pass a bloom or hand over the garden shears. The only words Ruby exchanged with her sister were to ask for another blossom, scissors, or for more floral tape. Mae's mother, Ella, the garden club president, arrived with more flowers, and together they filled every table with vases of yellow, white, and blue blossoms.

Robert came over, looking at Ruby and Opal with a hopeful expression in his eye. Ruby gave a slight shake of her head, and Robert sighed.

"Right on time," Ruby said, holding up the boutonniere she'd been working on to his lapel. The yellow rose, with a sprig of laurel, worked perfectly with the dark gray suit he wore with a cornflower blue tie.

"You look pretty as a picture."

Ruby accepted his compliment with a smile. She did feel pretty. She'd found time to sneak away to Greenwood in the midst of all the preparations and found new dress at a little boutique in town. The bright blue short-sleeved dress hugged her curves and had a flattering low scooped neckline. She added a pair of black patent pumps and a chunky colorful necklace to complete the outfit.

She secured the boutonniere on Robert's lapel and fussed with his pocket square. "I can't believe Reverend Collins refused to officiate," she hissed. "That man calls himself a Christian and doesn't act anything like it." She paused her fussing and looked into Robert's eyes, full of compassion. "It doesn't matter. Dan and Reid made the right choice to officiate."

"Thank you, honey," Robert said with a slight tremor in his voice. He gave her a quick kiss. "I think we're almost ready. Can I escort you to your seat?"

"Give me one minute to help clean this up and I'll be ready."

With four pairs of hands, the empty buckets and floral supplies were cleared away within minutes. Ruby washed her hands and returned to Robert's side. "I'm ready."

Ruby's heart skipped a beat when Robert took her hand and then held his arm out to her sisters. "Ladies, I'll escort you to your seats."

She sucked in her breath, waiting for Opal to snap. But there were no angry looks or sharp words. Opal nodded and fell in step next to Robert, with Pearl at her side. Ruby knew everyone in the room was watching as Robert seated them in the front row. On the other side of the aisle, Dan's Uncle Minh, along with his brothers and sisters and their families, filled five rows of benches. Callie sat next to Ruby with their baby girl.

Robert kissed her and whispered, "I'll see you in a minute," with a quick wink before he made his way behind the bar.

Dax came forward and asked the rest of the guests, who were still mingling, to take their seats. As soon as everyone was seated, Primus came in with Robert and Reid on each arm. Primus and Reid were both wearing dark blue suits. Reid wore a blue gingham tie with a matching pocket square. Primus's tie matched the blue of Reid's. The three of them made their way to the front of the room. Robert and Reid lowered Primus into a chair, plumping the cushions around him and making him as comfortable as possible. Ruby fought back tears, watching Primus give Reid a kiss on the cheek when Reid stooped to help him. He grasped Reid's hand tightly, looking up at him with pride. Reid took his place, and the music began.

The first notes of Stevie Wonder's *As* filled the room. Everyone stood as Dan appeared at the end of the aisle with his parents, wearing a suit and tie that matched Reid's. Dan's eyes locked on Reid's, and Ruby watched him walk toward his intended, buoyed by love and supported by his parents, with a pang of envy.

When Dan and his parents reached the end of the aisle, Robert greeted them with a smile and asked Dan's parents, "Who gives this man in marriage today?"

"We do," Dan's parents said, giving their son a hug and a kiss. They took their seats in the front row next to the other family members who'd come up from Biloxi.

Robert turned to Reid with a smile and then looked at Primus and asked, "Who gives this man in marriage today?"

Primus pulled himself up and straightened his shoulders. "I'd like to stand in for Reid's parents today and give my blessing, if that's okay with him." His voice was thin and frail, but his eyes were clear and bright when he spoke.

Ruby dabbed at her eyes, noticing her sisters doing the same.

Reid nodded and embraced Primus. Dan jumped forward, and both men helped him back into his seat. Primus squeezed their hands, whispering something before they turned to face Robert.

"Shall we begin?" Robert asked when the two of them returned to stand in front of him.

Dan and Reid both nodded.

"Dearly beloved, we are gathered here today to witness the marriage of Reid Ellis and Dan Nguyen," Robert said in a loud, clear voice with a slight tremor.

"For some reason, these two thought this gruff old man would make a decent officiant." His opening was met with laughter and a few nods from the friends and family gathered to witness the wedding. Robert sobered. "I have to tell y'all, this old man couldn't be more honored to be here today to join these two men in matrimony. Reid and Dan have their own vows to exchange. Those are the words that are important." Robert pulled a small book from his breast pocket and looked at Reid. "I've given you my fair share of wisdom over the years, but I won't do that today. I think this fella right here," Robert held up the book, "has better words than anything I can come up with." Robert cleared his throat. "From the poet and philosopher Rumi. 'Goodbyes are only for those who love with their eyes. Because for those who love with their heart and soul, there is no such thing as separation.' Dan and Reid, love each other well, love with your hearts, and every memory you share will be a blessing. Reid, would you like to say your vows to Dan?"

Ruby sniffed, fighting back tears as she watched Primus nodding along with Robert's reading.

Reid looked down at Primus, who nodded and let go of his hand so Reid could take both of Dan's in his.

"Dan Nguyen." His voice shaky with emotion as he brushing his thumb over Dan's knuckles. "I didn't want to love you when I met. I didn't want to love anyone. I was scared. And then I met you and I couldn't not love you. And in loving you, I learned to love myself. Thank you for always giving me the space to do that, to let me love and grow. I promise to do the same for you, in sickness and in health, for better or worse."

Dan nodded, his lips trembling. "Reid Ellis, the moment I met you, I knew my life had changed. You blazed into my life like a comet, so bright you blinded me for a minute. I thought I came to Colton for a case. I understand now that fate brought me here to find you. I promise to guard your heart, to love you in sickness and health, for better or worse. There is nothing I will do in this world that will be better than loving you."

Robert swiped at his eyes. The sound of sniffles and handkerchiefs being pulled out of handbags and pockets filled the room.

Robert cleared his throat, but his voice was still gruff with emotion when he pronounced Dan and Reid husbands.

Dan pulled Reid toward him and framed his face with his hands. Everyone in the room bore witness with a tear in their eye as he whispered, "I love you," before giving Reid a tender, heartfelt kiss.

The room erupted in cheers and applause with a few catcalls when Reid and Dan kissed again. Before they accepted congratulations from their guests, both men went over and knelt down in front of Primus and accepted his blessings.

Robert worked his way through the crowd toward Ruby. When he reached her, he slipped his arm around her waist and kissed her temple.

"Did I do okay?" he asked.

Ruby patted his heart. "Your brother would have been proud."

"I wondered what he'd think about Primus giving Reid away, when Reid asked me what I thought. He was the best father he could be, but Primus is the one who's here and who shepherded Reid through the aftermath of his birth father's deception."

"This wedding happened as it should." Ruby glanced toward Primus, his face pinched with pain despite the brave face he tried to put on for the boys. "It won't be long now."

"No, I expect not."

Gasps of surprise rippled through the crowd as Lucas Monroe walked in, strumming his guitar, his band trailing behind him.

"Sorry we're late, folks," he called out with a grin. "The drive from Atlanta took longer than we expected."

His stage crew began hauling in equipment. In less than twenty minutes, the benches that served as pews were moved out of the way and Lucas and his band were set up and playing.

Robert put out his hand. "Can I have this dance?"

Ruby let herself be swept out on the dance floor. "That's a nice surprise," she said, tilting her head toward Lucas Monroe."

"Dax called. He didn't even have to finish asking before Lucas said he'd move heaven and earth to get here."

Ruby looked around at everyone in the room. "Colton might not be perfect, but when it matters, this town can make magic happen."

"I don't know when I've ever been so proud," Robert said. He glanced toward Opal and back at her. "Have you had a chance to talk to your sister?"

Ruby shook her head. "No. And now isn't the time to hash out our problems. Today is a day to celebrate love."

On cue, Lucas announced Reid and Dan's first dance. He serenaded them with a new song he'd written for the occasion.

I see you standing in the light,
A little lost, but still so bright,
In your eyes, I find my home,
No need to be afraid, you're not alone.

Dan gently wiped away the tear that escaped Reid's eye. The lyrics were perfect, a song about strength, love, and loss. It told the story of their journey to this moment in time, putting the promises they'd made with their vows into a beautiful ballad that captivated everyone in the room.

The world can try to tear us down,
But we've got roots that hold our hearts,
I'll always be your shelter, be your guide,
My heart is safe when I'm in your arms.

"I can't wait until it's our turn to have our first dance as a married couple." Robert paused. "I'm not saying that to pressure you. You asked for time, and I'm going to give it to you."

"Robert, I—" Her emotions were a jumble. Ruby wanted nothing more than to start her life with Robert, but she liked the independence she'd claimed for herself.

"It's okay, darlin', you don't have to say anything. I just wanted you to know, that's all."

"I do know. And I want that first dance more than anything. But I also think I'm not done getting to know this version of Ruby Colton." She gave him a slight smile. "I like this girl. I think we're gonna be good friends. Will you be okay with that?"

"Sweetheart, you are the most precious jewel in my life, and I'll treasure every facet of who you are."

Ruby sighed. "I swear, Robert Ellis, you could charm the paint off a wall."

Robert chuckled and drew her in for a kiss.

"I'm going to need at least a hundred of those a day to make up for lost time," she said.

"Happy to oblige, ma'am," Robert said before capturing her lips with his once again

Chapter Fifteen

Primus passed away less than a week later, clutching a picture of his beloved Marcus over his heart, with Reid and Dan at his side.

While all of Colton mourned his passing, everyone recognized the blessing that his last years on this earth were spent surrounded by love and found family. Primus's passing also reunited the Jewels. Opal marched over to the clinic when she heard the news. Ruby told Robert how she'd burst into the waiting room, calling out for her little sister. In a rush, she searched the clinic until she found Ruby and Dr. Colton in a treatment room. They were finishing up with a little boy who had hurt his wrist. Opal pulled Ruby into her arms and told her how sorry she was and said she realized she didn't have any years left to be stubborn. Through her tears, she shared the story of their great-uncle and his lynching. Ruby sat frozen, listening, horrified and heartbroken. Understanding the fear behind Opal's actions didn't magically resolve their differences, but it opened a door toward a way forward. It was time to find a way beyond their fears and embrace the present.

Robert and Ruby were together at the funeral, with her sisters beside them, holding hands and listening to Reid recite the poem "Do Not Stand at My Grave and Weep" by Mary Elizabeth Frye.

"Do not stand at my grave and weep
I am not there. I do not sleep.
I am a thousand winds that blow.
I am the diamond glints on snow.
I am the sunlight on ripened grain.
I am the gentle autumn rain.
When you awaken in the morning's hush
I am the swift uplifting rush
Of quiet birds in circled flight.
I am the soft stars that shine at night.
Do not stand at my grave and cry;
I am not there. I did not die."

Reid finished by saying, "Primus will live on in all of our memories. Every glass raised in the Buckthorn will celebrate his memory."

Dan stepped forward and put his arm around Reid's waist. "Reid and I would like to invite you all back to the Buckthorn to raise a glass in celebration of the life and legacy of Primus Wallace."

Someone behind Robert whispered, "What do you think is going to happen to the Buckthorn?"

Robert suspected what Primus had done with the Buckthorn, and no one would be surprised when his will was read.

Robert and Ruby joined the long line of cars crossing Mockingbird Bridge and winding their way through the woods to the Buckthorn after the graveside service.

Once again, the floors of the Buckthorn were swept clean and the picnic tables were pushed aside. This time they were laden with casseroles, cobblers, and a rainbow of Jello salads that came through the door as friends and family arrived. Reid and Dan stood on the threshold, accepting condolences as they went inside.

Robert pulled Reid into a hug. "How are you holding up, son?"

Reid took a deep breath. "If I'm honest, I'm numb. I knew it was coming, but I—I wasn't ready. I was never going to be ready. I try to remind myself that I've been lucky to have two fathers in my life. But it still hurts." His voice broke and he let out a sob.

Dan reached for his husband. Taking him in his arms, he whispered words of comfort. Dax and Callie came over, and with Dan they formed a circle of love and support for Reid.

Robert exchanged a look with Ruby, both of them proud of the way Robert's nephews had grown to love and support each other. They mingled with the rest of the folks who'd come to tell stories, reminisce, and praise Primus. The president of the state NAACP arrived to pay his respects, along with the congressman from their district. There were others that Robert didn't recognize. Apparently, folks in Colton weren't the only ones who respected Primus's skills as a master distiller. A few industry bigwigs showed up to pay their respects, but Robert suspected they were really there to sniff around and see if they could get ahold of the recipes that were handed down through the Wallace family and kept as a closely guarded secret.

Speaking of family, Ruby leaned in to whisper in Robert's ear. "I can't believe out of all these people, there isn't a single member of Primus's kin."

"The only family that matters are those two boys right there." Robert nodded to where Reid and Dan were talking to one of the industry executives who'd come to pay their respects. His gut tightened as the man said something and Reid's jaw hardened and his expression turned thunderous. Reid leaned in and said something to the man between clenched teeth while Dan put a restraining hand on his husband's shoulder. The man blanched and quickly made his way toward the exit.

"Trouble," Robert said under his breath. Primus had warned him it was coming. He didn't believe it would be that quick.

"What is it, honey?"

Robert patted Ruby's hand that rested on his arm. "The wolves are already circling." He nodded toward Reid and Dan. "We won't know until the will is read, but I suspect Primus left everything he had to Reid, and that includes his recipes. Recipes a lot of folks have been wanting to get their hands on for a long time."

Ruby sucked in her breath. "Oh my."

Opal and Pearl appeared at their side.

"I can't believe some of these people," Opal said with a furious glare at another industry executive making his way toward Reid and Dan. "You should hear them plotting and scheming. I don't like people who come in talking big and throwing around money, thinking they can waltz in and buy whatever they can't take."

Pearl nodded in agreement. "They're still filling the grave over at the cemetery, and these men of privilege think they can come here and make demands."

"Oh, hell no," Opal said, leaving the group and heading toward Reid and Dan, where the man who'd come over to talk to Reid was pointing a finger at him with an angry frown.

Robert chuckled, watching Opal march up and poke her finger in the man's chest. Whatever she said had his face turning from red to purple before he marched out the door, and Reid pulled Opal into a hug.

"I have to admit, there are times when I don't mind it when my sister's mulish temper makes an appearance," Ruby said, shaking her head with a wry smile.

"I have to agree with you," Robert said with a worried glance toward his nephew.

As if reading his mind, Ruby gave his arm a gentle tug. "Reid's okay, Robert. There are lots of folks here looking out for him, a lot more than want to take advantage of him."

Robert nodded, and they spent the next hour saying hello to their friends and family who'd come to pay their respects. Eventually they made their way to the patio away from the crowds for a few quiet moments.

"Are you hungry? Can I get you anything?" Ruby asked, worry in her eyes.

"Naw. I'm good." He looked over the people milling around inside and then turned to Ruby. "You ever think about who will turn out when your time comes?"

"Sometimes. I wish I'd be sitting on the porch surrounded by my children and grandchildren."

Robert put his arm around her and kissed her temple. "I'm sorry, honey."

"There's nothing to be sorry for. We made our choices for good reasons, and I promised myself a long time ago that I wasn't going to live a life of regret. Look around, Robert. When our time comes, we'll be honored by the next generation. You've been Uncle Robert to more than your kin. All of the young folks in town appreciate you as a mentor and consider you family."

"The same goes for you, Ruby. Everyone considers the Jewels family. I see you spending time with Presley, and the way Callie and Mae look up to you." Robert stopped and took Ruby's hands in his. "Ruby, officiating at Dan and Reid's wedding, being here today, what are we doing? I don't want to waste any more days waiting for my life to start with you." Ruby's mouth dropped open and her eyes grew round when he dropped to one knee. "Marry me, Ruby. Let's be Uncle Robert and Aunt Ruby to these kids. Let's create memories together that will be stories our nieces and nephews tell on a day like today."

He let go of one of Ruby's hands and reached in his pocket. He didn't know why he'd carried the ring with him everywhere since he'd bought it with his first paycheck when he joined the Army. Over the years it had become more than a ring; it was his good luck charm, talisman, and a reminder to always have hope. His hands were shaking as he slid the simple diamond on her finger. "It was the biggest one I could afford at the time," he said, looking at it on her finger with a frown. It looked like nothing more than a chip on her finger.

Ruby grabbed his face and leaned in to give him a kiss. "It's perfect, and my answer is yes."

An excited yelp broke them apart. Presley was standing off to the side, bouncing on her heels and grinning at them. Robert looked around and realized their proposal had an audience. As he stood back up, applause broke out.

"Hardly appropriate for a funeral," someone muttered.

"Primus would approve." Reid came forward to shake Robert's hand and give Ruby a kiss on the cheek. "Welcome to the family."

The dam broke, and they were swamped with well-wishers. Callie and Dax were there, offering their congratulations along with Jason and Mae. Robert received warm hugs from Rhett and Jasmine, who whispered something in Ruby's ear that had her blushing and smiling. Opal and Pearl gave Ruby hugs, kisses, and words of congratulations that left Ruby with tears in her eyes. When Opal extended her hand to Robert with a smile and said, "Welcome to the family," Robert let go of the breath he didn't even realize he'd been holding. He shook her hand and then gave her a hug.

"I hope you'll save a dance for me at the wedding," he said.

"I'm going to want one too," Pearl said, with a hug for him as well.

"Of course, I'm going to dance with both of my sisters-in-law. Y'all had better get ready to cut a rug."

His answer brought a round of giggles from Opal and Pearl. A sense of contentment that he hadn't felt in…. ever settled over him. He was home with the people he loved. Colton would always have his soul, and Ruby would have his heart.

It wasn't until they made their way back to his cabin that they had a chance to celebrate alone. Ruby lay nestled in his arms, her head pillowed on his shoulder, holding her hand up and fluttering her fingers, admiring the sparkle in the moonlight.

She turned to her side and lifted her head. "You said this was the biggest one you could afford at the time. How long ago did you buy this ring, Robert?"

He scrubbed his face with his hand with a sigh. "Almost right after I left. As soon as I got my first paycheck, I went to the jewelry store."

"And you've been carrying it around ever since?"

Robert lifted her hand and twisted the band on her finger. "It's been my lucky charm. A reminder why I needed to keep myself alive, of what I wanted to come home to."

Soft lips pressed the spot over his heart, and Ruby looked up at him with a wistful smile. "I'm glad you had it with you."

"I am too, but I like it better on your finger." He picked up her hand again and studied the ring with a frown. The diamond seemed bigger when he bought it and the gold had dulled from being rubbed and scratched over time. "I'm sorry, honey, it needs a good cleaning. We can take it to a jeweler in Greenwood and get it cleaned up."

"We can get it cleaned, but that's all."

"You're sure you don't want something bigger?"

Ruby pressed her lips together and shook her head. "Absolutely not. I don't need a big fancy diamond. The ring isn't what makes a marriage, it's the two of us, together living, loving, fighting—" She pressed a kiss to his cheek. "—and making up. That's the stuff that matters."

"I love you."

"I love you too," she said, giving him a kiss that left no doubt about their love and their hope for the future.

"So, what kind of wedding do you want to have?"

"Will you think I'm corny for wanting to be a gazebo bride?"

"I'd be disappointed if you didn't."

Robert was sure that the wedding of Robert Ellis and Ruby Colton under the gazebo dome would set tongues wagging in Colton, and he was ready for a humdinger of a party.

Chapter Sixteen

RUBY DEBATED taking off her ring before going into the Catfish Café. There was no way anyone was going to miss it. She held her hand out, watching the glittering flash of deep red and white sparkles in the sunlight. She should have known Robert wouldn't be satisfied with having her ring cleaned and polished. While Ruby held firm on keeping the original diamond, Robert insisted on the rings of rubies and diamonds that sat nestled against each side of the single stone. The diamonds on the band were the same size as the engagement ring. Taking a deep breath, she straightened her shoulders and opened the door. There was no way she was taking that ring off her finger. It had taken too many years to get it on there. Besides, everyone in town already knew they were engaged.

Of course, this would be one of those days when the café was packed, and Tillie had an eagle eye. Ruby barely made it up to the counter before Tillie pulled out a large calendar and shouted out, "It looks like three of y'all picked June 12th. Jasmine Owens, Callie Colton, and… Nate Colton, y'all come on up and collect your winnings."

Ruby gaped at her cousin, who walked by with a cheeky smile on his way to the counter. Callie gave her a kiss on the cheek on her way past and Jasmine a little hug on her way up to collect her winnings.

Everyone else in the café came up to *ooh* and *ahh* over her ring except Marsha and Roberta Musgrove. Presley came over and put her arm through Ruby's. Lifting her chin, she shot the two of them a withering look while she leaned in close and whispered, "I'm gonna enjoy every minute of watchin' those two eat crow."

Suddenly Presley stiffened at Ruby's side.

"Congratulations, Miss Ruby. Uncle Robert sure is a lucky man." Isiah Owens came forward and gave her a hug.

"Maybe you'll find some luck someday," Ruby said.

She watched as Isiah's eyes darted quickly toward Presley. And Presley, who was usually a chatterbox, had become as quiet as a church mouse.

The door to the café opened, and the whole room went silent seeing Ruby's sisters in the doorway.

"Which one of y'all gets to be maid of honor?" Tillie shouted, pulling out a clipboard with a piece of paper.

"Please tell me you weren't betting on that too," Ruby said.

"I'm fixin' to buy myself a new fishin' pole if I win," Hank called out.

Opal glared at Hank with a thunderous expression.

"Don't let them pressure you, Miss Ruby," Presley whispered.

"Presley's right, stand your ground, Miss Ruby," Isiah said quietly.

Ruby could have sworn everyone in the café was holding their breath, waiting to see if Opal was fixing to pitch a fit.

Pearl leaned over and whispered something to Opal, and a second later her scowl morphed into a smile. "Unless some of you had co-maids of honor, all of you have lost this bet. You should all know by now, the Jewels don't play favorites."

Nate was still standing at the counter, and he held is hand out to Ruby with a grin. "I told you."

"That's not fair, he's family," someone called out.

"I didn't make the rules. I only played the game." Nate laughed.

"I'm sure you're going to get your cousin a nice wedding present with your winnings," Presley called out.

"Good job, honey." Ruby patted her arm.

Opal and Pearl came over. "Sorry we're late."

"That's okay, I'm glad you're here."

Opal drew her shoulders back. "Of course we're here."

Presley let go of Ruby's arm. "I'd better get back to work. Don't forget what I said, Miss Ruby, and you let me know if I can help with anything."

"I sure will."

She ignored the curious stares. No one would have taken a bet on her becoming friends with Presley Beaumont, but like Mae and some of the other folks in town, she was glad she'd given her a second chance.

"A table opened up." Opal scooted them toward the empty booth. As soon as they were seated, Tillie was there clearing the dirty dishes.

"I'll be right back to take your order." She pointed at Ruby. "Yours is on the house. It's the least I can do. But you know it's all in fun and because we care about you and Robert. Everyone wants to see the two of you happy."

Ruby couldn't help glancing at Opal to gauge her reaction. Had the tide really turned? Was Opal going to be okay with all of this?

Opal dug into her handbag and pulled out a pad and a pen. "We've got a wedding to plan. Let's get to planning."

As if she knew a storm was coming, Tillie stopped mid-stride on her way back to their table. Turning on her heel, she retreated back to the counter, watching them out of the corner of her eye.

"I've talked to Pastor Roberts and the church is free...." Opal paused to dig in her bag again and pull out a calendar.

"Hold on a minute. I'm not getting married at the church. I'm going to be a gazebo bride."

"At your age?" Opal scoffed. Pearl sighed, shooting Ruby an apologetic look. "You'll look like a fool. No. An afternoon wedding at the church. You can wear that pale pink suit and—"

Ruby slammed her hand on the table. "I said I'm going to be a gazebo bride. I'm going to wear a proper wedding dress and have a proper wedding, and if you don't care for it, then you don't have to come."

Heads swiveled and folks started whispering. The usual morning buzz took on a different tone. The Jewels were the talk of the town. All three of them squirmed under the scrutiny.

Nate appeared at their table. "Morning," he greeted the sisters with a solemn nod before speaking to Ruby directly. "Ruby, since your father is no longer with us, I'd like to offer to walk you up the stairs of the gazebo. I know there are others who'd like to claim the honor, and if you'd like to accept one of those offers instead of mine, I understand. But we're cousins, you're my kin, and it seems like the proper thing to do."

Ruby put her hand over her heart. Nate kept to himself. Even as children he was the quiet, serious one. His time in the military made him only more reserved. His restrained nature meant most folks didn't know how much it meant to him to serve the community he loved. They didn't get to see the side of Nate that loved a good corny joke and went to see every Marvel movie as soon as it came out.

Ruby scooted out of her seat to give Nate a hug. "I'd love that."

He patted her back before pulling out of her embrace. With another nod, he turned and left the café. Ruby sat back down and stared at Opal, daring her to challenge her on wedding plans.

After a minute, Opal made a little noise of disgust before she picked up her pen again. "What colors do you want?"

It was a small victory, and Ruby knew there were going to be other battles ahead.

"Why don't you tell us what you have in mind," Pearl said.

Ruby folded her hands on the table. "Nothing too fancy. We'll get married under the gazebo and have the reception—"

"You'll have the reception right here," Tillie said, setting three plates down on the worn Formica table. "I went ahead and made your usual order. Didn't think it was a good idea to interrupt your wedding planning to take an order when I knew what you were going to ask for anyway."

"Thanks, Tillie." Ruby pulled the plate with fried chicken, mac and cheese, and black-eyed pea salad in front of her. "And thank you for the offer to have the reception here."

"I figured we could do what we did with Taylor and Jo, and have a tent out front."

Taylor and Jo's wedding was a bit more extravagant than what Ruby planned, but a tent in front of the diner strung with lights, their friends dining and dancing in the moonlight, fit her vision perfectly.

"That would be wonderful."

Tillie pulled a pencil out of her bright red beehive and a small pad from the pocket of her bright yellow gingham shirt. "Now when are we going to have this grand affair?"

Ruby frowned. She hadn't discussed a date with Robert. "Hold on a minute." She pulled out her phone and sent him a quick text.

When do you want to get married?

The ping of Roberts reply came instantly. Ruby read it with a chuckle.

Tomorrow

She put her phone down and looked at her sisters and then Tillie. "Do you think we could put together a wedding in a month?"

"Color me surprised, I'd bet Robert would have wanted you to get hitched tomorrow," Tillie said with a knowing smile.

"Tomorrow," Opal sputtered. "My sister is going to have a proper wedding."

Ruby bit back a smile and exchanged a knowing glance with Pearl. Opal might object to some of the details, but at the end of the day, appearances mattered to her. And with that some of the tension left the room, and they had most of the main details for the wedding in place by the time they finished their lunch.

That night, she filled Robert in on the details while they sat on the porch at his cabin. Summer nights on Robert's porch had become one of Ruby's favorite things in life. Away from the lights in town, the sky swirled with indigo and midnight blue and large swaths of twinkling stars. Without Robert by her side, quiet evenings at home left her feeling restless, wanting something more. But with Robert, quiet evenings with only the squeak of their rocking chairs and the crickets chirping in the yard were precious.

"What do you think?" she asked, even though she already knew the answer.

As she suspected, Robert replied, "Whatever you want, honey. As long as it's you and me under the gazebo, I'll be happy."

"Since I have Pearl and Opal standing up with me, who do you want to have?"

Robert stopped rocking. "Dax and Reid. They're the closest I think I'll ever have to children of my own."

Ruby reached for Robert's hand. "I think that would be lovely. I've been so caught up in wedding plans, I forgot. How did the reading of the will go?"

"Hold on to your hat, honey. Primus left Reid over three million dollars."

"My goodness," Ruby gasped.

"Reid gets all of it, including the Buckthorn. It's a lot of money, and Primus also left him his recipes. Everything he knew about crafting spirits, years of notes in an old leather journal Primus kept in a safe deposit box at the bank. Those are priceless."

"None of it will heal Reid's grief, though."

Robert sighed. "No, it won't. That boy has lost two father figures now."

She squeezed Robert's hand. "I'm glad he's still got one. Do you think we'll ever know who Reid's mother is?"

"It's up to him if or when he wants to find out, or if she wants to be found. I don't know… I don't want Reid's heart to be broken any more than it already has been."

Ruby agreed. She felt the same way about herself. It was time to put past hurts behind them and embrace a bright new future.

Of course, as with many things, that was going to prove easier said than done.

CHAPTER SEVENTEEN

"Who here thinks I want to look like one of them *Real Housewives* hoochie mamas on my wedding day?" Ruby glared at the group of women from the pedestal in the bridal store. "I want to see a show of hands right now."

Presley started to raise her hand, only to have Mae push it down with a stern shake of her head.

"There is nothing wrong with a little sparkle. Y'all act like I'm tryin' to take you to Vegas," Presley said in a loud whisper.

Each of the women Ruby invited, or they'd invited themselves to shop for a wedding dress, had chosen something for her to try on.

Mae's choice was a tailored white suit that made her look like a lawyer in heaven. Callie had chosen a frothy dress with so many flowers scattered on the layers of tulle, Ruby thought she might be mistaken for a Rose Parade float. Leave it to Opal to choose a high-necked, long-sleeved dress that would have been perfect if she wanted to be a Victorian corpse bride.

Now she was standing in a skintight beaded number with a back so low you could see her ass crack.

Ruby eyed Emma and Pearl over in a corner, whispering together. When Pearl noticed Ruby watching them, she gave Emma a gentle push in her direction. "You show it to her, honey, you're the one that picked it out."

Emma looked down at the garment in her hand and back at Pearl. "But you're her sister."

Pearl gave Emma another nudge. "Emma found something, and I agree you should try it on."

The saleswoman swept in and carefully lifted the dress out of Emma's arms, handing it to her assistant to put in the dressing room. "Miss Colton, why don't we get you out of that dress," she said, ushering her off the pedestal.

Twenty minutes later, Ruby stood in front of the three-way mirror in the dressing room, twisting and turning with tears in her eyes. She turned to the saleswoman. "Will you ask my friend Emma to come back, please?"

"Of course," she said with a smile.

Ruby had made a point of including Emma on her dress-shopping trip. Sweet Emma was so quiet and introverted, she was often left out of things because she was too shy or because people forgot about her. It took some convincing to get her to come along today.

The door opened and Emma gasped, her cornflower blue eyes sparkling. "Oh Miss Ruby," she exclaimed, clasping her hands to her cheeks.

"Since you picked it out, I wanted you to be the first one to see it."

It wasn't a dress, but a two-piece set: a full tea-length satin skirt paired with a satin-lined lace top. The top featured three-quarter sleeves and a wide neckline, delicately designed so the lace edge grazed her collarbone. It buttoned up the back with small satin buttons. Both pieces were in a soft, creamy blush-white that made Ruby's dark skin glow.

"And look," she said, putting her hands into the side slits, "pockets."

Emma clasped her hands together, her eyes lighting up. "It's beautiful, Miss Ruby."

Ruby walked over to Emma and tucked her arm around hers. "Let's go show the others."

As soon as they walked into the showroom, there were gasps and *ooh*s and *aah*s.

Ruby stood on the pedestal beaming at her family and friends. "Well?"

Pearl nodded, dabbing her eyes with a tissue.

Opal turned to Emma. "Well done, sweetheart."

Everyone got up and circled Ruby on the pedestal, admiring the dress.

Presley eyed another display across the room and rushed over, returning with a pair of fuchsia pink kitten heel pumps with a rhinestone buckle.

"I know y'all will say these are tacky, but—"

Ruby snatched them out of Presley's hand before she could finish and slid her feet into them. They fit like a glove.

"Ruby's sparkle," Callie nodded with approval.

Everyone stepped back to give Ruby a clear view of the mirror. She wasn't the picture of the young bride she'd carried in her mind for all these years. This was better. The dress showed off the dips and curves that came with age, highlighting her toned arms and slim ankles. But it was the maturity in her eyes and the confidence on her face that made her feel more beautiful now than she would have felt at sixteen.

"I'm a bride," she whispered.

"Now, what are we going to wear?" Opal asked.

The room went silent for a heartbeat before everyone rushed toward the bridesmaid dress section.

Ruby gave the saleswoman an apologetic look "Oh Lord, here we go again."

After a great deal of debate and two arguments, Ruby declared she wanted her sisters to be her something blue. Pearl found a dress with a chiffon skirt and lace V-neck top in a beautiful deep robin's egg blue. The slim belt with a rhinestone buckle accented her waist, and the top even had a hint of cleavage showing. After rejecting every version of a dress that looked like it came from the set of *Little House on the Prairie*, Mae and Presley wrestled Opal into a satin suit with trim cigarette pants and a fitted jacket with a peplum in the same color.

"Miss Opal, I always knew you had a figure under those baggy gardening overalls you keep wearin'," Presley said, earning a sharp elbow from Mae. "Ow, I'm just sayin'. You said it too," Presley shot back with an accusatory glare at Mae.

Ruby watched her sister twist and turn, and saw a spark in her eyes she hadn't seen in, well... maybe never. The shawl collar on the jacket emphasized Opal's short hair and long neck, and the slim cut of the pants showed off how lean her body was from the hours she spent working in the garden.

"My, my," Opal said quietly, turning back and forth to look at her reflection in the mirror.

"You'll make a beautiful bridal party," Callie said.

"Now what about the rest of you?" Ruby asked. Callie, Mae, Presley, and Emma looked at her with matching expressions of confusion. "You didn't think I'd get married without all my girls at my side, did you?"

Presley's smile was so bright the sun was going to need sunglasses.

"Really?" Mae said.

"Are you sure?" Callie added.

Emma took a step back, her pale gaze clouded with worry. "I don't think folks would want me to—"

"What?" Ruby cut her off. "Outshine the bride, because you're so beautiful?" She marched over and grabbed Emma's hand, leading her over to the wall of dresses in a rainbow of colors. "Since my sisters are wearing blue, I was thinking green would be a lovely accent color."

Emma threw her arms around Ruby. "Thank you," she whispered in a teary voice.

Sweet Emma still carried the scars of her daddy's cruel deeds. Ruby was determined to help her heal, to draw her out of her shell, and to make sure Emma knew, without a doubt, that she was wanted and loved.

"What about this?" Callie asked, holding up a simple sleeveless, tea-length dress with a scoop neck and A-line skirt in a blue and green floral pattern with pink accents that matched Ruby's shoes.

Mae came forward, nodding with approval. "Doesn't the color remind you of—"

"Eucalyptus," Callie and Mae said in unison, with smiles that said they shared a secret.

The saleswoman came over. "You mentioned it's going to be an evening wedding. This could be a nice touch if there's a chill." She held up a cardigan in the blue color that matched the dress, with a scattering of pearls around the collar and pearl buttons. "I'd have to do a rush order, but I can have them here in time."

"That's perfect," Ruby said, already picturing adding eucalyptus to her bouquet.

There was a debate over shoes, with Presley's suggestion of silver and rhinestone platform heels soundly being rejected.

"There will not be stripper heels at my sister's wedding," Opal declared.

Pearl elbowed her sister. "Quit bein' so hard on Presley. At least she didn't suggest those clunky pumps you wanted."

Opal harrumphed, crossing her arms over her chest.

The debate ended when a more sensible kitten heel shoe in a soft gold, similar to the style Ruby would wear but without the rhinestone buckle, was agreed on by everyone.

Callie modeled the final ensemble, standing with the Jewels. Ruby studied their reflection. Pearl linked her arm through Opal's. Smiling at Ruby, she asked, "Well, what do you think?"

"It's perfect," Ruby said.

The dresses and accessories were ordered and appointments made for alterations. When Ruby went to pay, the saleswoman shook her head with a sly smile and handed her an envelope. "It's been taken care of, Miss Colton."

Ruby looked at her sisters and friends, who were all trying to appear innocent and failing.

Ruby opened the envelope and pulled out the sheet of cream stationery.

Miss Ruby,

>*Reid and I hope you will accept the gift of your wedding trousseau from your soon-to-be nephews-in-law.*

>*We are honored to welcome you into our family. You have made Uncle Robert happier than we've ever seen him, and no gift we could ever give could outdo the gift of your love to him.*

>*We know you will be a beautiful bride and can't wait to see you under the gazebo on your wedding day.*

With love,

Dax & Callie, Reid & Dan

Ruby looked up from the note at Callie, who was fighting back tears. It hadn't occurred to her until that moment that she'd be gaining nieces and nephews. She'd always loved Callie and Mae as if they were her own daughters. That feeling took on a deeper meaning. She reached for Callie and pulled her into a hug.

"Thank you, sweetheart."

"We love you."

"Now look at what you've done," Opal said, wiping her eyes. "I was determined not to cry today."

"I expect they'll be more tears before this is over," Pearl said.

That night, Ruby sat back in the armchair by the window with her feet up on the footstool and a cup of mint tea in her hand with a satisfied sigh.

She smiled when her phone rang and Robert's name flashed on her caller ID.

"How did the dress shopping go?"

"I had a wonderful day."

Even though Robert attempted using his interrogation skills, Ruby refused to give up any details about her wedding dress. But she did share how Emma was the one who found it.

"Well, I'll be," Robert said, his voice thick with emotion when Ruby told him about Dax and Reid's gift.

They talked late into the night about the next generation. Ruby shared her worries about Emma. She was so quiet and shy, Ruby wanted to make sure she didn't get left behind. Robert talked about Dan and Reid. Offers to buy Primus's recipes were pouring in. Some people were persistent to the point of being relentless.

"I want everyone to be happy and settled." Ruby sighed.

"Like we're going to be."

The certainty in Robert's voice soothed away Ruby's worries. That night Ruby dreamed of standing in the gazebo with Robert, only this time she didn't dream of them the way they were. This time she saw herself in the dress she bought that day, a bouquet of peonies and eucalyptus in her hands, surrounded by the people they loved. Far off in the distance, a woman stood by one of the oak trees smiling, and a voice whispered, "It's about time."

Chapter Eighteen

Robert stepped into the Buckthorn and immediately froze. He'd been expecting a meeting with Reid to go over some of the proposed improvements to the old bar, maybe chat about a few changes here and there. Instead, the familiar clink of glasses and buzz of conversation hit him like a wave. As his eyes scanned the room, the sight of his nephews greeted him along with a half dozen of the town's familiar faces. A good chunk of the men from Colton all greeted him with raised glasses and shouts of congratulations.

Before he could fully process it, the first clap on his back hit, followed by another, then another. The friendly hands seemed to pull him deeper into the warmth of the room, and before he knew it, someone had shoved a glass of whiskey into his hand. He blinked, realizing in a haze of surprise that this wasn't a casual get-together. Everyone gathered was here for his bachelor party.

"Well, I'll be," he muttered, his voice trembling slightly as he wiped at his eyes. The room, full of old friends and younger faces, family by blood and family by choice, truly touched him.

Dax appeared at his side, slapping him on the shoulder with a grin. "You didn't think we'd let you get married without a proper bachelor party, did you, Uncle Robert?" he said, his eyes gleaming with that familiar mischievous spark. "We were never gonna pass up an opportunity to throw the best damn bachelor party Colton has ever seen."

Robert shook his head, still trying to wrap his mind around it. "I hadn't even thought about it. Hell, I guess I figured at my age, a bachelor party was more of a… a young man's game."

"Hogwash!" a booming voice called from behind him, so loud it rattled the glass in his hand.

Robert turned, with a jolt of surprise at the familiar voice.

"I'll be damned," Robert said, grinning at the man.

Blake Richardson, General Blake Richardson, stood in front of him, looking like he'd stepped off a military base but without the full dress uniform. The goofy grin he had when they first met all those years ago in boot camp was still there, although now it was framed by a face that had weathered with time. His hair, once dark and thick, was still close-cropped but now peppered with gray. His eyes still twinkled with that same irreverence. But there was no mistaking the man before him. Blake had risen through the ranks to become a three-star general, a brilliant strategist, and an intelligence expert respected around the world.

But to Robert, Blake was simply Blake—the guy who'd saved his ass more times than he could count.

Robert pulled him into a bear hug. Blake drew back and grinned even wider. "Well, your nephew Dax tracked me down. I was about to head out on my boat, you know, fishin' the Keys for a bit before your big day and all that, but you think I'd miss your bachelor party? Hell, I wouldn't miss it for all the marlins in the Gulf."

Robert laughed, still in shock. "I didn't think I'd see you until the wedding. This is a damn fine surprise. I'm glad you've finally made it here. I hope you'll stay until the wedding."

Blake's expression softened for a moment. "Been wanting to make my way here for years, Robert. I never seemed to find the right time, ya know?" He dropped his gaze to the floor, then back up with a half smile. "Betty's been gone over a dozen years now, and... well, the boys are out in the world living their own lives. I've been kind of rootless, to be honest. When Dax called, I couldn't get here fast enough."

A deep silence passed between them, a rare moment of shared understanding. Robert placed a hand on Blake's shoulder, his voice quieter now. "You did everything you could for her, Blake. Those last few years with Betty… you made sure she was taken care of. You made sure she was loved."

Blake exhaled sharply, a little grin tugging at the corner of his mouth. "The boys were there too. The doctors and the nurses… I was the guy holding her hand through it all." His expression softened even further. "Caleb's overseas, following in our footsteps. Chance—well, he's in Dubai somewhere, last I heard. He's working the pit crew at the Abu Dhabi Grand Prix."

"Formula 1?" Robert said, a note of awe in his voice. "Who would've thought?"

Blake laughed. "Well, thank God Chance isn't driving. I don't know if I could take the stress. But working the pit crew—now that's enough pressure for anyone. At least he's not in the thick of it. You've seen the wrecks those guys get into. It's a nightmare."

Robert chuckled, shaking his head. "I'm proud of both of them."

Blake nodded, his eyes reflecting the kind of pride only a father—or in this case, a father figure—could have. "They've both done good for themselves. But tonight, Robert… tonight's all about you." He slapped Robert on the back, hard enough to rattle his teeth. "Let's make sure Colton really knows how to throw a bachelor party."

"Remember that speakeasy we found in New Orleans, and we decided it was a good idea to drink some of that horrible absinthe the bartender convinced us to try?"

Robert groaned with a wry smile. "We must have chased that green fairy for three days before we sobered up enough to figure out where in the heck we were."

A cheer went up from the crowd when Lucas Monroe arrived with his guitar slung behind his back. He sat down on one of the bar stools and started strumming. Someone else joined in with a fiddle and Hank pulled out a harmonica, surprising a few folks who didn't know the town barber could play a mean tune on a mouth harp. Dax had reappeared, thrusting another whiskey into Robert's hand, and the entire room seemed to swell on a wave of music and laughter and faces that had been a part of his life for as long as he could remember.

It felt good to be surrounded by so much love and friendship, by men who'd been through battles together, both literal and metaphorical, all gathered to raise a glass to his new beginning.

Robert introduced Blake to everyone. Of course Blake instantly gravitated toward Dan and Jacob, recognizing fellow members of the intelligence community. When Blake and Dan made their way toward the bar for another round, Robert took the chance to check in with Reid.

"How you holding up, son?"

Reid gave him a half smile. "Honestly? Married life is great, but…." He rubbed the back of his neck. "I have to say, life at the prosecutor's office back in Chicago was less stressful than trying to run a distillery everyone wants to buy."

"Any offers you'd consider?"

"Hell no," Reid answered with a steely glint in his eye. "I want to carry on Primus's legacy. Grow it into something even bigger that will benefit the community and give him the recognition he deserves."

"I'll support you. Whatever you need, you know I'm there."

"Thanks, Uncle Robert. There'll be plenty of time to figure out what we're going to do. For now, let's focus on getting you married."

"I'm ready."

He'd never been so ready for anything in his life. If it were up to him, Robert would sling Ruby over his shoulder and run off to Vegas that night. But there was something to be said for getting married surrounded by the people you considered family.

"Where are y'all going on your honeymoon?" Reid asked.

Robert froze. "Aw, hell. We've been so busy I didn't even think about it."

"Think about what?" Dax asked.

"The honeymoon."

Dax's eyebrows shot up. "You haven't planned anything for your honeymoon?"

"I've been busy," Robert shot back.

"Busy gettin' busy with Ruby every chance you get." Isiah slapped him on the back with a smirk. "Your truck's been parked in front of the Barton Building so many nights, I told Dax we should make you a designated spot with a sign to make it official."

"Ruby and I've heard you coming home late often enough."

Isiah gave him a side-eye. "I'm the sheriff of a small town with only two deputies and a whole lot of ground to cover. I'm stretched too thin to be having as much fun as you two seem to be having these days."

"Your time will come, son," Robert said.

"Not anytime soon."

Robert frowned, instantly going on alert. "Anything specific got you runnin' around like a cat chasing its tail?"

Shaking his head, Isiah took a sip from his glass. "I spend most of my days writing speeding tickets instead of dealing with White supremacists, and I intend to do everything I can to keep it that way."

"Glad to have you here. I was worried we might not be exciting enough around here compared to the big city."

Isiah chuckled. "I've got plenty to keep me entertained here. Chicago was great, but I didn't have that sense of community that I've got here. And now, with my sister settling down in Colton, I have no plans to go anywhere else."

"You okay with that?" Robert asked, taking in the note of worry in Isiah's eyes.

"Rhett's kind of a tough guy to get to know. I'm always worried I'm going to say the wrong thing around him. He's...." Isiah's gaze flickered toward his future brother-in-law talking quietly with Jacob Winters in a corner of the room. "He's a good man. A hero, but his bravery caused a lot of damage. How did you deal with it and come out unscathed?"

Unscathed? Robert bit back a bitter laugh. Did he want to share his secrets with Isiah? No one did the kind of work they did without coming out with scars. Robert had learned to hide his better than most.

"Go over and talk to him," Robert urged. "All that stuff you said about him? He's feeling the same way. Rhett's worried you don't approve of him as his future brother-in-law. Y'all are family now. You should be good friends too."

"You're right. I hadn't thought of it that way. Thanks." Isiah raised his glass in salute before he made his way over to Rhett and Jacob.

Robert rubbed his chest where a small pang of... regret? took up residence. It was an emotion he tried to avoid. Regret could pull you under and drown you if you let it. These last few weeks, he missed his brother, Landon, more than ever. He missed the camaraderie they should have shared. They should have toasted Dax and Reid at their weddings and celebrated birthdays, Christmas, and all life's milestones together. Robert took in the scene in the room, a small kernel of hope in his chest that his brother's face might magically appear in the crowd. This was why he refused to let regrets take up space in his heart. It hurt too much. He would always have to live with his failure. It took too long for Robert to recognize how troubled Landon's family life really was when he came back to Colton. He did his best to make up for his brother's failings and set his wayward nephew, Dax, on the right path. But he'd failed to see the layers of lies and deceptions that would eventually shatter his family. Being able to see the patterns others couldn't was what made him a valuable asset to his government. But he hadn't read the clues that were right under his nose, and that would be one of the two greatest regrets in his life.

"You okay?" Blake asked, pulling Robert out of his unexpected bout of self-pity.

Robert blinked. "Thinking about my brother." He took a drink, letting the whiskey burn a trail to his gut. "I don't think I'll ever figure how to make peace with loving someone and being so damn disappointed in them at the same time."

"You've done a fine job stepping into his shoes and being a father figure to Dax and Reid." Blake scowled. "I'll never understand how he could have let Dorothy abuse those boys the way she did. Smothering one with love and control, while withholding her affection from the other."

"I'll never get over my brother hiding the truth about Reid from me. It was bad enough that he had an affair, but asking Dorothy to raise his love child in secret makes it worse. I can't excuse how she treated him, but I suppose I understand why she was so bitter and angry all the time."

"I don't blame you." Blake studied him for a moment before he slapped him on the back. "Come on, this isn't a night for thinking about the past. We're here to celebrate your future." Blake tipped his head toward the bar. "Let's get you another glass of the finest damn whiskey I've ever had."

Robert followed his friend into the crowd. Blake was right. It was time to leave the past behind and step into a bright future with the woman he loved at his side.

Chapter Nineteen

THE WAITING room at the clinic was full all day: twisted ankle from sliding into home plate; an unfortunate incident with a box cutter; and two brothers, one with a broken arm from helping the other one move that ended up in a fight with black eyes and scrapes on both of them. Mixed in with the regular appointments, Ruby and Dr. Colton were run ragged by the end of the day.

Ruby was about to put her feet up when Presley called.

"Miss Ruby," Presley said in a teary voice, "I think I've ruined it."

"Ruined what, sweetheart?"

"I painted the front hall," she wailed. "I was trying to make it like a faux finish I saw on TikTok. It's supposed to be all swirly like clouds, but Ashton says it looks like someone threw up strawberry milk."

"Well, it does," Ashton could be heard muttering in the background.

"Can you please come and look?"

Ruby looked down at her comfy pajama bottoms and slippers. As much as she wanted to say no, Presley had been a good friend to her in her quest for independence.

"Of course, honey. I'll be over in a minute."

Ruby hung up and, with a sigh, got up and changed into a pair of jeans and a pretty new pink floral blouse she'd bought on her shopping trip with Presley. Slipping her feet into a pair of ballet flats, she grabbed her purse and headed down the block to the Beaumont house, formulating a plan to give Ashton a piece of her mind when she got there for being so mean when Presley was genuinely trying to do better.

She rang the doorbell, frowning when she heard hushed voices and a giggle. A second later the door few open and Presley stood on the threshold, her face crumpled with teary eyes.

"Oh, good, you're here," she said a little too loudly, her voice more eager than miserable. She hooked her arm through Ruby's, practically yanking her through the door and into the hall.

The walls didn't look like someone threw up strawberry milk. Instead, they were painted an elegant magnolia color, white with a hint of green with a soft sheen finish. An elegant Queen Anne-style table sat in the center of the entryway on top of a beautiful Persian rug in pastel shades of cream, brown, and green. A large floral centerpiece in a classic urn vase decorated the center of the table. The entryway that used to look like a bordello now welcomed guests with classic Southern grace. Taking in the change, it took Ruby a moment to notice the balloons or the banner at the railing on the staircase with *Congratulations* spelled out in gold glitter. Ruby's eyes lifted to the top of the stairs where her sisters stood, along with everyone from the garden and knitting clubs smiling down at her.

"Surprise!" The shouts and confetti rained down on her.

Ruby's purse fell to the floor as she clapped her hand on her cheeks. "Oh, my heart," she said in a shaky voice.

"Surprise, Miss Ruby!" Presley threw her arms around her.

"Oh, sweetheart. This is… I'm overwhelmed."

Ashton came forward looking festive, wearing a pair of trim plaid pants, a pale lavender dress shirt and one of his trademark bow ties. He handed Ruby a glass of champagne and gave her a peck on the cheek. "Sorry for the ruse, Miss Ruby. But you gotta admit, Presley put on a pretty convincing show," he said with a wink. "Now if y'all will excuse me, there's another surprise for your intended at the Buckthorn tonight I've got to get to." With a quick hug, Ashton turned to leave, calling out, "Ladies, y'all behave yourselves tonight" as he headed out the door.

Presley gently pushed Ruby into the large living room, where a few of Tille's apprentices from the culinary school were already circulating through the room with trays of canapés. Tillie supervised with a cocktail in her hand, nodding with approval.

"Presley thought drinks with garden club themes would be fun," Pearl said, pointing to the bar that had been set up in the corner. "That girl is so clever. We've got the 'Thirsty Tulip'—it has elderflower and lime in it—and the 'Basil's Kiss.' That one is my favorite. And there's lots of champagne, of course."

"I still can't believe it," Ruby said in awe.

Pearl leaned in and whispered, "Opal insisted on doing all of the flower arrangements herself. She wouldn't let anyone from the garden club lift a finger."

Ruby blinked back tears at her sister's loving gesture.

A few hours later, the drinks were still flowing, and gift wrap littered the floor. Ruby looked around with a full heart at the generosity her friends had shown. Emma had given her a beautiful basket full of her homemade lotions, shampoo, conditioner, and other skincare products. Callie gave her a signed set of books from Aliyah Burke, her favorite romance author. Mae presented her with a gift certificate for a couple's massage at a fancy spa in Memphis, while Presley gave her a gift certificate to a fancy restaurant in Memphis and a beautiful cream silk nightgown and robe with a note of congratulations from Madame Cecile.

Pearl's gift was a pair of ruby and pearl earrings, saying, "It's not something blue, but I thought you could wear them on your wedding day."

Opal handed her a slim box. "This is something borrowed."

Ruby's hands trembled as she opened the box, slightly faded with age. Inside, she found the bracelet their father had given to their mother on their thirtieth wedding anniversary, a strand of rubies, opals, and pearls."

"Mama always said she hoped we'd each wear it on our wedding day." Opal's face crumpled and a tear escaped, sliding down her cheek. "We made her wait too long. You should have worn this years ago, saying your vows under the gazebo with Robert." Her voice broke and she put her head in her hands, her shoulders shaking as she cried. Ruby jumped up and pulled Opal into a hug. "I feel like we've let Mama down," she said in a choked whisper.

"I think Mama is pleased that we're finally finding our way." Ruby gestured to Pearl. "Come on, girl, this needs to be an official sister hug."

They formed a circle, arms wrapped around each other, foreheads touching. "Love you, sister," they said in unison.

There were sniffles and tears around the room when they parted. Mae watched with her head on Callie's shoulder, her eyes shining bright. Presley had Emma's hand clasped in hers. Thank God she wore waterproof mascara, otherwise they would have had a Tammy Fae incident on their hands. Sweet Emma's nose and eyes were red from crying. Even the usually stoic Tillie was wiping away a tear.

Ruby took in the scene and declared, "Oh no, we can't end the party with everyone crying." She called out to the bartender, "We're going to need a round of those Blackberry Brambles, please." He nodded and started working his mixology magic. Ruby turned to her sisters.

"Since this is such a festive occasion, I think we need to do something we haven't done in a long time."

A slow smile spread over Pearl's face. "Do you mean…?"

"Oh Lord no, we're too old for that now," Opal declared.

Pearl shot her a look. "Speak for yourself."

"Maybe you don't remember," Ruby goaded her sister.

Opal drew her shoulders back. "I've never heard so much foolishness." She turned to Presley. "You got anything that will play music around here?"

Presley's eyes lit up. "Yes ma'am."

Within minutes the wrapping paper was swiftly cleared away, and another round of Blackberry Brambles was served as the sounds of the Supremes filled the room. The crowd fell silent for a beat, then gasps of surprise echoed around the room, followed by shouts of encouragement and enthusiastic clapping as Opal, Pearl, and Ruby struck their first pose in the center of the floor.

"All right, girls!" Opal said, dramatically swinging her arm out like she was on stage at a sold-out theater. "Let's show 'em what we've got!"

Ruby fought back tears, this time of pure happiness at having her sisters at her side and the memories of doing this same performance using hairbrushes for microphones in the living room of their childhood room.

Mae shouted, "Get it, girl," when Opal kicked her leg up with dramatic flair. Pearl did a spin that was half graceful, half awkward, but charming in the way only Pearl could pull off, and Ruby? Well, Ruby stepped up too, even if her own high-kick wasn't as impressive as Opal's. She still managed to pull it off without tripping over her feet.

They finished with Opal holding her pose like she was auditioning for *America's Next Top Model* and Ruby and Pearl back-to-back in a *Charlie's Angels* pose.

Someone shouted out, "Encore," and of course all that singing and dancing made them thirsty. That's the excuse they would use to would use to explain what happened next.

Chapter Twenty

Robert noticed Blake out on the Buckthorn's deck, leaning against the railing and staring out at the shadowed trees in the woods behind the juke joint. He grabbed a bottle from the bar and went out to join him.

"You doin' okay?" Robert joined him at the railing, nestling his drink in the slight groove on the top rail, worn down from folks who'd done the exact same thing for decades.

Blake waved his hand at the Southern pine trees in the distance. "Admiring the view. It's nice here, peaceful."

"Most days, yes. But we've had our fair share of dust-ups from time to time."

"I have to say, all these years you've been telling me about how much you love this place, I can see why now that I'm here. The minute you cross over Mockingbird Bridge, it's like you've come to another world. Kind of reminds me of that old movie, what was it called?"

"*Brigadoon.*"

"Yup, that's it."

"It's a good place to live, but we don't appear out of the mist once every hundred years like in the movie. We have the same struggles other small towns face. Infrastructure, making sure we have the goods and services we need. Things have gotten better thanks to the next generation. Dax and Reid coming home along with the others did a world of good. But we've had our share of bad with the good."

"No disrespect, but that business with your sister-in-law…," Blake shook his head with a frown. "That woman was bat-shit crazy."

Robert took a sip of his whiskey and nodded in agreement. His sister ran Colton as her own kingdom. She was the queen and the sheriff her first knight. Corruption ran rampant while they were in charge.

"Is the Klan still giving you trouble?"

"Things are pretty quiet now. Don't get me wrong, they're still around, trying to fool folks by dressing up in khakis and polo shirts. Don't get me started about the ones wearing the red trucker hats. You can try to dress it up any way you want. Hate is still hate."

"Ain't that the truth."

The two men sipped their whiskey in silence, each lost in the memories of battles they'd fought that no one would ever know about to keep their country safe.

"Reid seems to be doing well after everything that happened."

Robert glanced over his shoulder watching Reid and Dan laughing with Isiah. "That kid is remarkable." He turned to Blake. "Imagine finding out your existence was a lie."

Robert gripped his glass tighter. When his nephew Dax started a relationship with Callie Colton, no one was prepared for the depths of Dorothy's hatred. That wasn't reserved for those who had a different skin color but for her stepson as well, Dax's brother Reid.

"Dorothy trying to kill Callie and Reid was…." Blake shook his head. "As bad at that was, I will never be able to wrap my head around what your brother did. What was he thinking, bringing home a baby he had from an affair and asking Dorothy to raise him as her own?"

"I ain't saying it's right, but he did love his son."

"Not enough to shield him from his stepmother's malice," Blake spat out.

"He never should have kept the truth of Reid's birth from him."

"It's a good thing you were here to help deal with the fallout."

"I'm glad you're here, Blake. You'll be able to tell everyone who thought I'd never settle down you were a witness when Ruby and I said our vows."

"It's an honor. I gotta say, I wasn't sure I'd ever see it happen."

"Someday I hope I can do the same for you?"

"Naw." Blake refilled his glass. "I'm a confirmed bachelor."

"Maybe if you'd stop trotting around the world and settle down, you'd have an opportunity to change that status."

"I've been thinking about that. I haven't decided where I want to land yet."

"I hope you'll let me know when you figure it out. Ruby and me would be glad to come and visit."

"Boy, you sure are smitten."

"Have been since the first time I laid eyes on her."

"Glad you finally worked it out."

"It ain't clear sailing yet. Ruby's got two sisters, and the three of them have always been joined at the hip. Ruby's the youngest."

"Uh-oh. You came in and snatched the baby sister."

"That sums it up pretty well. I think her middle sister Pearl is coming around. But the oldest of the Jewels, Opal…." Robert grimaced. "That woman can hold a grudge like nobody's business."

"I'm sure you'll win her over with time. That Ellis charm has never failed you."

Robert wanted to agree, but it had been over forty years, and Opal Colton was as stubborn now as she'd been back then.

"You're not good enough for her and you'll never be. You'll get her killed if you keep hanging around makin' moon eyes at her."

Opal's words still hurt. They hit him hard right in the gut, because she'd been right. He had been putting Ruby in danger, and the only way he could keep her safe was to leave and take the assignment he'd been offered. An assignment that would help keep everyone he loved safe.

"I'm looking forward to meeting your bride after hearing about her for so long," Blake said, rousing Robert from his memories.

"Tell you what, why don't we meet you for breakfast tomorrow? Where are you staying?"

"I hadn't figured that out yet. I wasn't sure I was going to be able to make it until the last minute. Didn't see if your town had a hotel when I drove through."

"Aw hell, I should have offered. You'll come and stay at my place."

"Thank—"

"Baby? Where's my man!" A drunken voice called out, cutting off Blake's answer.

Robert froze. It couldn't be.

He got up and peered through the french doors into the Buckthorn, his eyebrows disappearing into his hairline at the sight of his fiancée and her sisters standing in the middle of the room with their arms linked, swaying side-to-side as if they were trying to keep their balance on a ship navigating stormy seas.

Blake snorted a laugh and gave Robert a gentle push. "You better go to your intended before she loses her voice calling for you."

Callie came rushing forward. "I swear we tried to stop them, but I was afraid if we didn't give them a ride, they'd try to walk here and fall over the edge trying to cross Mockingbird Bridge." She leaned forward and whispered, "The Long Island iced teas after the Blackberry Brambles weren't a very good idea."

Robert gave Callie's shoulder a reassuring pat. "It ain't your responsibility, and I don't think anyone could have kept those three in check."

As soon as Robert crossed the threshold, Ruby started to gyrate her hips, belting out the first lines of "Love to Love You, Baby" in what he supposed was meant to be a sultry serenade. Her sisters were doing something that must have been intended as a backup dancer routine that in reality was the two of them bumping hips until they almost fell over.

Blake chuckled next to Robert while Callie clapped her hand over her mouth, covering a squeak of shock. The rest of the bachelorette party had crowded in behind them. Mae and Presley were hanging on to each other, laughing with tears streaming down their faces.

"Robert, I hope you'll take this how it's intended, but you are one hell of a lucky man," Blake said, slapping him on the back.

"Yes." Robert's gaze raked over his bride-to-be as she started to stumble toward him. "I am a very lucky man."

Ruby lurched into his arms, her eyes bright with a mixture of alcohol and love. "Love to love you, baby," she slurred against his lips before giving him a sloppy kiss with the taste of sweet tea and lemon on her tongue.

A low rumble of thunder echoed in the distance, or it might have been the rumble in his heart, knowing the day after tomorrow Robert would finally be able to call the woman in his arms his wife. Too many nights he'd whispered that in his dreams, his heart calling to Ruby from around the world and back again. Someone cleared their throat, and Robert realized their kiss had turned into a bit of a spectacle.

"What are you laughing at?" Opal's sharp voice broke them apart.

"When three sexy, beautiful ladies crash a bachelor party, isn't that what you're supposed to do?" Blake said, looking Opal up and down with an appreciative gleam in his eye.

"I am not s-sexy," Opal hiccupped.

Pearl giggled, eyeing Blake. "But he sure is."

Opal bumped her sister's hip so hard she almost fell over. "But we don't want him to know that." She clapped her hand over her mouth. "Did I say that out loud?"

"Oh Lord, I'm gonna pee my pants." Mae laughed, gasping for breath.

Opal let out a loud belch, and her sway became a little more exaggerated.

"Uh-oh." Blake dashed forward in time for Opal to fall into his arms.

Opal straightened for a moment. "Don't be fresh—" she slurred. She drew in a sharp breath, her face going pale. "I don't feel…."

Blake half held, half carried Opal out to the deck, where she promptly emptied the contents of her stomach.

Ruby wrinkled her nose. "That's not very ladylike…."

Robert watched her face turn green and rushed her out to the patio to join her sister, calling out, "Somebody better grab Pearl."

Judge Beaumont brought out Pearl, who was insisting she was fine before joining her sisters at the railing.

Robert, Blake, and the judge stood by while the Jewels proceeded to pay the price for those Long Island iced teas.

"If you'd bet me a million dollars, I'd never think I would have seen the day," Reid said, bringing over bottles of water.

"I take it this isn't normal behavior for these three," Blake said with a wry smile.

Opal turned her head and slowly unbent. "I'll have you know I'm an uptight… I mean, upstanding Christian woman." The comment would have been withering if she weren't burping between each word.

Blake chuckled despite the warning glance Robert tried to give him. Robert sucked in his breath when Opal jabbed her finger at Blake's chest.

"You—"*Jab.* Opal bent her finger a couple of times with a frown and poked Blake again. "Your chest is very… firm." Opal wrinkled her forehead. "But that don't matter. Don't be imp—impermanent."

With the next poke, Blake picked up Opal and threw her over his shoulder. "Where are we taking them?" he asked, ignoring Opal's sputtered protests.

"Hey, you put my sister down!" Ruby exclaimed.

"When she can behave herself, I will."

Ruby looked at Robert. wide-eyed. "Don't worry, darlin'. Blake is a brother-in-arms. I trust him with my life." Robert bit back a laugh. "Your sister's in good hands."

"Those hands better not come anywhere near my butt," Opal hollered.

"I think we can declare this shindig officially over." Dax slung his arm around his wife as Callie's mouth stretched open in a yawn.

Who knew drunk Ruby was a dangerous combination of handsy and horny? The drive back to his place was like having an octopus in the passenger seat.

"Ooh baby, baby." Ruby crooned an unrecognizable tune, batting her eyelashes at him.

Robert pressed his foot on the gas, worried they might not make it before the alcohol that remained in her system hit her stomach and decided to stage another rebellion. He got her out of the car and steered her toward the porch, but before he could get her inside Ruby let out a loud belch, her eyes growing wide-eyed with alarm.

"Baby, I don't—"

He grabbed her in the nick of time, holding her hair back and pushing her toward a patch of lavender growing along the porch railing while she emptied the contents of her stomach.

He managed to get her inside before she started heaving again. Eventually, when she had nothing left in her stomach, he got her into the shower, made sure she brushed her teeth, drank a glass of water, and put her to bed.

"You're gonna be the best husband ever," she sighed, her eyes drifting shut.

"That's my plan, darlin'," he said, pressing a cool washcloth on her forehead.

She hiccupped and a tear escaped, rolling to the pillow. "I'm gonna be a terrible wife," she wailed.

"What makes you say that, sweetheart'?"

Her brown eyes popped open. "I'm stubborn."

"That's a good thing," he said, settling himself on the edge of the bed.

Ruby ripped the towel off her forehead. "I'm too set in my ways."

Robert's lips quirked as he refolded the towel and settled it back against her skin. "I wouldn't say that. You've made an awful lot of changes in a short amount of time lately."

"Robert, I'm terribly jealous." She hiccupped again with a grimace. "I swear if that heffa Marsha Musgrove keeps batting her eyelashes at you after we're married, I'll thump her harder than a bible at a revival.

I'll do it in the middle of church too," she said with an earnest pout that Robert found charming in its own drunken way.

Robert bit the inside of his cheek trying not to laugh. "That's okay, honey. It would be an honor to have such a valiant champion defending me."

"Robert?" Ruby's voice was childlike, her big brown eyes still teary. "I love you so much."

He shifted back against the headboard and drew her into his arms. "I love you too," he whispered, as her breathing deepened into a soft, steady snore.

CHAPTER TWENTY-ONE

Robert watched with an amused smile as Ruby cracked an eye open.

"Oh Lord," she groaned, squeezing both eyes closed tighter.

Robert chuckled, and Ruby's eyes flew open. She scrambled to sit up, clasping the side of her head with one hand. "Oh, that hurts." Her eyes darted around the room. She peeked under the blanket, seeing nothing but her lacy underwear on her body. "What in the world—how did—what in the world happened?" she groaned, flopping back against the pillows. "I did something foolish last night, didn't I?"

Robert chuckled with a twinkle in his eye. "Here, drink up and take these," Robert said, handing her a glass of water and a couple of aspirin.

"Coffee." It wasn't a question or a request, but more of a plea.

Robert jumped up. "I've got a fresh pot ready for you."

Ruby rested her head on his shoulder as they made their way into the kitchen, her movements slow but steady. He gently guided her to a seat at the table and poured her a cup of coffee, adding a splash of milk exactly the way she liked it. Robert joined her moments later with his own cup in hand, sitting across from her. He watched quietly as Ruby slowly came back to herself, the soft shift in her expressions something he cherished. The subtle play of emotions across her face as she gradually came back to life was better entertainment than any blockbuster movie.

Ruby took another sip from her of coffee. "You know, I've never noticed before. Why don't you have any pictures in your house?"

"Sure, I do. Got that Walter Anderson painting over the fireplace and the one over the bed in my bedroom."

"The paintings you have are beautiful. But you don't have any family pictures scattered around."

Robert froze. No one had ever noticed that before. "I…."

Ruby's eyes narrowed. "What are you not telling me?"

"Nothing." Robert schooled his expression. "I don't like being reminded of…. You know I've got kin crazier than a bag of cats."

Ruby eyed him for a moment. "I hope it's okay if we add a few when I move in."

He tried not to wince. "I want you to make this place your home. You can gussy it up however you like."

"Are you sure you don't mind?"

"As long as I'm waking up with you every morning, I don't care," Robert said, dropping a kiss on top of her head. "Speaking of moving in, we need to bring some of your things over here. You must be dying for a shower and fresh clothes. How about I take you back to your apartment, you can freshen up, and I'll buy you breakfast at the Catfish?"

Ruby groaned, squeezing her eyes closed. "The whole town is going to be talkin' about last night."

"Wish I could say I'm sorry." Robert chuckled. "But that was the best performance I've ever seen."

Ruby pressed her palms against the table and stood up with a slight wince. "Might as well get it over with."

An hour later, Robert opened the door of the Catfish Café for Ruby. As she predicted, all eyes were on his bride-to-be when they walked in. But the diner was unusually quiet. When Robert saw the other occupants of the worn red vinyl booths, he understood why. Most of the women who'd attended Ruby's bachelorette party filled half the diner. A few of them lifted their coffee cups with wry smiles and bloodshot eyes in silent salute as Ruby walked by and they slid into a booth.

Tillie appeared at their table, her green gingham shirt matching her green pallor. She winced when the coffee cups in her hand clanked as she put them on the table with one hand and filled them with the other. "Everybody's getting the hangover special today," she muttered as she shuffled away.

Robert looked around, biting back the amused laughter that threatened to erupt. He didn't dare make a peep. Tillie would banish him from getting pie for the rest of his days. He let Ruby drink her coffee in peace, content to take in the scene surrounding them.

A few moments later, Tillie returned with two plates filled with sunny-side up eggs, extra crispy bacon, grits, and biscuits.

A commotion made every head in the café swivel toward the front door.

Robert jumped up, seeing his friend Blake trying to usher Opal through the door while Pearl leaned on his side, wearing sunglasses and clearly green around the gills.

"Unhand me, you—you—brute!" Opal's loud voice elicited groans from the other diners.

"Woman, I'm trying to get some food and coffee in you so you'll stop acting like a banshee," Blake said, yanking her through the door.

"Help him," Ruby said in a hushed voice, with a panicked shove.

Robert slid out of the booth and went to the front of the café. "Opal. You and Pearl come on over and sit with your sister."

Pearl sagged with relief and pushed her way past her sister, making a beeline for Ruby. Opal glared at Robert for a moment before she lifted her chin and turned away. Her retreat would have been more dignified if she hadn't wobbled a bit and wasn't wearing the same clothes from the night before.

Robert raised an eyebrow at Blake. "Want to tell me what's going on here? How is it you're escorting Pearl and Opal to the café this morning?"

Blake rubbed the back of his neck. "Well, since I spent the night at their place—"

"You what?" Robert's voice rang out.

His outburst received a chorus of *shh*s and groans.

He jerked his head toward the counter. Blake followed. While Blake sat down, Robert took the liberty of slipping behind the counter and pouring them a couple of coffees, figuring Tillie was too hungover to mind, before he joined Blake at the counter. They sat at the far end, as far as possible out of earshot of the Jewels, who were all whispering among themselves. Every once in a while, Opal shot an angry glance in their direction.

"What the hell happened?" Robert asked.

"I didn't feel right dropping them off and leaving them there on their own. What if they got sick or something happened? So I slept on the couch." Blake sighed. "You should have heard the commotion when Opal found me there." He tugged on an earlobe. "My ears are still ringing. That woman sure does have a set of lungs on her. She would have made a great drill sergeant.

Robert took a sip of coffee to hide his grin. "You're a brave man, I'll grant you that. I'm surprised you didn't have the sheriff on their doorstep."

"In all my years, I've never had to do so much fast talking."

"Remember that time in Kenya?"

Blake snorted. "That was a cakewalk compared to this."

Robert let out a low whistle. "That's pretty bad."

"Good Lord, that woman," Blake muttered, downing the rest of his coffee.

"We'd better get some food into you too."

"What's good on the menu?"

"Ain't gonna be ordering off the menu today. Tillie's got a hangover special goin'." Robert leaned over and whispered, "Between you and me, I think she's too hungover to keep track of different orders today."

Sure enough, a few minutes later Tillie slid two plates with the identical fixings as the ones she'd served Robert and Ruby earlier. "Pearl ate your breakfast," she said before retreating behind the counter again.

Robert and Blake tucked in. "Damn, this is good." Blake said.

"Ain't gonna find a better breakfast than the Catfish," Robert said around a mouthful of biscuit.

When they finished eating, Robert went over to take the temperature at the Jewels' table.

"How you doing, honey?"

Ruby answered with a loud belch. "Oh Lord." She clapped her hand over her mouth. Tillie reappeared, wordlessly setting a packet of Alka-Seltzer and a glass of water on the table. "I think I'd better go home and lie down for a while."

Pearl and Opal nodded in agreement.

"I'll walk you back to your apartment, and Blake can—" All three women glowered at him. "No, I guess that's not a good idea."

"We can get ourselves home, thank you," Opal said with a dismissive wave.

Ruby scooted out of the booth and grasped Robert's hand. "Tillie, put it all on my tab," he said. "Blake, why don't you come with us, and I'll give you a ride back to your car."

Blake followed, waiting on the sidewalk while Robert delivered Ruby to her apartment, and then they made the quick drive to the Jewels' house where Blake left his rental car.

"Want to come back to my place and we can catch up a bit?"

"I'd like nothing better."

Blake followed Robert back to his cabin, pulling into the yard and parking his rental car next to Robert's truck. He got out and grabbed his duffle bag out of the backseat.

"You still carrying that thing around?" Robert chuckled. "I'd have thought you would have upgraded by now."

Black patted the faded canvas. "Darla's been around the world and back again with me. Ain't no way I'd ever leave her behind. Mind if I grab a shower and change?"

"Make yourself at home. I'll grab you a couple of towels."

"You sure you don't mind my bunking with you? I didn't think to ask." He let his bag fall to his feet and rubbed the back of his neck with a sheepish smile. "I shouldn't have assumed, now that you've got a fiancée keeping you warm at night. I don't want to take away from your time with Ruby."

"If I want a little alone time with Ruby, I can go to her place. Besides, with the wedding coming up, I doubt there'll be too much of that, anyway. Get your ass in here and make yourself at home."

After Blake showered and changed, they spent some time on the porch, catching up and revisiting old times. Blake was one of less than a handful of people in Robert's life he could talk shop with. Robert loved his nephews, both by blood and the other young men in Colton who had become his chosen family. But he'd forgotten how nice it was to sit and talk to someone his own age who'd shared long nights in dark caves and countless days tracking down those who committed heinous crimes in the name of hate.

Robert was making a pot of chili for dinner while Blake got some shut-eye to make up for the sleepless night on Opal and Pearl's sofa when a sharp knock on the door caught him by surprise. He grabbed his phone and frowned at the image caught on the high-tech camera most folks never noticed tucked in the porch soffit. A cold grip of dread crept over him when he saw the man and woman standing at his door. Their faces were unfamiliar, but their clothing and demeanor were all too familiar and spelled nothing but trouble.

He steeled himself and opened the door. "Robert Ellis?" the young woman, with blond hair pulled into a ponytail and light hazel eyes, asked. Her unofficial uniform of khakis and an Oxford shirt declared her status even without the government ID she held up. Neither she nor the man next to her, a young Black man with close-cropped hair and thick eyebrows slashed across his dark brown eyes, could have been much older than thirty.

"I think you know the answer to that," he said with resignation in his voice. He stepped back from the doorway. "Come on in."

They hovered on the doorstep. "We should talk outside," the woman, whose ID said she was Nicolle Evers, suggested.

Robert glanced over his shoulder, where Blake had emerged from the guest room, taking in the scene with a grim expression.

He followed when Robert stepped out on the porch.

"I'm Agent Evers," the young woman said, "and this is Agent Lee." The young man, shook his hand.

"This is General Blake Richardson. Anything you've got to say to me, you can say in front of him. We have the same clearance."

Agent Evers clearly recognized the name, pulling her shoulders back as if she were about to give a salute. "It's an honor, sir."

Blake nodded, joining them on the porch. Agent Evers gestured for them to follow her. When they reached the middle of the yard, she stopped.

"What's brought you to my doorstep this afternoon?" Robert asked.

The agents exchanged telling glances. It was easy to see neither of them were eager to deliver the news, and that meant it wasn't good. Eventually, Agent Evers cleared her throat. "Sir, the new president issued pardons when he came into office. Several of the people he pardoned had cases you were involved with. We have intelligence that indicates your name is being shared on a list."

Blake muttered an oath, pulling his phone out of his back pocket. His thumbs flew over the screen. A second later he pressed it to his ear and barked, "Richardson," as he walked away from the group.

The wheels in Robert's head turned faster than a race car careening around the track. The list of people who held grudges against him was long. And the new president surrounded himself with scum. Men and women who didn't care about the rule of law or honor the Constitution.

He sighed. "It was nice you to deliver the news in person."

"Sir, we've been asked to sweep the premises and make sure your security is up to standard."

Robert narrowed his eyes. "On whose orders?"

Agent Lee looked him in the eye. "We can't say."

Robert turned toward the house. "You think the house is bugged?" he asked, already kicking himself for getting too comfortable and lax with his security measures. He'd been so focused on Ruby he didn't do a quarterly sweep.

"You have friends in the agency who want to make sure you aren't being monitored," Agent Lee said.

Blake came back, his phone clutched tightly in his hand, his jaw rigid. "That bastard is unfit for office," he spat out.

Agent Evers folded her arms in front of her, dropping her chin to hide her smile. Agents were supposed to remain neutral, but it wasn't always possible to hide their reactions.

Robert rubbed the back of his neck "I'm figuring you are staying in Greenwood?"

"Yes, sir," Agent Evers said.

"You can start first thing in the morning, There ain't nothin' that's gonna be said tonight that will make any difference if someone's listening in. If they are, they know where to find me."

As soon as the taillights of the agents' car turned onto the main road, Robert rested his hands on his hips, blinking at the sky with a heavy sigh.

Blake's hand landed on his shoulder. "It's gonna be okay."

"These kids think I can't check my own home for bugs. And when they're finished, then what? We don't have any backup on this one, do we?"

Blake shook his head slowly. "The agency's been compromised."

"Do we trust those two?"

"They're jeopardizing their careers coming here to warn you. It's likely the director didn't authorize it. Nothing can be taken for granted, and we can't assume anything."

Robert's chest tightened. He'd learned to work with his fear instead of against it, but this time, his fear couldn't be contained. "Come on, I could use a hand in the barn." Nothing he was about to see would surprise Blake. Inside the weathered barn, Robert walked over to the hay bales stacked at the back. No one ever thought to question why Robert kept so much hay when he didn't have any animals other than a few chickens running around. Most folks didn't see what was right in front of them, and he'd used that to his advantage. He reached between two hay bales and pressed in the code. With a soft click and hiss, the bales swung open, revealing a small room.

Blake peered over his shoulder. "Nice to know you haven't changed," he said with an appreciative nod.

The firearms he kept in the cabin offered plenty of protection under normal circumstances, but the criminals the president set free were the type who ran around with high-powered firearms, trying to make up for having tiny dicks with big guns.

He went over to a black metal tool cabinet and started opening drawers methodically, pulling out scopes and ammo.

"Grab the top two on the right," he said, jerking his thumb toward the wall of guns behind him.

"Got it."

Blake's presence offered some comfort. There wasn't anyone he trusted more, and he knew Blake wouldn't question his actions.

They walked back to the cabin, each carrying a gun bag in silence. Inside they used hand signals while they unloaded the bags into the compartment Robert built into the living room floor. Then Robert checked his security system.

"We're clear," he said, putting away his sweeping equipment.

Blake exhaled. "Good. Do you want some privacy so you can call Ruby, or did you want to head over and tell her in person?"

Robert shook his head. "Not until tomorrow. I'll let the agents do their job. When they've cleared out, I'll tell Ruby."

"I'm sorry, friend."

"Not as sorry as I am."

How was he going to face Ruby and tell her the wedding was off?

Chapter Twenty-Two

"The house is clean, sir," Agent Lee said, jogging down the porch steps.

Robert nodded, hearing confirmation of what he already knew. Even though he'd done his own sweep, he wanted confirmation with their more sophisticated and up-to-date equipment.

Dan and Blake flanked him. He wasn't happy with Blake for reaching out to Dan behind his back, but he also understood why he did it. Dan was one of them, and Blake already respected him as much as Robert did. If he was under threat, that meant Colton was in danger. Dan had a right to know what was going on. He'd have to tell Isiah too. He was already stretched thin, running the sheriff's office with limited resources; this was only going to make Isiah's job more challenging. The three of them stood in the yard with the same stance, feet apart, arms folded across their chests, alert and ready.

The young agent's phone buzzed. "Yes, sir," he answered, eyeing Robert. The two agents were both curious and in awe of him. In Robert's opinion, that made them useless. He suspected Blake and Dan thought the same thing.

"Do you want me to make a call and get rid of them?" Dan offered.

"Sorry, son, their orders come above your clearance," Blake said.

Robert muttered an oath, kicking the dirt at his feet. He walked away toward his fields, ignoring a shout to wait from the agent. He heard Dan telling him to stand down. Robert walked until he was lost in the corn before he stopped, taking his cap off and throwing it to the ground with a string of epitaphs.

"I know what you're thinking," Blake said quietly.

"I'm not gonna to put her life at risk. Not only Ruby—Pearl, Opal, Dax, and Callie and my granddaughter. Reid and Dan."

"Do you realize you've listed half the town?" Blake asked when Robert finished naming all the people he felt responsible for. "Robert, you can't protect everyone."

"Dammit, don't you think I know that? Don't you know every mission that failed still haunts me? How do you think I feel right now, knowing we put a man in the White House who spews nothing but lies and hate?" Robert's jaw ticked. "I've been thinking I should go back in. Maybe I can—"

Blake grabbed his arm, squeezing painfully tight. "Stop." The word was an order, not a request. Blake put his face in Robert's, bringing a flashback to his boot camp days. "You're spiraling. We've served our time. Folks are going to have to learn the hard way what happens when you let a fox into the henhouse. We can't save the world. You'll lose all those people on your list, including the love of your life. Ruby deserves better," he spat out.

Robert jerked back at Blake's comment about Ruby. His friend said out loud what Robert kept as his deepest secret, one that he'd never shared with anyone. He'd buried the secret so deep he'd stopped admitting his fear to himself. He dropped his chin to his chest.

Blake loosened his grip on his arm, understanding no other words needed to be said.

The sound of a throat being cleared ended the moment. Robert saw Agent Evers hovering nearby. His earlier annoyance at their presence turned into sympathy. The young woman standing in front of his was at the beginning her journey. Her bright and alert gaze didn't yet have the shadows that would come.

"Sir, we've done a sweep of the house and the grounds, and everything is clear. We'd like to make a few upgrades to the security measures you already have in place. It should only take a day or two."

Robert nodded, fighting back the urge to argue and tell them he could do it himself. "Sounds good. I'll tell Tillie Reynolds at the Catfish Café to put your meals on my tab. Make sure you mind your manners, and you'll get an extra-large slice of pecan pie."

"Thank you, sir. The agency will cover—"

Robert put his hand up. "It's on me."

"Thank you, sir."

"Anything else you need?"

"No, sir."

Robert picked up his cap, pulling the bill down low over his eyes. "All right, then."

Robert and Blake made their way back to his cabin. He scrutinized every inch of his home, the barn, and the yard, checking sight lines, scanning for any weak points. Dan stood on the porch leaning on the railing, waiting for them. Robert saw his own worry reflected in Dan's dark eyes.

"We need to have a talk," Robert said. "I'm gonna call Rhett and Jacob. I—I'd like to talk to folks who will understand."

Dan nodded and pulled out his phone. "I'll take care of it."

As the sun started to set, and the shadows grew long in the yard, Robert sat on his porch surrounded by Blake, Dan, Rhett, and Jacob. It was part strategy session, part therapy session. In the last hour, Robert had shared more of himself and the secrets he'd kept close to his heart than he'd ever been willing to before.

"You've got to tell Ruby."

Robert bowed his head and sighed. "I know."

"Tonight," Dan said, getting up from his rocker. "Call her now."

Robert pulled out his phone and made the call he'd been foolish enough to believe he'd never have to make.

He spoke for a few moments and hung up. "She's on her way."

"I'll stay in a hotel tonight," Blake said.

"Reid and I have room at our place, and if you don't mind, I'd like to pick your brain on a couple of cases I've been working on."

Blake accepted Dan's invitation, and one by one everyone left, until it was Robert and Rhett alone on the porch.

"I almost lost Jasmine because I didn't tell her the things that gave me nightmares. I thought I was keeping her safe. You can't love her and keep lying, saying everything's okay. If you love her as much as you say you do, you have to let her share the nightmares as well as the sweet dreams."

Rhett's wisdom hit him like a punch in the gut. Robert took a lot of pride in being the one to dole out wisdom. What Rhett was saying humbled him.

They parted with an embrace and Rhett reassuring him they would all work together to keep the people they loved safe. He didn't say everything would be okay, and Robert was thankful to him for it.

Ruby arrived a few minutes after Rhett left. Robert took a deep steadying breath as he left the porch and met her at as she got out of her car.

"Hello, darlin'," he said, swallowing past the lump in his throat as he pulled her into an embrace.

"Robert?" Ruby drew back, searching his face. "What's going on?"

"Come on into the house. I need to…. I've got a story I want to tell you." He led Ruby into the house and settled her into the oversized chair next to the fireplace.

He stood in front of her, uncertainty making him hesitate before Rhett's advice came back to him.

"I—" He started pacing in front of her, stopping at the painting over the fireplace. "Yesterday, you asked me why I didn't have any pictures." He turned from the painting to face Ruby. "I don't have any pictures because it's a security risk."

Ruby's brow furrowed. "Why would having pictures be a risk?"

"Because if someone broke into this house, they could find another target, another way to hurt me by hurting the ones I love."

"Who would try to hurt you, Robert?"

He sat down on the footstool, clasping his hands tightly. "Ruby, I've put many people in prison for trying to take America back to a time when women, Black folks, and anyone they didn't think met their standards of purity didn't have rights. Some of those people have friends in high places. Now, one of them sits in the White House, and he's freed people I put away." Robert sighed, rubbing his forehead, trying to lessen the tension. "A couple of them might try to get their revenge."

Ruby's fingers dug into the armrests. "No," she breathed out in a shaky whisper.

"I—I owe you an apology. I wasn't going to tell you any of this. I almost slipped back into my old habit of thinking I could protect you by keeping you in the dark. Last night I was ready to leave." He shook his head with a pained smile. "I told Blake I was going back in."

Ruby's expression morphed from shock to anger.

Robert grabbed her hands. "I know, honey, I know that was wrong, and I'm not leaving you." He rubbed his thumb over Ruby's knuckles, taking a minute to breathe. "Rhett said I have to share both the nightmares and the sweet dreams with you."

Ruby pulled one of her hands out of his grasp and cupped his cheek. "How many nightmares have you had, Robert?" she asked in a hushed tone.

He shook his head, biting the inside of his cheek. "Too many."

"Oh, baby." Ruby put her arms around him.

He exhaled a long, shuddering breath, letting himself sink into the comfort of her embrace. Robert didn't recognize the sobs as his own at first. The last time he'd cried like this was the night he left Colton and Ruby the first time.

In Ruby's arms, he finally let go, sharing his fears and the memories that gave him those nightmares. He didn't protest Ruby helping him into bed, continuing to hold him.

When he opened his eyes, a beam of sunlight painted a wide stripe across his bed. He pushed up on his elbows, blinking against the bright light, and cocked his head at the quiet murmur of voices coming from the kitchen.

He stopped short as he rounded the corner. For a moment it felt like the entire town had taken over his home. Ruby and her sisters were bustling around the kitchen, their quiet chatter blending with the clinking dishes. The smell of coffee and grits wafted toward him. Dan and Reid, Jacob and Mae lingered in the living room along with Dax and Callie, Presley and her brother, Ashton. At the kitchen table, Isiah, Nate, Blake, and the two agents studied a map. Their hushed conversation carried a note of seriousness. The cabin was bursting at the seams.

In all the time since he'd come home, Robert never had so many people crowding his space. Under normal circumstances, it would have irritated him. But this morning, as he took in the faces around him, filled with care, determination, and an unspoken bond, his heart swelled. They weren't there invading his privacy; they were standing with him. It was a show of force. Colton had changed, more than just a small town. They were a community united in their determination to fight against hate and division. The pride he felt in that moment would stay with Robert for the rest of his days.

Everyone froze when he came into the room. Ruby rushed over, giving him a kiss. "I bet you're ready for some coffee."

"What's going on here?" he murmured.

"I hope you don't mind." Mae stepped forward, handing Robert a cup of coffee. "We all wanted to come and see what we can do to help."

"Rhett wanted me to let you know he'll check in later. Jasmine is having a rough time with morning sickness," Jacob said.

"Did you put out the call?" he asked Ruby

"It wasn't only me."

"When Jacob told me, I asked everyone you see to meet me here. This isn't only about you, Robert. This is also about our town. We've fought against hate before and we'll do it again, but we need to have a plan." Mae looked around the room with pride. "Everyone here has played a big part in bringing Colton back to life. Everyone here has a personal stake in keeping our town safe. We've all experienced the evil of White supremacy. The threat won't impact you alone, Uncle Robert. If one of us is threatened, our entire community is in danger. This is the first planning session to form a Colton Safety Committee."

"It's not about just handling domestic threats, either. We need to have plans for natural disasters and anything else that might come our way," Isiah said.

"That seems like a sensible idea," Robert said, his voice gruff. The message was clear; the weight of the world didn't rest on his shoulders alone.

He wrapped his arm around Ruby, pressing a kiss against her temple. "Thank you," he whispered.

The love and compassion he saw in Ruby's eyes when she smiled at him took his breath away.

Two hours later, the meeting broke up. He and Ruby stood on the porch alone for the first time since he'd broken down in her arms the night before.

"How are you feeling?" Ruby asked.

"Honestly? Pretty raw. Like I've been turned inside out."

Ruby squeezed his hand. "That's understandable."

"Do you.... Maybe we should postpone—"

"Robert Ellis, don't you dare." Fire flashed in Ruby's eyes.

Chapter Twenty-Three

Ruby vibrated with anger. She was not going back to being treated like a child who couldn't make her own decisions.

Was she scared? Lord yes, but she had enough strength and knew herself, who she was as her own woman, to stand on her own two feet now.

"We're not postponing anything, Robert Ellis. Do you hear me? When have you ever let fear control your life?"

"Every day," he confessed, his voice softer than she'd expected.

Ruby reached out, her fingers brushing his cheek. "Let me ask it a different way, then. When have you ever let fear stop you from getting up every morning and living your life?"

"Never," he answered, the words a little firmer this time, a spark reigniting in his eyes.

"And that's exactly what we're going to do now," she said, her voice resolute. "But this time, we're doing it together. It's you and me, Robert. Those are the only terms, and they're not up for negotiation."

Without another word, he pulled her to him, his kiss firm and reassuring. When he pulled back, a smile curved his lips. "I accept your terms."

"Good," she whispered, lifting her face for another kiss.

An hour later, Ruby curled up against Robert's side with a yawn. "We should get up. Blake must be coming back soon."

"I suppose so but, in the future I want plenty of lazy Saturdays together where we spend all day in bed."

She sighed. "That sounds wonderful."

Reluctantly, she left Robert's bed. They made sandwiches and came out to the porch with their plates and glasses of sweet tea when Blake returned.

"Y'all good?" he asked.

Ruby nodded at Robert. "We're good."

"Are you hungry?" Robert asked. "I can make you another sandwich."

"I'm good." Blake waved him off. "I had some barbecue with Reid and Dan. They're fine men, Robert. You must be proud."

"I am."

"They told me about Primus and his will and the folks showing up trying to buy his legacy from Reid." Blake's jaw tensed. "It made me wonder if any of those buyers have connections to any of the names on the threat list. I have Agent Evers and Lee checking into it."

Ruby froze. "Would they go that far?"

"All bets are off when it comes to those folks," Blake growled. "You've got a good security plan, and enough folks aware of what's going on to keep an eye on things. I envy you folks. You've built something special here in Colton."

Ruby reached for Robert's hand. "Yes, we have."

RUBY COULD see the conflict in Robert's eyes. She knew how hard it was for him to go against his protective instincts and let her go. But he understood she needed to check on her sisters. She parked her car at the Barton Building and took advantage of the warm evening weather, walking across the park toward her childhood home. She didn't bother knocking, even though she didn't live in the little white bungalow anymore.

"I figured you'd stop by," Pearl said when she waked through the front door.

"I wanted to check on you. It's been a long day."

"It sure has." Pearl shook her head with a sigh. "You start to think there's hope… well, I suppose there's always going to be someone who lives in hate." Pearl sat forward. "Do you think you should—"

Ruby held up her hand. "The rest of that sentence better not be about postponing the wedding. I already had to talk Robert off the ledge."

"Absolutely not." Opal came in with a book tucked under her arm and a plate of 7up cake in the other. "The little slice is for you, Ruby. You've got a wedding dress to fit into."

Ruby's hand hovered over the plate Opal set down on the coffee table. What in the world had come over her sister? Instead of her usual dour expression, there was a fire in her eyes Ruby hadn't seen in a long time.

Opal handed her the book she had tucked under her arm. "We've got to get organized. I've been thinking about your flowers. I think we should see if we can order some orange blossoms."

"I've already gone over the flowers with Ella."

"According to this book, orange blossoms are the proper flowers for a wedding."

Ruby turned the slim cream volume with gold lettering that had faded with age over in her hand.

Wedding Embassy Yearbook—Maison Blanche

She opened the cover and started flipping through book. Her eyes grew wide when she realized what it was. "This is a wedding planner from 1955."

Pearl clapped her hand over her mouth, trying to stifle a giggle.

Opal nodded, clearly proud of herself. "I found it in a vintage bookstore over in Greenwood."

"You know she's always shopping for vintage romances," Pearl added.

Opal shot Pearl a look before turning back to Ruby. "Well, this time I found exactly what we need."

"I don't think we need a wedding planner from 1955." Ruby eyed the book in dismay. She flipped through the pages again, her finger landing on a sentence. "It says here, the bride needs to give the groom's family her health certificate. What in the fresh hell misogynistic bullsh—"

"Ignore that part." Opal waved her hand as if she were swatting a fly. "There's important information in there we need to know." Opal drew her shoulders back. "My baby sister is going to have a proper wedding. Now, I've found a glove maker in Memphis who—"

"Stop." Ruby pinched the bridge of her nose. "I can't deal with any of this right now." In a petty act of defiance, she snatched another piece of cake and stalked out.

She took a few deep breaths before walking down the block. Ruby wondered which was worse, Opal disapproving of her wedding or taking charge?

"Evening, Miss Ruby. Care to come up and sit for a spell?" Presley called out when she passed the Beaumont house.

Ruby paused. It had been a long day, and she was exhausted. But lush ferns swayed gently in the breeze, their green tendrils spilling over the iron hooks above. The wicker chairs, with their timeworn frames, sat waiting, draped in plush chintz cushions patterned in soft floral hues.

"Sure, honey," Ruby said, climbing the stairs.

"Can I get you some sweet tea or wine?"

"A glass of water would be lovely."

Presley jumped up and went into the house, returning a minute later with a tall glass of ice water. Ruby accepted it with thanks. Taking a sip, she eyed the stack of papers and open laptop on the wicker loveseat Presley occupied.

"What are you working on?"

Presley shuffled the papers, stacking them into a neat pile. "Homework and organizing the notes for the updated town emergency plan. I've taken a map of the town, and I'm going to work with Dax on where we can put up more cameras. I found a program, the Conrad-30 Waiver Program. Mississippi can request J-1 visa waivers for foreign physicians. In exchange, the physicians agree to work in a rural or underserved area for three years. The doctor gets a chance to earn citizenship, and we could get another doctor."

"Dr. Colton could sure use the help," Ruby agreed.

"If we had an emergency, we'd be in trouble. Our community should have more than one doctor." Presley sighed and pushed her papers aways. "Mainly I've been sittin' here thinking about how much I love this town. I know folks in other parts of the world think a small Southern town doesn't matter, that we're nothing but a bunch of racist hillbillies." She winced. "Well, I was. But we're more than that, aren't we? I went to the Two Mississippi Museums in Jackson a couple of weeks ago. And this time I paid attention. Did you know they have some of Callie's grandpa's things in there? They've got little plaques on them and everything."

"Callie's grandpa played an important role in Mississippi history."

Presley's expression became pained. "I didn't know about how he worked with Medgar Evers on the Emmitt Till case. I can't believe he was in a gunfight with the Klan. I—" She wrinkled her forehead, shaking her head. "I had no idea."

"A lot of people don't know. And there are folks out there who want to keep it that way."

"I was never—I thought that stuff didn't matter to me. But now… when I was sittin' in Mr. Ellis's living room, it all became so real. This is our town, our home, my family and friends. I've never felt this scared and angry before."

Ruby moved over to sit beside Presley on the loveseat. Without a word, she wrapped her arm around the younger woman's shoulders. Presley's head leaned naturally against Ruby's, the weight of the day settling between them in quiet understanding.

"There's a lot to be afraid of in life," Ruby murmured, her voice soft but firm. "But you can't let fear keep you from living it."

Presley was quiet for a moment before she spoke again, her voice smaller this time, unsure. "Miss Ruby… can I ask you something?"

"Of course, honey."

Presley hesitated. "Do you regret not having children? I mean… I'm scared. I want to have children one day, but I'm scared that… I won't find anyone who will love me."

Ruby's heart tightened. She gave Presley a little squeeze. Beneath all the sparkle Presley wore, there was still a scared little girl searching for reassurance.

"Oh, honey," Ruby said softly, her voice steady. "There were times I wished I'd had a child. I won't lie about that. But there was only ever one man I wanted to have a child with."

"Robert?" Presley asked.

"Robert." Ruby's smile was bittersweet. "Once I gave my heart to him, there was no getting it back. He had it, all of it."

Presley stayed quiet for a beat, then spoke again. "I'm sorry you didn't get to have kids."

Ruby tightened her hold on Presley, pulling her a little closer. "Oh, but we have, honey. We have. Callie, Mae, Emma, and you. Dax and Reid too. All of you kids. Maybe not by birth, but no parent could be prouder than Robert and I are of all of you. You've brought us so much joy." Her voice wavered a little, but she steadied herself. "You know, Robert and I always thought of you young ones as our own. All of you. Don't you forget that."

Presley's eyes softened, and she chewed thoughtfully on her bottom lip. "Miss Ruby, for a long time, I thought of Dax's mama like a mother. You know, before...."

Ruby's stomach tightened at the mention of Dax's mother. She had a lot of words and none of them kind about the woman, the one who'd cast such a long, dark shadow over their town with her hatred and cruelty.

That woman who'd never been a proper loving mother to Dax and Reid. But she kept her silence, letting Presley finish.

Presley twisted her fingers in her lap, avoiding Ruby's eyes. "I don't think of her that way anymore. I hope you don't mind, but… I wish I had a mama like you. Someone to sit here with on the porch, talking about life, going shopping together. Even with Ms. Dorothy, we didn't do things like that."

Ruby felt her heart constrict, an ache deep inside her chest. She had known grief in many forms, but the weight of this quiet confession from Presley was something entirely different. Her tender words threatened to shatter Ruby's heart.

She swallowed hard, her voice shaky. "Oh, sweetheart… I would have been proud to have you as a daughter.

"Even with all the mistakes I've made? How hateful I was?"

"That's because you didn't know any better. Think about everything you've accomplished. You're the mayor's right-hand woman. You've gone back to school, and here we are sittin' on this porch, together, because that's what friends do."

"I'm glad we're friends, Miss Ruby."

"Me too, honey. We've got to be the best friends and neighbors we can be, especially now."

"Is there anything I can do to help with the wedding."

"All I need you to do is to make sure you're on time to stand up with me as one of my bridesmaids."

"I'm still pinchin' myself that you asked me."

"I can't get married without my girls, my honorary daughters by my side."

Presley sat up, her eyes sparkling with excitement. "It's going to be a beautiful wedding, Miss Ruby. Everything you've ever hoped for. We're all going to make sure of that. Just think, in less than two weeks you're going to be Mrs. Robert Ellis."

Ruby patted her heart. "Lord yes, I guess I will."

Chapter Twenty-Four

Two days later, Ruby burst through Robert's front door and announced, "I've changed my mind. We're going to Vegas."

Robert and Blake both looked up from their game of chess in surprise.

"I'm gonna take myself for a walk while you two talk," Blake said.

"What's the matter, honey?"

"My sister has lost her mother-loving mind," Ruby snapped.

Blake chuckled as he walked out.

"What now?"

"She's turned into a Bridezilla. You'd think this was her wedding. We're saying our vows in a week, and she's decided she doesn't like the flowers I picked, and she wants to have another cake tasting. Tillie's going to have a conniption fit. She… she…." Ruby pressed her hand over her heart and burst into tears.

Robert wrapped his arms around Ruby, patting her back while she cried.

"All I care about is us gettin' married. We don't need all the fuss."

"Yes, we do, sweetheart. You deserve to have the wedding you've always wanted. We both do. Of anyone in Colton, don't you think we deserve to say our vows in the gazebo?"

Ruby nodded as she wiped her eyes.

"Do you want me to talk to Opal?"

"Lord no," Ruby said with a teary laugh. "I'm not gonna have a family dust-up when Opal is finally coming around to having a brother-in-law. We've got enough troubles as it is."

"I'm sorry for bringing my past down on us when we're about to move forward. I don't know when I've ever been so unsure of so many things, but the one thing I know with absolute certainty is we're gonna stand in the gazebo together, and Judge Beaumont is going to pronounce us man and wife."

"Can we just… let's go for a walk."

Robert reached for his coat and grabbed Ruby's hand.

"I missed this so much." Ruby voiced exactly what Robert had been thinking.

"I'd dream about sneaking out and taking walks with you. I'd be in the dirtiest, foulest-smelling hole on earth, and I'd remember nights like this so clearly, I could smell the corn stalks and the red dirt."

Ruby took a deep breath and exhaled, her shoulders relaxing. "I feel better, thank you."

"I don't think your sister is trying to take over your wedding. People deal with stress and fear in different ways. I think Opal is trying to take care of her little sister the best way she can. The wedding is the only thing she can control right now."

Ruby stopped, tilting her head she smiled softly, taking his face in her hands. "How did you get so smart?"

Robert kissed her palm. "I'll never be as wise as you."

"I love you so much, Robert."

"And that's all that matters," he said when he finished kissing her.

"Hey, you two," Taylor Colton called out.

"Looks like you had the same idea we had," his wife Josephine said. "I love evenings like this, when there's a golden glow and the air is sweet."

"How are things at Halcyon?" Robert asked.

"Our new group of interns is doing well."

"We've had so many requests from people who want to come to work and study, we're thinking about expanding," Josephine said.

"Glad to hear it." Instead of turning Halcyon, the old Colton plantation house, into a wedding venue or stereotype of plantation life, Taylor and his wife Josephine turned the grand old house into a living museum and trade school, preserving the history of the enslaved people whose skill and craftsmanship created the house and grounds. It was a damn fine idea, and Robert couldn't have been prouder of his relative from the tangle of vines that made up the Colton family tree.

Taylor's smile faded. "We've heard about the list you're on. I hope you know Jo and I are on board with whatever plans the town has to keep our community safe."

"We are not going back to what Colton was before. We've all worked too hard to let that happen," Josephine said.

"Thank you. I—I'm—" He squeezed his eyes shut for a moment and took a steadying breath. "I appreciate y'all's support. I'm wish I hadn't put us in this position, but—"

"Uncle Robert, if it wasn't you, it could have been Rhett or even me. Do you know how much hate mail I get for marrying a Black woman? For including Black history on my show?" Josephine grasped his arm as Taylor kicked the ground. "There's always somebody who chooses hate because they think it gives them power. This isn't your fault."

Josephine nodded at her husband's side. "Taylor's right."

Robert let go of Ruby's hand and hugged Taylor and then Josephine. He'd never find the words to say how much their support meant to him.

"I expect next time we see you, you two will be standing in the gazebo saying your vows," Taylor said, the bright smile that earned him a loyal following for his home improvement show returning.

Robert put his arm around Ruby's shoulder. "Come hell or high water."

They said their goodbyes to Taylor and Josephine and continued down the road for a while before the crickets started chirping, signaling it was time to head home.

"I want to stay, but…."

"You've got to deal with your sister," Robert finished for her.

"It'll keep me up at night if I don't. Now that I understand why she's acting like Martha Stewart with OCD, I can deal with her better. I'll talk to Pearl first and come up with a plan."

Robert pressed a kiss to her forehead. "Let me know if you need backup."

With a few more kisses, they finally said goodbye. Robert waved as Ruby drove off in her little red Mini, watching her disappear down the road. He stood there for a moment, hands resting on his hips, his gaze lingering on the last traces of daylight slipping behind the trees. For years, he'd trained himself to keep his emotions in check—but now? He bit the inside of his cheek, already raw from the effort to hold it all together. Deep down, he knew the feelings bubbling to the surface couldn't stay buried forever. He'd seen the consequences—what happened to Rhett, and to others—when you didn't let it out.

Since sharing his past with Ruby, he'd felt lighter, freer, though the fear for her safety still gnawed at him. Having the whole town know about the threat he faced was strange, like standing exposed in a way he hadn't expected. But there was something else too—something that caught him off guard.... Support. And... love.

Blake sent a text letting Robert know he was having dinner with Reid and Dan at the Buckthorn. He considered driving over and joining them, but his rocking chair and a quiet evening on the porch beckoned.

He'd settled in with a turkey sandwich and a cold beer when Rhett pulled into his yard. Robert's stomach sank when he saw the haunted shadow returned to his eyes.

"Rhett? What's wrong, son?"

Rhett climbed the porch stairs as if his feet were made out of sandbags. He leaned against the porch railing, gripping the wood, the skin stretched taut over his knuckles.

"I want to help," he started out in a strained voice. "I don't want to let you down. I don't want to disappoint folks, but... it's too soon. I'm not strong enough to go back in."

Robert put his plate down and slowly rose to his feet. "Son, no one is asking you to. This isn't a fight that you have to let rest on your shoulders. It's okay if you want to stay home with Jasmine. Take a step back and let others have a turn. You've done your part."

Rhett took a deep, shuddering breath. His chin dropped, his long blond hair creating a curtain hiding his face. "But I want to help."

"Those who can't do, support. We all value your experience. You can share what you've learned and offer advice."

Rhett looked at him, a spark of hope returning to his eyes. "I—I can do that."

"You and I both know this new threat isn't so new. It's been around for a long time." Robert put his hand on Rhett's shoulder, giving him a little shake. "It's gonna take more than you and me to fix it. Until folks stop trying to make excuses and pretend like there's exceptions that make prejudice okay, we're gonna be part of a long list of people who have fought the good fight.

"It feels like were losing right now. Every day more people try to deny the Holocaust even happened. They're trying to rewrite history and to make people believe slavery was a good thing." Rhett lowered his head, clasping his hands tightly. "When all the history books are rewritten, who will be left to tell the truth?"

Robert leaned back, blinking up at the stars. "Your children someday, Callie and Dax, Jacob and Mae's kids. You'll teach them what they don't learn at school. Every time you take your kids to play in Ada Mae Colton Park, you'll remind your kids that she was more than a woman kept as a slave. You'll teach them what a remarkable woman she was, how she helped her kin to escape and taught others how to read and write. When I got the news I'm on a threat list, there's a song that popped into my head from the musical *South Pacific*. 'You've Got to Be Carefully Taught.' It was about how kids learn to hate from their parents. Some kids do, but others learn about love and empathy. They grow up in homes with parents who teach history at the dinner table. That's the kind of home I know you and Jasmine are working to have. The strongest weapon we have is education. Teaching folks the truth. You sharing your story, your experience is a powerful thing, son."

"Thank you." Rhett blew out a shaky breath. He tapped his temple. "I got all caught up in my head and… I panicked."

"I get it. I'm glad you came over."

"Jasmine told me to. She said I need to talk to someone who would understand."

"You were there for me, and I'll always be there for you. That's the way it works. We're family."

"I appreciate you."

"Can you sit a spell?"

Rhett gave him a shy smile. "Jasmine—"

Robert held his hand up to stop him. "You don't have to say anything more. Go home to your fiancée."

Rhett pulled him into a hug. "Thanks again, Uncle Robert."

"Y'all come back anytime you need."

"I will." Rhett jogged down the porch steps with a bounce in his step he didn't have when he arrived.

Content, Robert returned to his rocker. The worry and fear would never go away, but the burden he'd always carried within him felt a little lighter now. He hoped Rhett felt the same. The empty chair next to him taunted him. Jealousy was a funny thing. It had a way of creeping up on you before you noticed it. But that pang he felt in his heart thinking of Rhett, Dax, Reid, and Taylor all happily settled was that little green-eyed monster poking at him. For too many years he took solace in his time alone on the porch. Now the empty chair next to him made him angry. The time when he and Ruby were sitting out here together couldn't come soon enough.

Chapter Twenty-Five

TIME SLOWS down when you're sitting on a porch waiting to have a serious conversation with someone. Ruby stopped rocking and stood up, her shoulders back and head held high, prepared for battle when Opal pulled her ancient gray sedan into the driveway.

"Good, you're here," she said when she got out. Opening the rear door, she started gathering packages in her arms before heading toward Ruby. "I finally found the perfect unity candle, and wait until you see the rhinestone and pearl clips I found for your updo. And the gloves finally arrived—"

"Opal, stop. Let's put these packages down." Ruby gently pulled the bags out of her arms, setting them down on a side table. "Sit down. We need to talk."

"You're right, and now is a good time, while we have some privacy," Opal said, her voice dropping to a hushed tone as she sat down in one of the three rocking chairs on the porch. She leaned in close when Ruby sat down. "I wish Mama were here for this part, but as your oldest sister, it's my responsibility. Ruby, honey, marital relations aren't always easy at first—"

"Sweet Jesus, are you seriously trying to give me the talk?" Ruby exclaimed.

"Hush!" Opal fanned her hand at her. "The neighbors will hear."

"Opal Louise Colton, how is it you are the only one in this town who doesn't know Robert and I have been having sex? What in the world do you think we've been doing when I go out to his place or he comes to mine?"

If she'd been wearing pearls, Opal would have clutched them. "I thought you were… canoodling."

"Good gravy." Ruby rolled her eyes.

"I'm trying to do what the book says. I want everything to be proper."

Ruby reached for her sister's hand. "Opal, this isn't about the wedding and doing things the right way. You're scared. Right now the world, our world, feels unsteady on its feet. We don't have any control over what folks are gonna do. And you can't fix that by trying to control my wedding."

Opal's shoulders slumped as her face fell. When her chin started to quiver, Ruby moved to perch on the arm of Opal's rocker so she could put her arm around her. "It all feels so… unsteady. Like I'm on a ship in stormy seas, and I don't have a life jacket."

"We're your life jacket. Pearl, me, Robert."

Opal sniffed and wiped her eyes. "I got a little out of hand, didn't I?"

"A little?" Ruby raised an eyebrow.

"I wanted to make up for the wrong I did to you and Robert."

"We can't go back, only forward."

"I suppose so." Opal sighed. "But do you think between now and the wedding we can hang out more, like we used to?"

"Of course. I expect we'll see each other every day. We've got a wedding to organize."

Opal patted her arm. "Yes, we do. And I'm gonna make sure your big day goes off without a hitch."

The sound of raindrops tapping against the window jerked Ruby from her dreams. A low rumble of thunder followed, pulling her fully awake. She glanced at the charcoal-gray clouds gathering outside, thick and heavy in the sky.

With a quick scramble, she jumped out of bed and rushed to the window, her eyes widening as another rumble of thunder vibrated through the air, much closer now.

"Mother Nature, don't do me like this," she muttered, her voice a mix of disbelief and pleading. "Not today."

Mother Nature was too busy wreaking havoc to listen. A clap of thunder brought a torrent of hail that quickly coated the ground, creating a winter wonderland. A bright flash, followed by another boom a few minutes later, brought a deluge of rain.

Ruby sagged against the window frame. "Well, hell."

The week before her wedding had gone by in a flash and blissfully without any incident, lulling Ruby into a false sense of security.

A knock on the door pulled her away from the gloom outside her window. She opened it to find Presley on her threshold.

"Mae gave me the code to get in the building," she said, bustling inside. "Now don't you worry, Miss Ruby. It's gonna be okay. I sent Ashton to Greenwood to find as many umbrellas he can find in your wedding colors. And I have these." She held up a pair of white rain boots with a look of triumph. Presley took Ruby's silence as disapproval. "Don't worry," she continued, digging into the tote bag on her arm. "We can gussy them up," she said, pulling out a glue gun and a bag of rhinestones.

Bless her heart. "Thank you, honey."

Presley set her things down on the kitchen island and pulled off her raincoat. "Gosh almighty, I'm drippin' everywhere," she exclaimed, water puddling on the floor under her feet.

"I don't think that can be helped on a day like today." Ruby sighed.

Isiah was the next one to show up on Ruby's doorstep wearing his rain gear, his sheriff's hat covered in plastic. "Miss Ruby." He tipped his hat. "I wanted to reassure you everything's going to be all right. According to the weather service, this storm should blow through before the wedding."

"But what if it doesn't? We still need a contingency plan," Presley said.

Isiah's face morphed into a scowl. "There's no need to be so negative."

Presley put her hands on her hips. "And there's no reason not to be proactive and have a plan B."

"Are you the wedding coordinator? Is that your job?"

Ruby watched with a mixture of amusement and alarm as the two argued. They moved forward until they stood toe- to-toe. "I'm not useless. I'm good at organizing things. You can ask Mae. And I'm a good friend, but you wouldn't know that because all you ever do is tell me what I'm doing wrong." Presley poked Isiah in the chest.

Isiah grabbed her finger. "That's because you... you...."

He was either going to kiss her or arrest her, but today wasn't the day for them to figure that out. "Children!" Ruby clapped her hands, using her stern nurse voice. "Behave yourselves."

"Sorry, ma'am."

"Sorry, Miss Ruby."

Isiah and Presley said in unison. Isiah realized he still had Presley's finger in his grasp and let go.

Mae showed up in Ruby's open doorway breathless, her raincoat completely soaked. "Isiah, good, I'm glad I caught you. Mockingbird Creek is rising fast, and I'm worried about the bridge. Presley, let's be ready to activate our emergency plan, if we need it."

Presley shot Isiah an *I told you so* expression, and Ruby half expected to see her stick her tongue out at the sheriff. She put her coat her back on and came over to give Ruby a peck on the cheek with a stern look in her eyes. "Don't you worry, Miss Ruby, you're gonna have a beautiful weddin' day." Presley brushed past Isiah on her way out with one more angry glance.

Isiah nodded. "I'm on it," he said to Mae and followed Presley down the stairs.

"Are you doing okay?" Mae asked. "I'd stay with you if I could, but…."

"That's all right, honey, you take care of what you need. I'll be fine."

"We're here," Pearl announced breathlessly with Opal behind her, panting with her hand on her chest.

Mae's eyes narrowed. "What did you do? Please tell me you didn't run up those stairs."

"We were worried about Ruby." Opal gasped like a dying catfish.

Mae's phone rang, and they all watched as she answered, her eyes grew wide, and she muttered "shit" under her breath. She hung up and turned to Ruby. "Do. Not. Panic," she said before she turned on her heel and ran out the door.

Ruby's phone rang next, and a wave of relief washed over her at seeing Robert's name flash on her screen.

"You okay, honey?"

"I think so. Everyone keeps telling me to stay calm and everything will be all right." She barked a laugh that sounded a little too high-pitched and slightly panicked to her ears. "I think I'm too numb to panic," she confessed.

Another clap of thunder shook the windows and made her jump. The sound of the fire engine siren echoed out through the town square.

"I don't know, Robert. We may need to postpone for a day."

"Absolutely not. I said come hell or high water when we were talkin' to Taylor and Josephine, and I mean it. We're saying our vows today."

"You're right. We're not wasting one more day."

Robert chuckled softly. "I'm glad to know you're as eager to seal the deal as I am." There was a pause. "Sweetheart, I've got to go. I'll see you in the gazebo, okay?"

"Okay. Love you."

"Love you too."

Even if she wanted to, Ruby didn't have time to panic. Over the next hour, the wind picked up and the rain fell harder.

Opal peered out the window with a frown. "It's fierce out there."

Chapter Twenty-Six

Robert hung up with his bride-to-be with a heavy sigh.

"This is a hell of a way to start a wedding day," Blake said, watching the rivulets of water run through Robert's yard.

Robert checked the weather app on his tablet. "The wind's shifted. We should only be getting the edge of the storm now." He slapped the table. "Today of all days."

Blake shot him a sympathetic look. "We've been through worse, and we're gonna get through this."

They'd come so far to get to today. Was it too much to ask for the sun to shine? "Let's head into town. Ruby is trying to sound calm, but I can hear in her voice, she's worried as hell."

They grabbed their suit bags and toiletries and headed toward town. One of Isiah's deputies was at the other end of Mockingbird Bridge when they pulled up. Robert rolled down his window and leaned out to peer at the water rushing below with a grim expression.

"Don't know when I've seen the creek this high."

"Mr. Ellis," the deputy called out. "You better get across now. I might have to close the bridge down. If the levee upstream breaks, we're gonna be in trouble."

"Got it." Robert rolled up his window and turned to Blake. "Bet you wish you were on your boat in the Keys right about now, don't you?"

"Absolutely not. Let's get into town and see what needs to be done," he replied. His tone let Robert know he'd already switched into military mode.

Robert had to dodge a few fallen branches on the road into town. Ruby and her sisters were huddled together in their rain gear on the sidewalk across the street from the Barton Building when they pulled up.

They got out of the truck, and Robert ran over to Ruby. He couldn't tell if it was rain or tears in her eyes when he reached her.

"What are we going to do?" she asked, squinting at the gray skies. "Even if this rain lets up, it's going to be a muddy mess."

He cupped her cheek, brushing away the rain or tears on her cheek. "I'm here. We're okay, and today is our wedding day,"

"Some wedding day," Ruby sniffed. "We can't get married like this."

Robert grasped her shoulders. "We've waited too long for this day. We *are* getting married. We'll figure it out."

"I've got a plan," Presley shouted, marching toward them in a bright translucent raincoat, carrying the clipboard she always had on hand on farmers' market days to check in vendors. "I need you two out of this rain. We can't have the bride and groom coming down with colds before the wedding, It'll spoil the honeymoon. Go back to Ruby's apartment," Presley ordered, pointing across the street.

Blake chuckled. "She's got gumption. I like it."

"We didn't get to meet before. You had your hands full." Presley realized what she'd said, and her cheeks turned pink. She leaned toward Opal. "Sorry."

Opal glared at Blake, the rain dripping off her hood making her seem like an angry kelpie.

"What do you need us to do?" Pearl asked.

Presley opened her mouth to speak and then frowned at Robert, pointing toward the Barton Building entrance. "I said git."

Robert looped his arm around Ruby's waist with a chuckle. "Come on, honey. It seems our wedding coordinator has everything under control."

They shook their coats out and left their rain boots outside Ruby's door before going in. Ruby paced inside the apartment. "I feel so useless. I'm not sure what we should be doing with ourselves."

"I have an idea." Robert waggled his eyebrows, pulling Ruby into his arms. It was easy to lose himself in kissing Ruby, but another clap of thunder broke them apart.

"Have you eaten anything?"

"Coffee this morning," he admitted. "What about you?"

"I haven't had anything. Presley was on my doorstep before I'd barely woken up, trying to reassure me the day wasn't going to turn into a disaster."

"You got eggs and cheese? I could make us a couple of omelets."

"Sounds good. I'll make some coffee."

Their wedding day might still be up in the air, but Robert was thoroughly enjoying working alongside Ruby in the tiny kitchen of her apartment. This was the kind of simple, everyday moment he envisioned for their future. He paused, spatula in hand, hovering over the eggs he'd poured into the pan.

"I realized," he said, breaking the comfortable silence, "we've never talked about where we're going to live. I figured you'd move out to the farm with me."

Ruby raised an eyebrow, glancing up from chopping vegetables. "I thought the same."

Robert hesitated, turning the eggs gently in the pan. "But you've always lived in town. Will you miss it?"

Ruby's gaze swept around the apartment, lingering for a moment on the small, cozy space. "I've only been here a short time, but yeah... I think I'll miss this place."

Robert caught the wistful look in her eyes and smiled, his voice softening. "Then let's keep it. Or maybe we can find a little house nearby. That way, if something's going on in town and it's too late to drive back, we'll have somewhere to stay."

Ruby's eyes lit up. "I like that idea. But are you sure? It's an extra expense."

"Home is where we're together. I like the idea of having a place in town. Now that I've got a grandniece, and with everything Reid and Dan are going through right now, I think it would be a good thing to stay close by."

"What about the farm?"

"I can hire someone to run it." He wrapped his arm around Ruby's waist and gave her a kiss.

"It's a lot of money, Robert."

There was one last thing he needed to share with Ruby. It wasn't exactly a secret, but their wedding day wasn't the best timing. He pulled the pan off the stove before he burnt the eggs and took Ruby's hands in his.

"There's something I need to tell you," he said, his voice tentative. "It's not a bad thing," he added quickly when he saw the flicker of alarm in her eyes. "Sweetheart, we don't have to worry about money. I've lived a pretty frugal life, and I had a good investment broker." He gave her a sheepish smile. "We've got enough to live however we want for the rest of our lives, and we'll have enough left over to make a healthy endowment to the town."

Ruby drew in a sharp breath, her mouth pressed into a thin line for a moment before she blurted out, "We can't get married, Robert, not without a prenup. It wouldn't be right."

"You've got to be kidding me. Ruby Anne Colton, what's mine is yours. The material things don't matter. You've always had my heart, so you get everything else that goes with it. Besides, are you thinking this marriage isn't going to work out?"

She swatted at his chest. "Of course not."

"This is it, Ruby. I'm the man for you and you're the woman for me."

She leaned into him with a soft sigh. "That's what we used to say to each other."

He held on with one arm and returned to the stove, putting the pan back on the burner to warm up the omelet with his other hand. "It took us a lot longer than I ever thought it would, but we're doing it now."

Robert let go of Ruby and slid the omelet onto a plate and set it on the counter. The pan sizzled as he added more egg mixture and started making one for himself.

"Mine will be ready in a minute. Eat up before yours gets cold," he said, waving his spatula toward the plate.

A few minutes later he sat down at the island next to Ruby, noting she'd only taken a couple of bites of her food.

"You don't like it?" he asked.

Ruby smiled and patted his arm. "It's delicious. How lucky am I that my future husband is a good cook."

"I wouldn't go that far. I don't know how to make much, but what can make usually comes out pretty well."

He coaxed her into eating every bite, knowing her anxiety about the storm outside took precedence over her hunger. Robert felt the same way but forced himself to clean his plate too. They were washing up in the kitchen when there was a knock on the door and Presley poked her head in.

"Are y'all decent?" she asked, covering her eyes with one hand.

Robert's amused chuckle earned a sharp elbow jab from his fiancée.

"Come in, Presley," Ruby said.

Presley came in, her raincoat leaving a small puddle around her feet. "The rain is starting to let up. If we delay for an hour or two, we can make this work."

"The ground is going to be soaked. We can't ask our guests to tromp through the mud."

"We won't. I put the word out we won't be setting up chairs and for everyone to wear their galoshes. The wind died down and the tent is going up in front of the café, and we have extra heaters going to dry everything out."

"I doubt we'll have much of an audience. Who's going to want to come out and stand in the mud to watch us?" Ruby sighed.

"Lots of folks, you'll see, Miss Ruby. Mr. Ellis, I sent your friend Blake over to my brother's apartment. You head over and get ready over there. Miss Ruby, your sisters will be up in a minute. I've got to get back out there. I've got work to do."

With that, Presley whirled around and left.

Robert raised an eyebrow. "Did you ever think you'd live to see the day?"

"Can't say that I did, but I sure am proud of that girl. She's got gumption."

Robert took Ruby's hands in his. "Come on, Miss Colton, it's time for us to get ready to say our vows." Robert pressed a gentle kiss on Ruby's forehead and left for Ashton's apartment.

"You ready?" Blake clapped Robert on the shoulder when he walked in.

"I've been ready since I first set eyes on her."

Blake gave him a sympathetic smile. They'd spent their fair share of sleepless nights in caves and safe houses where Robert regaled him with stories about a girl back home that he'd given his heart to when he was a boy.

"She's a wonderful woman." Blake snorted a laugh. "Ruby and her sisters. The Jewels are priceless."

Robert raised an eyebrow. "You see somethin' you like?"

Blake avoided making eye contact. "Maybe."

In all the years they'd been friends, Robert could count on one hand the times his friend wouldn't look him in the eye.

"I think it's only fair to warn you, Opal Colton could give a mule lessons on stubbornness."

Blake grinned at him with a twinkle in his eye Robert hadn't seen in a long time. "That's what I like about her."

Robert threw his head back and laughed, the sound echoing off the brick walls.

Ashton came through the door, not as rain-soaked as Robert expected.

"It's clearing up out there," Ashton announced, shucking out of his raincoat.

"Good to hear. Thanks for offering up your place for us to get ready."

"Happy to play a small part in your big day. Now, what can I do to help out?"

"I think we're good." Robert reached up to check his tie.

"I'll get showered and changed in a jiffy. I expect the rest of your wedding party will be knocking on the door any minute."

Sure enough, there was a knock and Dax and Reid poked their heads in.

"Y'all ready for company?" Dax asked with a grin.

"Come on in."

"Jacob is on his way. He's finishing up a few things."

A sunbeam broke through to brighten the room.

"Well, that's a good sign," Blake said.

Ashton's apartment overlooked the park. Robert's jaw dropped when he saw the transformation. "Y'all have worked wonders. Ruby's gonna be tickled pink when she sees what you've done."

Dax came up behind him and clapped him on the back. "Everyone wanted to help. We've had quite a few weddings in Colton in the last few years, but this one is the talk of the town."

Jacob arrived, and a bottle of whiskey was brought out.

An hour later, once Dax made sure the coast was clear and there was no chance of Robert seeing his bride before she walked down the aisle, Robert and his groomsmen went out to the park and took their places in the gazebo.

Chapter Twenty-Seven

As soon as Robert slipped out the door of Ruby's apartment, Opal and Pearl rushed in, shedding their raincoats and boots with practiced ease. The sound of wet leather hitting the floor was quickly drowned out by the bustle of activity that followed. Callie and Mae entered right behind them, each holding garment bags that swished as they moved.

"Where's the glue gun?" Mae asked. "I have strict orders from Presley to make those rain boots... glittery."

Ruby barely had time to register their arrival before the whirlwind of activity enveloped her. She could feel her apartment transforming into a hive, buzzing with voices, laughter, and the soft rustle of fabric. Callie ushered her into the bathroom, insisting she soak in a hot tub overflowing with bubbles. The steamy warmth helped soothe away any remaining pre-wedding jitters.

Now, settled at the kitchen island in a bathrobe, Ruby sat under the careful hands of Emma, who was gently dabbing cream onto her face, and Callie, who deftly curled sections of her hair with her fingers. Mae thrust a glass of champagne into her hands with strict instructions that Presley said she could have only one before the wedding.

Ruby sighed softly, trying to make sense of the whirlwind of preparations. "Don't think I don't appreciate the fuss," she muttered, her gaze drifting over the frantic motion around her. "I do. But I don't imagine many folks are gonna want to come out and stand in the rain for a wedding." She couldn't help the flicker of concern in her voice, though she tried to hide it. The rain had been relentless, pouring down in sheets for hours, and she could already picture the waterlogged guests huddling under umbrellas, the whole thing feeling less like a celebration and more like a soggy inconvenience.

Emma paused her gluing with a smile that was warm despite the weather's gloom. "Don't worry," she said, her tone light but with a confidence that was rare for Ruby's quiet friend. "A little rain never hurt anyone. Besides, we've got glitter and gumption on our side. It'll be perfect, you'll see."

Ruby couldn't help but laugh despite herself. This crew was nothing if not determined, and she loved them all for it.

The atmosphere in the apartment buzzed with the energy of people who were willing to do whatever it took to make the day perfect, no matter the weather. Though Ruby still had her doubts about the rain, one thing was clear: the wedding was going to be unforgettable—rain or shine.

By the time she donned her dress, the rain had stopped and the sun burst through the clouds.

"I knew Mother Nature didn't stand a chance against Presley Beaumont."

The woman herself burst through the door as Ruby was putting on the earrings Pearl gave her at her bridal shower.

Presley stopped with a gasp. "Oh, Miss Ruby, you're beautiful." She bit her lip, her chin quivering slightly. "I appreciate you asking me to be a bridesmaid, Miss Ruby. It's an honor, it really is, but… I won't have time to get ready."

"Nonsense."

Presley jumped back as Ruby came toward her. "Oh no, I don't want to get raindrops on your dress."

Ruby stopped her advance. "I am not getting married without my full wedding party."

"Miss Ruby, there isn't time to go back home, change, do my hair and makeup."

"Your brother dropped your clothes off, and we can help with your hair and makeup," Mae said.

"Come on, honey." Opal shooed Presley toward the bathroom. "Jump in the shower real quick and we'll get you fixed up."

In under an hour, Ruby circled Presley, smiling and nodding with approval. Presley reached up, fingering one of her blond curls nervously. "Are you sure I'm okay like this?"

Ruby and the other women all exchanged glances in silent agreement. Presley's appearance was much improved without her blown out, teased up hair and heavy makeup. Beneath all the heavy foundation, Presley had a beautiful complexion. Her cheeks had a natural rosy glow. Callie and Mae convinced her the faint smattering of freckles across her nose didn't need covering up, and her eyelashes were long enough with a light coat of mascara instead of adding false eyelashes.

She put up the biggest fuss about her hair. Ruby practically had to bar the door to keep Presley from making a break for it when she was told she couldn't use a hairdryer. Without all that heat, her hair fell in loose curls that framed her face.

"Honey, you are beautiful," Ruby said. "I'll be proud to have you standing with me when I make my vows."

Presley's eyes became bright with tears. "If anyone ever said to me I'd be here—" She looked around at the women surrounding her and then back at Ruby. "You've been such a good friend to me. All of you, but Miss Ruby, you've been… well…." Her voice trembled. "You've all given me a second chance when a lot of folks—"

"Now, none of that. You'll have us all weeping, and I can't walk down the aisle with red eyes," Ruby said, pulling her into a tight embrace. She chuckled, patting Presley on the back. "I suppose it will be more like wading down the aisle."

Presley pulled out of Ruby's embrace, her eyes now bright with excitement. "You won't be wadin', Miss Ruby. You can put on your fancy shoes. You'll see when we get downstairs."

Opal and Pearl linked arms with her as they descended the stairs, following Callie, Mae, Emma, and Presley, all looking radiant in their green dresses. At the bottom, Mae's mother, Ella, waited with bouquets of roses, peonies, and eucalyptus for each of them.

"You all look lovely," she said to the bridal party. She handed Ruby her bouquet. "Ruby, you are breathtaking."

Ruby thanked her, holding the bouquet to her nose and inhaling the natural perfume created by the blend of flowers in her bouquet.

Nate came in. His smile grew when he saw Ruby and her sisters. "I don't believe I've ever seen the Jewels sparkle so bright."

Ruby took his arm. Ella, who'd graciously stepped in to be the coordinator for this moment, arranged the rest the rest of the bridal party ahead of her.

Ella held up a finger, and when everyone stilled, she opened the door of the Barton Building.

Mother Nature had redeemed herself in spectacular fashion. The sky was clear, the sunset coordinating perfectly with the dresses Ruby's bridesmaids wore.

A wood thrush, the first to greet the dawn with its song, now heralded the arrival of the wedding party. Ruby stepped into the soft evening light, taking in she scene with wonder. A path of pavers led the way to the gazebo, glowing in the fading warmth. It seemed there wasn't a single string of lights left in Mississippi that hadn't been woven into the golden web of light in the park. Rows of chairs, placed on sheets of plywood to keep the guests' feet dry, stood at attention. Not a single seat was empty, despite Ruby's worry that the rain might keep people away.

"I see skies of blue...."

Louis Armstrong's distinct, gravelly voice filled the air. Everything else faded away when Ruby locked eyes with Robert. He stood at the top of the gazebo steps, looking every inch the groom of her dreams in a dark suit with a crisp white shirt, with a pink tie and pocket square.

Ruby handed her bouquet to Opal, and Nate put her hand in Robert's.

Robert leaned in and placed a tender kiss on Ruby's cheek. "Evenin', Miss Ruby. Seems like a nice night to get married, doesn't it?"

"It sure does, Mr. Ellis."

Hand in hand, they turned to stand in front of Judge Beaumont, who peered at them over the rim of his glasses.

"Dearly beloved...." He paused, looking at them for a moment and then sighed, shaking his head. "I don't think the traditional vows are suitable for this occasion." He gave Robert and Ruby a wry smile. "To say this day has been a long time coming would be an understatement."

A ripple of laughter went through the guests.

"We are gathered here this evening to witness a wedding. This is more than a joining of two people. Robert and Ruby, standing here before you, are a testament to the power of love. Love can heal old wounds. Love can right the wrongs of the past. Love is the most powerful weapon we can wield. Martin Luther King said, 'Hate cannot drive out hate. Only love can do that.' Do you have rings you'd like to exchange as a token of your love?"

Robert turned to Blake, who pulled out a simple gold band and handed it to him.

Opal stepped forward to hand Ruby its match.

"Robert, do you promise to love and cherish this woman at your side? Do you promise to make Ruby your partner, facing any trials life presents together, united in love?"

Robert cleared his throat and locked eyes with Ruby, his bright with unshed tears as he slid the band on her finger. "I do."

"Ruby, do you promise to love and cherish this man at your side? Do you promise to make Robert your partner, facing any trials life presents together, united in love?"

Ruby squeezed Robert's hand before she put his band on his finger, never more sure of her answer to a question in her life. "I do."

Looking down at their hands, she felt like they'd finally put the last piece of the puzzle in place. Ruby's heart was whole.

When they turned to face their guests, a broom draped in so many flowers that the bristles were barely visible was placed before them. Hand in hand, they jumped.

There were shouts and cheers as they danced their way back down the aisle to Earth Wind and Fire's "Got to Get You into My Life." Ruby's Mini was festooned with flowers and ribbons, ready to whisk them away to their reception.

Chapter Twenty-Eight

THE DELUGE of rain required a change of venue. It was too wet to have their reception outside the Catfish Café the way they'd planned, but once again Presley worked her magic, and with Dan and Tillie's help they'd moved the entire reception to the Buckthorn.

White tablecloths covered the picnic tables, and the usual wooden benches had been replaced by rows of gold banquet chairs with plush white cushions, rented for the occasion. Garlands of peonies, roses, and delicate greenery ran the length of each table, with tea lights woven in their soft glow creating a touch of romance in the rustic charm of the venue. The tables were arranged in a way that left the center of the room open, creating a spacious dance floor where guests could get their groove on.

When they arrived, Tillie was standing near the cake table, inspecting the delicate sugar blossoms that adorned the wedding cake. She complimented the culinary students who had taken on the ambitious task of creating the towering three-tiered cake. Its white fondant exterior gleamed in the soft light, and sugar roses, peonies, and—to make Opal happy—orange blossoms trailed down one side of the cake in a graceful spiral. The students had outdone themselves, and Tillie's admiration was evident as she continued to examine every detail of the cake with a satisfied nod.

It was almost two hours of greeting guests and accepting congratulations, dinner, and toasts, before Robert was able to get his bride to the dance floor.

He spun Ruby into a twirl and pulled her back into his arms. "Well, Mrs. Ellis, the day may not have gone the way we planned, but all things considered, I wouldn't change a single thing. What do you think?"

Ruby smiled at him. The canopy of twinkle lights made her eyes sparkle even brighter than they already were, filled with happiness and love. "It was a glorious day."

They took in the scene around the room filled with friends and family dancing, drinking, and laughing, and then at each other. "Mrs.

Ellis, I think I've loved you my entire life, but I don't think I've ever loved you more than I do right now." Robert pulled her into a kiss, tasting the champagne and sweet lemon filling from the cake on her lips.

"Get a room," Blake chuckled, dancing by with Opal in his arms.

"Mind your manners," Opal said, swatting at Blake's chest.

"I'm warning you, Ms. Colton. I have no intention of doing any such thing," Blake said with a mischievous twinkle in his eye.

As they moved out of earshot, Robert watched them continue to bicker out of the corner of his eye, unable to hear Opal's response.

"I don't know when I've seen my sister so riled up by a man," Ruby said.

"I think it's good for her. For both of them."

Ruby raised her eyebrows. "You're not trying to play matchmaker, are you?"

"Absolutely not. I'm not gonna interfere if nature takes its course."

Ruby eyed Emma and Presley standing alone next to the punch table. "Well, I've decided Mother Nature might need a little push." She grabbed Robert's hand, dragging him with her toward the two wallflowers. "I don't know what to do about Emma," she muttered under her breath. "But Presley…." She stopped when they reached the two women.

"Emma, honey, you stay right there for me." Ruby grabbed Presley with her free hand. "Presley, you come with us."

"Miss Ruby, I mean Mrs. Ellis, what are you—" Presley sucked in her breath when they reached Isiah, standing with Ashton by the bar.

She gave Presley a little shove towards Isiah. "I'm an old married woman now, and I know what's best."

"Mrs. Ellis, you've only been married for a couple of hours," Ashton said with a sly smile.

"Yes. But I'm old and I'm married," Ruby shot back. She pushed Presley into Isiah's arms. "Y'all need to stop dancin' around each other and just start dancing."

"I'd do what she says or you'll never hear the end of it," Robert warned.

Isiah looked down at Presley's upturned face. "It is a wedding reception—"

"And people are supposed to dance," Ruby said, pushing them both toward the middle of the room. "Now shoo, get."

"Mrs. Ellis, I applaud your matchmaking skills." Ashton laughed.

"Don't get smart with me, young man. Your turn will come." Ruby's expression softened. "In the meantime, do me a favor and ask Emma to dance."

Together, the three stole a quick look at Emma, who stood alone, watching the dancers with longing in her eyes.

"Yes, ma'am," Ashton said.

"Happy now?" Robert said, sweeping his bride back onto the dance floor.

"Very," she said, resting her head on his chest.

The dance floor was filled with couples swaying to the music. Enveloped by the happiness and joy around him, a feeling of rightness and contentedness settled over him. The Jewels were giggling and toasting each other. His nephews danced by with their partners, happy and in love. Robert took it all in, bursting with pride.

Blake came over to stand next to Robert, observing the crowd.

"You've got a good thing going here, Robert."

"Sure do. I'm looking forward to staying on and watching what the next generation is gonna do."

"I think I'm ready for something new," Blake said, his gaze tracking Opal on the other side of the dance floor. "I might stay for a bit longer."

"It's a big change from Florida. What about your fishing boat?"

Blake shrugged. "Honestly, it's more work keeping up the maintenance than the pleasure I get from taking it out. I'd be as happy with a fishing pole over at your Turtle Pond."

Robert nodded, studying his friend. He sensed Blake was lonely and looking for…. He glanced at Opal. The energy that arced between them could light up the entire town square. Blake was looking for a battle. He was a soldier at heart, and he needed a challenge. It looks like he might have found one.

"Tell you what. You can stay in Ruby's apartment while you're here. I'm sure she won't mind."

"Won't mind what?" Ruby asked, wrapping her arm around Robert's.

"Blake here is thinking about sticking around for a while. I told him he could stay at your place."

"If you don't mind," Blake added.

"Of course not. I'll be staying at Robert's farm. We decided going to hold on to the apartment to have a place in town if we needed it. You are welcome to stay as long as you'd like."

"Thank you. I figure I can lend a hand and help with the town's emergency plan and shore up security."

Robert failed to hide his smile. "That's as good an excuse as any other."

Blake waggled his finger at Robert. "Stop trying to stir the pot."

"You seem to be doing that all on your own." Robert grinned at his friend.

"All right, you two. Stand down," Ruby said, stepping between them. "You can work this out when we get back from our honeymoon. Blake, I'll make sure Dax has a key to my place for you. Make yourself at home."

Ruby turned to Robert. "Mr. Ellis, are you ready to sweep me off my feet and take me on our honeymoon?"

"Mrs. Ellis, there's nothing I'd like to do more. Let's start saying our goodbyes. You know it's going to take another hour before we can make our escape."

Their honeymoon began with a town car and driver waiting to take them to Jackson, where they spent their first night in a suite atop the historic King Edward Hotel. The next morning they would fly Paris for a week, staying at the Four Seasons, followed by another week in Bordeaux touring wineries. When Ruby mentioned that she'd always wanted to see the Eiffel Tower, Robert's honeymoon dilemma was solved. It happened that he had a former colleague in French intelligence, and they'd stayed in touch over the years. One phone call to his friend, Sebastien Durand, and he had a perfect itinerary. Thanks to Sebastien's connections, they toured vineyards with a private guide and even enjoyed a dinner at a chateau with Sebastien, his new wife Amanda, and a duchess.

Now they stood side-by-side, wearing the plush robes from the hotel, relaxed and content, their bodies sated as they gazed out at the city lights below.

Ruby slipped her arm around his waist. "You know, if we'd gotten married when we originally planned, we wouldn't have been able to stay here."

Robert kissed the top of her head. "I have to admit, it feels a little rebellious."

"Like we're giving the middle finger to all those people who were against mixed marriages."

"You think Richard and Mildred Loving would approve?"

Ruby wrapped her arms around his neck and kissed him softly. "I do."

"What do you think, Mrs. Ellis, are you up for spending the rest of your life loving me no matter what the world tries to throw at us?"

She laughed softly and kissed him. "Every damn day, Mr. Ellis."

Keep Reading
for an excerpt from
Pavia's Legacy
by Eliana West

CHAPTER ONE

PAVIA JACKSON stared at the letter in her hand. She rubbed her thumb over the heavy paper with the name of the lawyer's office printed in bold type at the top. She'd never received an official document like this before. Reading it for a third time, she still didn't understand it. Why in the world was she invited to come to the reading of Antonio Conti's will?

When she'd heard the patriarch of the Conti family, one of the founding California wine families, was giving a lecture at her alma mater, Pavia made the three-hour drive to see him speak. Antonio Conti made a point to find her after his presentation "Clones and the Art of Propagation" at Washington State University, making his way through the crowd of admirers to introduce himself to her. Well into his nineties, his blue eyes still sparkled with his love of farming and the craft of winemaking.

"You're Pavia Jackson." His voice held a hint of wonder and his eyes searched her face as he smiled wistfully.

Pavia shook the callused hand he offered. "I am. I'm sorry. I don't mean to be rude, but how do you know me?"

He shook his head, his smile falling. "The Jackson family is one of the finest winemaking families in the country. Your father"—his voice faltered—"and your grandfather are two of the best vintners I've had the honor to know."

Was that a sheen of tears in his eyes?

"I'm so pleased you and your brother are following in their footsteps," he said.

Pavia noticed the other students and faculty watching their exchange with curiosity. She was just as curious as everyone around them. Why had this man sought her out?

"Thank you, sir."

"No, my dear, please call me Antonio."

"Oh, I don't think I can do that. Can we compromise with *Mr. Conti*?"

He patted her arm. "Yes, of course." Mr. Conti waved off the professors and the president of the program hovering nearby and tucked her arm through his. "I'd appreciate it if you would give me a tour of this facility."

Pavia looked from the shocked staff to Mr. Conti. "I—"

"Please." He cut off her reluctance. "I'm an old man who might not see another harvest. I'd like to spend some time with someone who reminds me of the hopeful days of my youth."

She couldn't say no to such a heartfelt request. Mr. Conti exuded both strength and weakness, and Pavia could see in his eyes a man looking at the arc of his life.

She nodded. "I'd be happy to show you around."

Mr. Conti's eyes brightened. "Now, tell me about your master's degree in molecular plant sciences."

Pavia spent the rest of the afternoon with him touring the viticulture and enology facilities at her alma mater, discussing winemaking methods. The experienced winemaker didn't scoff at her ideas about sustainable and organic production like some of his generation did. He asked probing questions, offering his thoughts and advice.

It had been an amazing experience. She returned home excited to share with her father and brother what had happened. Her older brother, Robert, shared her wonder and enthusiasm for the encounter, while her father sat stone-faced.

The door opened, pulling Pavia from her impressions of that day. A large silhouette of a man was shadowed by the bright snow behind him. Pulling off his heavy work gloves, he rubbed his hands together and stomped the snow off his feet.

"Days like today make me wonder if we'll ever see spring again," he said in his deep, rich baritone.

Pavia held up the letter. "Dad, come look at this. Someone must be playing a joke on me."

Her father moved to her side, peering down at the piece of paper. With a trembling hand, he pulled it out of her grasp. His dark brown skin took on a grayish hue that startled her.

"Throw it away," he finally said.

"Dad?" Pavia grasped his arm. "I don't understand."

Instead of answering, Anthony Jackson wadded up the letter and threw it in the garbage as he stormed out. Pavia stared at his retreating form in shock. He didn't bother to put his hat or gloves back on before going outside into the bone-chilling cold again. She went over to the doorway and watched her dad march through the vines, his breath coming out in tiny puffs, his figure hunched against the cold. He looked small. It was unsettling to see him this way.

Anthony Jackson was a towering figure, both physically and in the wine industry. At just over six feet, years of working the land kept his sixty-year-old body fit. The only hint of his age came from the gray hairs on his close-cropped hair and beard. As a vintner, he was an esteemed figure and a pioneer in the Washington wine industry. Her dad was always encouraging and steady, her rock. She'd never seen him like this before. He'd never said anything bad about the Contis or any vintner. That wasn't in his nature, so to see him react so strongly made her pause.

Should she run after him? Pavia debated what to do, watching her dad's figure grow smaller and smaller. She stepped back inside and closed the door. Whatever had made him upset, he wasn't ready to talk about it yet. One trait everyone in her family shared was a stubborn streak, and Pavia knew from experience her dad wouldn't talk until he was ready. Instead of following him like she wanted to, she closed the door against the cold, went to the garbage can, and pulled out the letter. Placing it on the counter, she smoothed out the wrinkles and read it again.

Her dad's response had puzzled her when she told him about meeting the legendary winemaker a few months ago. He seemed more annoyed than impressed. Now there was no mistaking his anger.

The wine industry was a tight-knit community, and it was rare for there to be any major disagreements. Why would her dad be so angry with Antonio Conti?

With the memory of her day with Mr. Conti fresh in her mind, Pavia folded the document and tucked it in her pocket. Hopefully her dad would be ready to talk by the time they sat down for dinner.

When he didn't appear, Pavia knew exactly where to go. He stood in front of the one stained glass window with a grapevine design in the small stone chapel that overlooked the vineyards spread across the sloping hills below. The chapel had been there when the hills were a sea of wheat farmed by Pavia's great-great-grandfather. It was the place the workers prayed for a good harvest. Others would come to ask for the rain to fall or the sun to shine. The tiny stone chapel was the place where her parents had exchanged their vows. It was also where they'd held her mother's funeral when cancer stole her life. Her family wasn't particularly religious, but the small chapel gave comfort to anyone who sought refuge inside its stone walls. Her dad always came to this spot when he struggled to make sense of whatever burden life had placed upon his broad shoulders.

"*Papà?*" Pavia stood next to him. "*Qual è il problema?*" she asked in Italian, the language they used when they spoke from the heart.

Her father released a long sigh. "Your mother said that it is impossible to keep a secret forever, as it will eventually bloom and expose itself to the world."

She rested her head on his shoulder. "What did Antonio Conti do to make you so unhappy?"

Her dad stiffened. "Nothing. He did nothing, and that's the problem."

"I don't understand."

"The only thing you need to know is that there's nothing the Contis can give you. I've worked hard for all these years to make sure of that. I can provide for you and your brother. You don't need anything from him."

Pavia turned to face him. Suddenly, he looked older. Grief when her mother died had aged him, but this was different. She looked down at their hands: his, dark brown, callused, with a few scars here and there from a lifetime of field work; hers, softer, lighter, a golden brown hue, a mix of her father and mother. She'd inherited the faint smattering of freckles across her nose from her mother and shared her dad's warm brown eyes. A lump formed in her throat seeing the pain in them now.

"Dad, I'm not a little girl anymore. You can't just tell me to ignore the letter without giving me an explanation."

His jaw ticked. "I can't… I don't know if I'll ever be ready to talk about the Contis."

"*Papà, devo andare.* I have to go," she told him.

The same pain Pavia saw in her father's eyes had flashed briefly in Antonio Conti's when she met him. She needed to know what had caused it, and something in her gut told her she'd find the answer at the reading of his will.

"I want to go, Dad. I—I wish I could just let it go, but I can't. There's a part of me that needs to know why Mr. Conti wanted me there."

Her dad's shoulders slumped. "I suppose I knew you would." He reached out and tugged one of her curls with a wistful smile. "You were always my curious child. You'll wonder if you don't go. Just know"—his voice quavered—"you'll find out what this is all about, and we'll go from there."

A WEEK later, Pavia watched the tiny sailboats dancing with the cargo ships on the blue-green waves of San Francisco Bay. She pressed her hand against the large floor-to-ceiling windows in the conference room of the law offices of Hendricks, Jamison, and Steele, craning her neck to take in the breathtaking view. When she squinted, she could just make out someone on a paddleboard bobbing up and down in the bay. Her stomach dipped and rolled along with the waves. Pavia glanced over her shoulder at the other people in the room and sucked in her breath. She'd taken refuge by the window, wishing her father had agreed to come with her.

She should have been with her father and brother. Her brother, Robert, was born to be a farmer and loved being out in the fields, tending the vines and the few acres of wheat and alfalfa that remained along with an apple orchard. All of them helped in the winery, but it was Pavia who spent the most time with their dad, honing her skills as a winemaker. She was at home in the lab, and in the barrel room, looking for just the right balance of acid, sugars, and yeast needed for a perfect bottle of wine. Her interest focused on enology, the craft of turning the fruit into wine. They were a team, and Pavia felt valued but not necessarily needed. It was her father's wine, and his vision. Lately she'd been thinking about her goals, to produce wine using cutting-edge organic production. She wanted to experiment with different methods than what her father used. Pavia loved him, and never took for granted how special it was to work alongside one another, but she was sheltered at home, and she wanted to challenge herself.

Today she missed the security of the familiar feel and smells of the winery back home. Instead of setting up to bottle their Battalion Blend, she was feeling out of place standing in this fancy lawyer's office wearing the only suit she owned that she'd had to dig out of the back of her closet. Pavia ran her hands over her pants, trying to smooth away the wrinkles from sitting on the plane. She eyed the reflection in the window of the people sitting at the conference table. They didn't seem uncomfortable in their expensive suits.

The two Conti brothers, Alex and Nick, looked just like the pictures she'd seen on social media. But instead of smiling as they had in photos with their grandfather, both of their faces became marred with angry glares in her direction as soon as the receptionist introduced her. It was obvious Mr. Conti's family didn't know why she was there either. The digital images hadn't prepared her for the real thing. The Conti brothers were a Brooks Brothers ad brought to life. Tall with dark blond hair, Alex, the older brother, had blue eyes that matched his mother's. The younger brother, Nick, had hair a little darker, and his eyes were deep brown. Alex wore his hair short with a close-cropped beard, while Nick could have just come from the beach with his longer, wavy hairstyle.

Between them sat their mother, Sarah Conti. She didn't have the same social media presence as her sons, so Pavia hadn't been able to find out much of anything about her. Mrs. Conti wasn't glaring at Pavia, but looking at her with an expression that looked almost like longing. When she'd first walked into the room and seen Pavia, her steps faltered, and Alex gently guided her into a seat at the table while Nick poured her a glass of water. She took a sip, eyeing Pavia over the rim of her glass. Even though she'd retreated to the window, she felt the older woman's gaze on her the entire time.

Overwhelmed by the urge to call her dad, Pavia turned away from the window, but before she could escape the stifling confines of the room, the door opened. An older, balding man walked in looking at them over the tops of a pair of tortoise shell reading glasses perched on the end of his nose.

"Ladies and gentlemen, should we begin?"

HE WANTED to hate her. Alex watched Pavia Jackson sitting across the conference table, looking scared. He wanted to paint her as some kind of gold digger who'd conned his grandfather. Alex didn't know what his grandfather had left her, and it didn't matter. He resented having an outsider at the reading of the will. More than anything, he didn't want anyone there to witness their grief… his grief.

He was surprised to find Pavia there alone. Alex assumed that her father or her lawyer would accompany her. Within minutes of their arrival, she'd gotten up and retreated to the large bank of windows overlooking San Francisco Bay. Her back straight and her head held high, the only sign of her nervousness was the way she held her hands clenched tightly in front of her.

The receptionist had introduced her when he led them into the conference room, but an introduction wasn't necessary. Alex knew who Pavia Jackson was. He'd looked her up the minute their family lawyer, Mr. Hendricks, informed them she would also be at the reading of his grandfather's will. There was a vast difference between reading about Pavia and actually meeting her. His research hadn't prepared him for the way her hair fell in light brown curls that rested between her shoulder blades, or how the charcoal gray pantsuit she wore showed off a figure with gently rounded hips and long legs. She wore a silk blouse in a shade somewhere between pink and orange that reminded him of a sunset sky. The color made her light hazel eyes stand out even more. Large and framed with long lashes, those big eyes had been sneaking glances at him since he walked in. His research on the Jackson family revealed that her golden brown skin tone resulted from a union between her Black father and her mother, who was half White and half Native American.

Alex's gut told him that, no matter how much he wanted it to be true, she was not a gold digger. And his body responded with an unexpected attraction that made him feel even more off-kilter than he already did.

His mother's hands trembled as she took another sip of water. Her physical response to seeing Pavia was another surprise. It was almost like she had encountered her before. To Alex's knowledge, they had never met. His mother's gaze seemed to be filled with longing, leaving him more perplexed as to why Pavia was there.

The Jackson family had an excellent reputation in the industry, but they ran in very different social circles. Alex's grandfather had produced one of the first California wines to be honored in the Judgment of Paris wine competition. Everyone knew the Conti vineyard for the quality of its fruit, and Antonio Conti's knowledge of farming and winemaking had made him an icon among his peers. The Jacksons made a quality product, but Brothers in Arms was minuscule compared to the hundreds of thousands of cases his family produced in a year. What was the connection that brought her to the reading of his grandfather's will?

His brother raised a questioning eyebrow at their mother's visceral reaction to Pavia's presence. Alex shrugged with a slight shake of his head.

He reached over and gently grasped his mother's hand. "Are you okay?"

She sucked in her breath and nodded. She kept her head bowed, the silver strands of her chin-length hair hiding her face.

The lawyer walked in, and Alex stiffened, his heart rate going up. He glanced at his brother, trying to gauge his reaction to this moment. Alex knew he and Nick would each inherit equal shares of the family business. Antonio had never kept secret his intentions for its ongoing growth and development. So why hadn't he ever mentioned Pavia Jackson before?

His grandfather's lawyer assumed the position of the head of the table. His gaze shifted to Pavia. "I'm Mr. Hendricks, Mr. Conti's attorney. Thank you for coming today."

Pavia gave a nod of acknowledgment as she clasped her hands together in front of her.

Mr. Hendricks opened a folder and read in a dry, emotionless tone, "I, Antonio Michael Conti, being of sound mind and body…."

Alex closed his eyes, pinching the bridge of his nose while the lawyer read his grandfather's words of love for his family. He'd known this day would come eventually, but he wasn't ready. He would never be ready to lose the man who'd been both a grandfather and a father to him. Without him, he felt lost. There were a million questions he still wanted to ask. He hadn't realized he should have counted the time he had left with his grandfather in minutes instead of years. He died in his sleep just as the vines had gone dormant, ready to rest and recharge for the winter. They would reawaken in the spring, but his grandad would not. Alex swallowed, trying to fight back his tears. He didn't want Pavia Jackson, a stranger, to witness his family's grief. As much as his heart hurt, his mother and brother were hurting as well. Antonio's death had affected them all, and their grief wasn't for public display.

"To Miss Pavia Jackson, I leave the fifteen acres known as the Brothers Block, the cottage and surrounding land, and"—the lawyer cleared his throat—"five million dollars."

"What?" Pavia exclaimed, clutching the edge of the desk.

Everything stopped as the words the lawyer had just read registered in Alex's mind. He jumped up from his seat. "What the hell do you mean she gets the Brothers Block?"

Nick pounded on the table. "He can't do that!"

The lawyer raised his hand. "Please, allow me to finish," he commanded in a stern voice.

The sunlight that streamed through the windows turned cold. He couldn't do this. His grandfather couldn't take away the only thing he'd ever wanted.

"This is ridiculous! Grandad wasn't in his right mind. He never would have done this to me… to us!" he continued to rant, unable to control the hurt and betrayal that swept over him.

His heart thundered in his chest. Alex looked down at his clenched fists, the skin over his knuckles stretched taut and pale. He took a deep breath, trying to regain some equilibrium before he confronted Pavia.

"How much do you want for it?" he asked.

"I…." Pavia's eyes were wide.

Mr. Hendricks jumped up. "Mr. Conti, sit down! I have not finished, and you need to hear this."

Alex was so wrapped up in his thoughts that he hadn't realized he had risen to his feet and was leaning across the table in a way that may have seemed intimidating. He sank down into his seat, glaring at Pavia.

"We're going to fight this," he said in a cold, firm voice.

Mr. Hendricks fixed them with a stern gaze before he resumed his seat and continued. "Any attempt to contest the terms of my bequest to Miss Jackson will cause the entirety of my estate being conferred to Miss Jackson." The lawyer held his hand up in silent warning. "Miss Jackson may not sell the land known as the Brothers Block for five years. If, after that time, she decides to sell, Alex Conti will have the first right of refusal."

"I'll never forgive him for betraying our family like this," Nick spat out.

"Enough… ENOUGH!" Their mother turned to Alex, tears streaming down her cheeks. "Respect your grandfather's wishes," she said in a strangled voice, then directed her attention to Pavia. Alex felt a wave of sorrow emanating from her that left him breathless.

He rested his hand on his mother's arm. "Mom, we can't allow some stranger to—"

The lawyer frowned, shuffling through his paperwork. "The rest of the estate is to be divided between Mrs. Conti and her sons," he said, looking at Alex and Nick. "There are no other bequests."

His mom rose and began heading toward the door, one step in front of another, almost in robotic fashion. Alex rushed after her, with Nick on his heels, but paused in the doorway, staring at Pavia for a moment. Her face was pale, her gaze darting between him and Mr. Hendricks, her mouth turned down. She was just as shocked as he was by his grandfather's bequest, but that didn't stop him from being mad and resenting the hell out of her.

His mother was silent and stone-faced in the elevator down to the parking garage. Alex exchanged a worried look with his brother. He hadn't seen her like this since…. A wave of nausea hit him, his stomach plummeting faster than the elevator. They were all silent until they were in the car and on their way out of the city.

Midway across the Golden Gate Bridge, his mother said in a shaky voice, "He didn't do it to hurt you."

Alex gripped the steering wheel tighter as he glanced at her in the rearview mirror. "But he did."

Nick looked over his shoulder at her. "He didn't have the right to give it away."

"I know you don't understand, but he thought he was…." She shuddered and looked out the window, pressing her fist against her mouth.

"What is it you're not telling us?" Alex frowned, observing his mother's distress in the rearview mirror.

"I'm not ready to talk about this now. But I need you, both of you, to understand what your grandfather did wasn't any kind of punishment or done to cause you pain."

"Did you know?" He asked the question knowing deep down his mother would never keep something like this a secret from him.

"No, of course not. I don't disagree with what your grandfather did, but he shouldn't have let you find out this way. He should have told you… told all of us what he was planning."

What wasn't his mother telling them? What secret was she harboring? "How do you know Pavia, Mom?"

Her forehead wrinkled. "What makes you say that?"

"It seemed like you recognized her when we walked into the conference room."

His mother took a deep, shuddering breath. "I never met Pavia Jackson, but her father was one of the most important people in my life."

Nick shifted in his seat to face her. "What does that mean?"

Her expression became resolute. "It means that we're not going to fight this, Nick. Your grandfather did what he thought he needed to do, and I support his decision."

Even if it means taking away the one thing I've always wanted, Alex thought, flexing his hands on the steering wheel. He glanced at his brother. With the passing of their grandfather, the change they knew was coming, and both dreaded, had arrived. Guilt sat heavy in his gut. He wanted to believe that his brother would finally step up and assume the role of the business partner Alex had desperately wanted and needed him to be. Until now, Nick had been more interested in the perks of a successful business than doing the work to earn them. When they arrived home, they would come together as a family and devise a plan to make sure every inch of the Conti vineyards remained in the family, as it was always meant to be.

Scan the QR code below to order

ELIANA WEST, the recipient of the 2022 Nancy Pearl Award for genre fiction, is committed to embracing diversity in her writing. That means she doesn't limit herself to a single genre. Instead, Eliana welcomes every story that comes her way with open arms. She aims to create characters that reflect the diversity of her community, with a range of social backgrounds, ethnicities, genders, and sexual orientations. Eliana loves to weave in historical elements whenever she can. She believes everyone deserves a happy ending.

From small towns to close-knit communities, Eliana West loves stories that bring people from different backgrounds together through the common language of unconditional love and acceptance. Eliana is a passionate advocate for diversity within the writing community. She is the founder of Writers for Diversity and teaches classes and workshops, encouraging writers to create diverse characters and worlds with an empathetic approach.

When Eliana isn't plotting her characters' happy endings, she can be found embarking on adventures with her husband, traversing winding country roads in their beloved vintage Volkswagen Westfalia, affectionately named Bianca. Whether it's traveling abroad or exploring locally, Eliana and her husband are always willing to get lost and see where the adventure takes them.

Eliana loves connecting with readers through her website: www.elianawest.com.

THE WAY Forward

MOCKINGBIRD BRIDGE

BOOK ONE

ELIANA WEST

Mockingbird Bridge Book One

The small town he couldn't wait to leave is calling him home….

Dax Ellis returns to Colton, Mississippi, a changed man. He traveled the world, earned a fortune, and made a lifetime of memories, but now he longs to put down roots. Time hasn't been kind to his hometown, and Dax wants to help—if only he can convince everyone he's not the same petulant boy he used to be. Especially the one woman who has every reason not to trust him.

Librarian Callie Colton cherished summers with her grandparents, in the town her ancestors helped build, in spite of the boy who called her names. Now that Colton is her home, life is quiet until Dax returns… and, along with him, threatening letters on her doorstep. He may still have the power to hurt her, but she's not the same scared little girl she used to be.

But as the danger escalates, Dax will have to face his past to find a way forward for the relationship they were cheated of once before.

Scan the QR code below to order

THE WAY *Home*

MOCKINGBIRD BRIDGE

BOOK TWO

ELIANA WEST

Mockingbird Bridge Book Two

A letter from the past will transform their future…

Taylor Colton always loved the crumbling plantation house passed down through his family for generations. Now he's bringing his popular renovation reality show to the small town of Colton, Mississippi, so he can bring the plantation house known as Halcyon back to life for the cameras.

After an ugly breakup, Josephine Martin needs a new start to heal her broken heart in peace. A hidden letter reveals a family secret that leads her to Colton to protect her family's history and honor a promise made before the Civil War… and to a house she didn't know was hers.

Suddenly, Josephine must decide if she's ready for the challenge of restoring a rundown mansion and its history, and Taylor's facing a challenge he can't charm away. Together, they must untangle a tragic history, a rocky relationship, and risk everything they love. Can they overcome the past to find their way home?

Scan the QR code below to order

THE WAY *Beyond*

MOCKINGBIRD BRIDGE

BOOK THREE

ELIANA WEST

Mockingbird Bridge Book Three

When she finds out his secret, will he lose her for good?

Jacob Winters has a secret: he's come to Colton undercover as an FBI handler. He didn't plan to stay, but the small town has charmed him with a sense of community that he hasn't felt in a long time. And his attraction to the beautiful Mae Colton complicates things even more. Jacob doesn't do relationships—he won't risk making memories he might regret.

Mae Colton loves her little town of Colton, Mississippi, and doesn't want to leave. In fact, instead of moving on to bigger things—namely a political career in DC—like she'd planned, she wants to run for a second term as mayor of Colton. But not everyone in town supports this choice, including the commitment-phobic Jacob Winters.

Mae is ready to make their secret relationship official and go public, but that would break Jacob's one rule. When a threat against Mae's life forces him to admit the truth of his feelings, he has to race to save the woman he loves before it's too late.

Scan the QR code below to order

A HIDDEN *Heart*

MOCKINGBIRD BRIDGE

BOOK FOUR

ELIANA WEST

Mockingbird Bridge Book Four

Rhett Colton has spent the last two years working deep undercover for the FBI. He's forsaken his friends and family to keep his community safe, but now that his mission is over, he's haunted by what he's done and is having a hard time returning to his previous life. Only two things are keeping him from becoming totally lost—his dog, Rebel, and the beautiful new town veterinarian.

Jasmine Owens is ready to start over in the charming town of Colton, Mississippi, by opening her own veterinary practice. Jasmine knows what it's like to constantly have her abilities questioned, but she's strong enough to persevere. When she agrees to board Rhett's dog while he's away in DC, they begin talking every night over the phone and she realizes Rhett isn't the man she thought he was. He's so much more and sparks quickly fly on both ends.

But when new threats surface, Jasmine and everyone in Colton's safety are threatened. Rhett will need to make a decision. He's always sacrificed everything for his job, but is he willing to risk their relationship too?

Scan the QR code below to order

ELIANA WEST
A
PARIS
WALK
A
PARIS WIDOWS
SHORT STORY

After three years of being a widow, Amanda Thompson is ready to venture out into the world on her own. A chance meeting with Sébastien Durand leads to a day of exploring Paris, remembering her first visit and considering what the future might look like.

Sébastien Durand is enchanted by the woman sitting alone at the café. When the opportunity presents, he offers himself as her tour guide. An afternoon leads to a day that becomes an evening falling to the magic of Paris's glittering lights.

Can Amanda overcome her own fears and doubts and the objections of others for a second chance at love? Will fate bring two souls together to meet for the first time again?

A Paris Walk is a seasoned romance about two people ready to take a risk of letting fate lead the way to love.

Scan the QR code below to order